French Twist

A Foreign Affair

French Twist

A Foreign Affair

A Novel by

Nancy L. Milby

A Word with You Press
Publishers and Purveyors of Fine Stories
310 East A Street, Suite B, Moscow, Idaho 83843

www.awordwithyoupress.com

Milby, Nancy
French Twist

ISBN-13: 9780988464650
ISBN-10: 0988464659

French Twist is published by:
A Word with You Press
310 East A Street, Suite B, Moscow, Idaho 83843

For information please direct emails to:
info@awordwithyoupress.com or visit our website:
www.awordwithyoupress.com

Book cover designed by Teri Rider from a photograph by Nancy Milby
Book interior design: Teri Rider

First Edition, February 2015

Printed in the United States of America

10 9 8 7 6 5 4 3 2 1   15 16 17 18 19 20 21 22 23 24

A Word with You Press
Publishers and Purveyors of Fine Stories
310 East A Street, Suite B, Moscow, Idaho 83843

Dedication

To all those free spirits who've traveled the back roads and villages of France with me in search of the perfect wine, the perfect cuisine, the perfect evening, and the perfect romance, this *foreign affair* is for you. *Amusez-vous!*

Prologue

The train was more than half full, but the boy knew the seat beside him would be the last one taken. He sat where he could keep an eye on the ancient bicycle. It was too small for him, and though he'd found it in an abandoned barn just the week before, he'd become attached to it nonetheless. It was the sign he'd been waiting for that it was time.

He took a deep breath and settled back into his seat as the train pulled away from the station. He trusted no one—could not let his guard down yet. Still, the tension that had gripped him since he'd started out that morning began to ease as the train picked up speed. He shifted his meager pack, leaned his bulky shoulders against the window and stretched out his long legs, cautiously assessing the people who moved between cars as they stowed their luggage and found seats.

The rocking motion of the train soothed him, gave him hope. He'd escaped, left the humiliation and punishment behind, and he vowed to keep the memory of that place contained, hidden in his heart until he could ensure justice was realized. For now, he needed to concentrate on his journey and keep his destination—and the promise of a new life—firmly in his mind. As the conductor strolled through the cabin calling *"Billets s'il vous plaît,"* the boy took another deep breath and forced himself to believe.

One

Village of Lacoste, France, some twenty years later

Louise Marcel whispered her way down the uneven stone steps that led from the Maison Forte at the top of the village to her apartment below. Frightened almost out of her wits, she wiped her clammy hands on her jeans before grabbing the rail as the stairway curved sharply downward to the left. She could still hear the muffled voices of the men above her. So far she'd passed undetected, but she wasn't taking any chances. What was it about Lacoste that attracted these lowlife thugs? It was the only thing she disliked about this assignment, but she was determined to not let them scare her away. She knew in her heart that she needed to be here in France, and this gig was her only option.

Beyond earshot of the upper terrace, she stopped to take a deep breath. She closed her eyes and tried to relax, willing the natural sounds of the night to calm her nerves. But before she'd let that first breath out, the bushes below her rustled, and she tensed, picking up some sort of low moan. She waited, and heard it again. It sounded like the whine of a wounded animal, only … not exactly. *What the heck?* She squinted down the slope, the only light coming from the moon that filtered through the clouds. Something was down there, a dark shape against a tree at the bottom. Another sound—only this time it was clearly a groan. *Crap on a crumpet! That's no animal!*

She forgot the men on the upper terrace as she swung herself under the railing and onto the steep dirt hillside. Hanging onto the edge of a step to gain her footing, she crawled and slid crab-like down the landscaped slope to the body of a man that she could just make out. Something reflected on his face in the moonlight. *Oh God, blood.* She looked up to the stairs and saw the gap in the railing near where she had just been standing, then back down at the unconscious man.

Even in the pale light, she could see dark bruises on his face, including a nasty black eye. *But holy Moses, what a face!* There were rips in his shirt, and she saw the glistening of more blood on his torso and smeared on the arm that was protectively hugged to his chest. Dried rivulets had seeped from a gash on the back of his hand down under the thick leather cuff on his wrist. He was tangled up in shrubs and practically wrapped around the tree—it must have broken his fall. She gingerly touched two fingers to his neck. His pulse was faint but steady.

Relief battled panic for top billing in her head as she tried to figure out what to do. She pulled out her cell phone but hesitated, glancing up toward the terrace. The closest *gendarmerie* was in Bonnieux; close, but not close enough. And besides, the guy needed a doctor more than he needed the police.

She put her hand gently on his shoulder. "I'll be right back," she whispered. "I'm going for help. Stay quiet as you can." She had no idea if he heard or understood her as she leaned down close. His breathing was shallow and labored, raspy, and she prayed he'd only bruised his ribs and not punctured a lung. A moment later, she was scrambling down to the narrow cobblestone path below.

The prone man waivered in and out of consciousness as he fought to hang on to the whispered words that echoed in his ear. *Merde!* He hurt everywhere. He opened his eyes but squeezed them shut at the stinging sensation of imbedded grit. It must have been his imagination—he was alone. An intense pain lanced through his ankle and seared his skull when he tried to roll over. *Putain de merde!* A wave of nausea swept through him and he broke out in a sweat, thinking he might puke, but then the fog rolled back over his senses and he let the lull of nothingness drag him back down.

In a dingy bar at the bottom of the village, Etienne Matisse grunted as one of his men dropped a worn wallet on the table in front of him. Matisse scooped it up and glared at the man when he hovered, sending him shuffling backward. After pulling out a thick stack of euros, he riffled through the rest of the contents. A French ID showed an old photo of Alexander Bouvier with a Les Eyzies address. His eyes narrowed thoughtfully as he studied another ID card: a California driver's license. The photo was more recent and the license was still valid, showing a San Francisco address. There was also a student ID for the local college and a BNP V-Pay card. After looking at every item in the wallet, including folded-up receipts, Matisse replaced everything but the euros, which he pocketed before tossing the wallet back to his man. "Drop it in the mail slot at the school office."

Two

Alex came out of the fog once more, this time determined to stay alert. He lay still, willing the darkness back. Opening his eyes, he blinked a few times to clear his vision and then looked around. The back of his bed was canted up so he didn't have to lift his head. A good thing, because it hurt like hell. The only light came from behind a drawn shade at the single window. Awareness sharpened. The faint beeping to his left and the bedrails at his sides were a dead giveaway as to where he was, and the slightly antiseptic smell of the room clinched the deal.

The fuzzy events of the day before—or whenever it was—came back to him. He'd spent the afternoon playing poker with that big ugly brute, Etienne Matisse. He'd won fairly, but Matisse accused him of cheating, loudly enough for everyone in the bar to have heard it. Then what? He'd gone to the photo lab and worked there until past midnight, and then … right. Then he'd been jumped. He winced at a stabbing pain behind his eyes. The rest was stuck in the fog bank somewhere. Someone must have found him, since he doubted he'd taken himself to the hospital.

He heard the muffled sound of people moving, and he shifted his gaze toward the sound coming through a partially opened door. There were two other beds in the room, but both were empty. He glanced down, realizing he wore nothing but his boxer shorts beneath a thin sheet that barely covered his bottom half. The lower part of his right leg was encased in a canvas cast that stuck out from the end of the sheet and rested on a large pillow. He tried to wiggle his toes and was rewarded with a jolt of pain in his ankle.

"*Aïe!*" Hissing air into his lungs had the same effect—bruised ribs or worse, he thought, letting out the breath out slowly as the pain and nausea subsided. *Merde.*

With eyes closed, he wiggled the toes of his other foot. Nothing wrong there. He opened his eyes and lifted his hands up in front of his face, turning them to survey the damage. Cuts, scrapes, and bruises—including one nasty gash that had a few stitches covered with a butterfly bandage, but other than that, nothing too serious. His watch was missing, and he stared for a moment at the tiny dots of scars that were still visible on the underside of his wrist. *That would feel good right now.*

He sighed and forced his thoughts away from that train wreck, instead continuing his self-examination. His right elbow was wrapped in gauze and, now that he noticed it, throbbed in pain. He brought a hand to his face and winced when he inadvertently poked a sore spot beneath the swath of gauze wrapped around his head. Experimentally moving his jaw back and forth, the ache confirmed his sketchy memory of being punched in the face. More than once.

He started looking around for his clothes and his cell phone when he heard a soft knock on the door. "*Entrez,*" he croaked in barely a whisper, then coughed and cleared his throat. "*Entrez!*" he said a bit louder, thinking nurses don't knock. A young woman peeked tentatively around the door. Hiding mostly behind it, her large blue eyes peered at him.

"*Comment vous vous sentez?*" *How are you feeling?* Her American-accented French was timid but held genuine concern.

"I've been better," he replied in English, thinking she sounded vaguely familiar. He cleared his throat again. "Come in."

She slipped into the room like a waif, hugging the door with her back. "I'm real sorry about your ankle," she said softly. "The nurse said it's a simple fracture, so it should heal up okay. You're lucky you don't have a concussion. I wasn't sure how bad you were hurt when I first, uh, when I found you."

Mid twenties, Alex thought, and her speech carried the gentle cadence of America's South. Her long blond hair was pulled back in a loose tie with wispy bangs falling softly over her forehead, and her pale blue eyes, fringed with thick lashes, looked luminous against her lightly tanned skin. She had a fresh-scrubbed look about her. She was wearing faded jeans and a ribbed cotton tank top that showed off her slender build and the toned muscles of

5

her arms. Alex regarded her silently for a moment before coming to a sudden awareness. *You're the one who whispered to me.*

"I was afraid to speak out loud because there were, um … I wasn't sure who might hear. I'm sorry I left you, but it was the only way I could get help."

Alex hadn't realized he had spoken the thought out loud, and he laughed softly, then winced at the pain. "Don't apologize, *mademoiselle,* please. Whatever you had to do to get me here—wherever here is—there is nothing to be sorry for. If not for you, I imagine I would still be bleeding in the dirt."

She looked startled and shook her head in denial. "No, no, I'm sure—"

"What is your name?" Alex interrupted her.

Her blue eyes widened again. "Oh gosh, I'm so sorry. Lou, my name's Lou. Louise Marcel, but my, ah, most people call me Lou." She was nervous, which he found oddly charming, but also curious.

"Well, Lou, it is a pleasure to meet you, although I would have preferred slightly better circumstances." Alex gifted her with an engaging smile. *"Je m'appelle Alex Bouvier."*

She responded with a smile of her own—it was impossible not to. *"Enchanté, Alex."*

He reached out his hand to her as if he wanted to shake hers. She moved cautiously to his bedside to take it. But rather than a perfunctory handshake, he clasped her outstretched hand and pulled her closer. Breaking into a mischievous grin that showed his dimples, he leaned up to lightly kiss her fingers. *"Le plaisir est le mien."*

She blushed, and he thought he saw a brief flash of fear in her expression. *Intéressant.* When she tugged her fingers from his grasp, he let her go.

"Can you sit with me a moment? I could use your help to figure out what happened."

For an instant she hesitated, then nodded, lowering herself to the chair beside his bed. "Do you remember anything? The RA made a report to the *gendarmerie* this morning, and they'll be here soon to talk to you."

"Pierre? Is that who brought me here? Where exactly am I?"

"Yes, I mean, well, no, not exactly. You're in Avignon. Pierre called an ambulance. You, uh … you looked pretty bad last night."

Lou paused as he watched her with his piercing gaze, unnerving her. Hazel green, she thought, but it was hard to tell in the dim light. But it wasn't too dark for her to see that he was every bit as gorgeous as she remembered, even with the bruises and butterfly bandaged cuts over his swollen left eye, compounded now by his half-naked state. She tried not to look at his wide chest and its sprinkling of dark curls. He was the kind of man that made her head spin and forget the danger. And he was waiting for her to continue. She cleared her throat, clasped her hands in her lap, and hoped her voice didn't shake.

"I stayed with you while he waited down the hill for the paramedics to arrive. You thrashed around some but never gained full consciousness. They gave you something to keep you under before they moved you. Pierre told me you have family nearby. He said he'd call them this morning."

As if on cue, they heard heavy footsteps in the hall a moment before the door pushed open. Lou turned to see a tall, handsome man with broad shoulders filling the doorway. She glanced at Alex before looking back at the newcomer. With a thick mop of dark hair peppered with gray and creases etched around his mouth and eyes, he looked like an older version of Alex. There was a look of concern on his deeply tanned face.

Alex groaned as his favorite relative stepped into the room, but his lips curved into a deprecating smile. The tall man's visage softened immediately upon seeing the smile. Meeting the man's direct gaze, Alex couldn't help making light of the situation.

"The last time we were in the same hospital room together, it was you in the bed and me gawking from the doorway."

Kaden Macallister laughed and his face opened into an affectionate grin that showed his own dimples. "You've got a good memory—that was twenty years ago and you were barely six years old." Turning serious again, he added, "Let's hope your recovery is easier than mine. How are you? And what happened? Your friend Pierre seemed to think you'd been mugged."

My friend? "I'm alive, as you can see, and I don't think there's any permanent damage. As to what happened, Lou and I were just about to sort that out." He looked at Lou, who'd been wordlessly watching the exchange. "Lou,

7

this is my uncle, er, cousin, Kaden Macallister. Kaden, this is Louise Marcel. Lou is …" he stopped. He had no idea who Lou was or what she was doing here.

Lou was astonished that they were speaking English, Alex with a barely discernible French accent and Kaden with a British one, and it took her a moment to pick up on the cue. *Odd family connection,* she thought as she turned to face Kaden. "I'm on staff at the art college in Lacoste, Mr. Macallister, working on the documentation of a property that they're getting ready to restore and renovate." She looked back at Alex. "*La maison Basse* project."

At that, Alex raised his eyebrows and opened his mouth to speak, but Kaden beat him to it. "Did you have some involvement in Alex's mishap?"

"She helped me, Kaden." Annoyance sparked in Alex's voice in defense of the young woman, whose eyes had gone wide with alarm.

Kaden rolled his eyes. "I wasn't implying otherwise. I certainly didn't mean to suggest she jumped you, Alex. You should be so lucky."

Voices and footsteps sounded from the corridor just before a nurse pushed open the door with two police officers on her heels. She surveyed the scene and frowned. "*Monsieur Bouvier, les policiers ont demandé de parler avec vous.*" She threw a pointed look at Louise and Kaden. "You will leave."

"*Excusez-moi, madame,*" Kaden said in flawless French, "but I am his closest relative and the *mademoiselle* has information regarding the incident last night. Please close the door on your way out, as the details don't concern you."

The nurse opened her mouth to protest but seemed to think better of it in light of Kaden's imposing presence and uncompromising glare. She looked to the officers for support but saw none. She put her hands on her hips and pinched her lips together. "Do not tire him. He needs another injection of pain medication in twenty minutes. I will be back at that time." With a haughty sniff, she whirled on her rubber-soled heel and marched out.

The remaining occupants of the room looked at each other for a moment before the lead officer cleared his throat and spoke. "*Madame, messieurs, je m'appelle capitaine Minot et il s'agit de major Leblanc. Nous sommes—*"

"*Veuillez attendre, capitaine,*" Alex interrupted as he turned to Louise. "How well do you understand French?"

She colored slightly. "I can follow along for the most part, but this about you, not me. When they're ready to hear from me, though, you may need to translate."

"Of course." Turning to the captain, he nodded. *"Pardon capitaine, veuillez continuer."*

The captain was apparently in charge of the investigation into the attack on Alex, and the major was assigned to the case as well. They had been notified of the attack as soon as their Bonnieux office opened that morning and had dispatched to Lacoste, where they were given what little details were known of the case so far. They also learned that his wallet had been recovered. The captain nodded to the major, who pulled a worn wallet out of his bag and held it up.

Alex acknowledged it was his, and everyone watched as he looked through it. Nothing was missing but his cash. The fact that his credit cards were still there and the other contents were shuffled a bit confirmed his suspicions about who was behind the attack. *Bastard,* he thought. He hadn't anticipated Matisse being such a sore loser. His only hope was that he didn't suspect Alex's involvement in anything other than poker.

Sensing they were all waiting for him to say something, Alex thought back to what had happened. "I left the photo lab late, close to midnight, and headed down the hill to my dorm room. They came from behind and slammed me into the side of a building. Face first." He shifted his jaw as if to punctuate that fact.

"How many were there?" This from the captain.

"At least two. One pounded me with his fists while the other held my elbows behind my back. There was blood in my eyes from bashing into the wall, so I didn't get a good look at them. I must have passed out. I don't remember falling down the hill." Alex glanced at his cousin before addressing the captain directly. "The streets are narrow. It's possible they were waiting behind a corner. I was preoccupied and obviously didn't hear them until they were on me."

The captain nodded. "Unfortunately these attacks are not uncommon. A simple case of being in the wrong place at the wrong time, it seems. Do you think you could identify them if you saw them?"

Alex shook his head.

The major, who had been frowning as he listened to the exchange, spoke up. "It is strange, *n'est ce pas,* that the thief did not take the credit cards, too. It is more than simple to use them."

Kaden disagreed. "Not necessarily. It can be risky as hell unless the thief knows what he's doing." He held Alex's gaze for a moment before addressing the major directly. "If there's enough cash, why bother?"

The major looked at Alex. "How much cash did you have?"

Alex kept his eyes on his canvas-wrapped foot. "A little more than five hundred euros."

The major looked like he might ask another question but then shrugged and stayed silent.

"Unless a witness steps forward, we have nothing to go on." The captain shook his head in regret but did not appear disappointed when Alex shrugged in acceptance.

Ignoring his cousin's laser-like gaze, Alex turned to Louise. "Can you tell us what you know?"

With a wary glance around the room, Lou began to explain her part, pausing to allow Alex to translate her story to the *gendarmes.*

Lacoste fit the pattern of most medieval château villages, wherein the château occupies the top of the hill and the rest of the village occupies the space between the château and the once-fortified walls. While the Château de Lacoste itself was left largely in ruins after the revolution, the Maison Forte—the main resident hall of the château—was one of the few remaining of its kind in the area. The village spilled down from the remains of the château in a maze of steep narrow cobblestone lanes, stone walls, arches, and tightly packed residences built shoulder to shoulder. The lower edge of the village was marked by a commercial street of sorts, which forms the main traffic route through the town. Just above the lower road at the base of the village proper sits a fourteenth-century church that anchors the north end of the lower section.

Now owned in large part by a private American college and used as a sat-ellite campus, the village underwent significant changes in the first decade of the twenty-first century as the buildings owned by the school were systematically restored and preserved by the school's architectural restoration department, of which Lou was a part.

She explained that she'd been in the Maison Forte, studying a particular masonry feature similar to one that had been discovered in partial ruin at Maison Basse, and had been caught up in the work, unaware of how late it had become. As she recounted her tale of exiting the building, encountering the group of men on the terrace, and then sneaking in silent fear down the stairs to avoid detection, all the men in the room stiffened.

"The only reason I discovered Alex was because I had stopped to get myself under control. I was shaking badly, trying to be as quiet as possible so those creeps wouldn't see me."

"Why were you so afraid of them, *mademoiselle?* Had you encountered them in the village before?" The captain watched her closely as Alex translated his question.

Irritation sparked in her blue eyes as she turned from Alex to her questioner. "I've seen them around the village."

"Have they approached you? Harassed you?"

She gave him an incredulous look that quickly turned to anger. "I'm plenty good at fending off unwanted advances, *capitaine*"—she stressed his title—"without making enemies. But I'm not stupid."

As Alex translated her answer, enjoying the sound of her thickening accent, he was puzzled by her reaction. The questions seemed reasonable in the circumstances.

"I haven't spent much time in France outside of Lacoste, but it seems to me it has more than its fair share of creeps lurking around in the dark. And have you forgotten that Lacoste is notorious for losing women? You might consider trying to figure out why."

The *gendarmes* exchanged glances as Alex translated her final remarks. Alex himself was aware of the accuracy of her observation about the creeps in town but was unsure about the second part of her comment. He elected to keep his mouth shut; he needed to speak with her privately to understand what she knew—it was plain she'd seen more than she was letting on. And her involvement with the Maison Basse was fortuitous. He needed to understand what was going on there, too.

He glanced briefly at Kaden and sighed. Alex sometimes swore his cousin could read his mind, and by the set of his jaw, he could tell Kaden wasn't fooled. But Alex didn't want him involved in the mess he'd gotten himself into. He steeled himself for the coming confrontation.

The odd tension in the room was broken when the nurse stormed back in. The captain handed Alex a card with instructions to contact him if he remembered anything else, and the two officers left. The nurse tried to get Lou and Kaden to leave as well, but Kaden outmaneuvered her again. She huffed and stomped around, but in the end, her only recourse was to dose Alex with his pain medication and hope that he fell into the sleep that he needed.

After the nurse left, Lou wanted to get out of there as well. In truth, she didn't know Alex at all beyond what she had learned in the last thirty minutes, and she was afraid she may have said too much. It appeared that his cousin intended to stay with him, and she didn't want to inspire any more questions. On top of that, she felt flustered, and that wasn't like her. She hoped it was just the natural female reaction to being in such close proximately to a beautiful man—one who looked at her as if he could see inside her soul. She rose from her chair, willing calm into her voice.

"I've gotta go, Alex. You need rest, and there's nothing more I can do. I'm glad you're okay. Maybe I'll see you when y'all get back to Lacoste."

Alex couldn't think of one rational thing to say that would keep her there, even though he hated to see her leave. "Thank you," he said simply. "You were brave to help me. Most people wouldn't have bothered. I don't know when I'll be back in Lacoste." He glanced at Kaden. "But I hope to see you soon."

His words pleased her. In her experience, most men wouldn't have thought beyond themselves. Before she could do or say something she might regret, she forced herself to leave. *"Au revoir, Alex. À bientôt."* With a nod to Kaden, she was gone.

Three

Kaden studied his young cousin, whom he loved like a son. His eyes were closed, but Kaden wasn't fooled. The pain meds would kick in soon, but he knew Alex was still awake.

Even though they were technically cousins—the boy's father was Kaden's first cousin and best friend—Alex had called him Uncle Kaden his whole life and they were close. Much closer than Alex was to his own father. Kaden understood Alex's rebellious nature and the bitter resentment it had stemmed from, and he forgave his transgressions without judgment. The time that Alex had spent in America seemed to have settled him down, before it ended so badly. Alex's work visa had expired six months after he'd lost his job, and he'd been forced to head back home. He'd stayed for a while in London with his college friend Jonathan Spencer, and Kaden had expected to hear he'd found a position there. But then he'd asked to come to Rasteau and use Kaden's estate there as a home base while he sorted out what he wanted to do next.

As he watched his cousin feign sleep, Kaden wondered if Alex had somehow involved himself in one of Spencer's investigations. Despite their separation after graduation, the young men had remained close. The two European nationals—Alex from France and Spencer from the UK—had attended university together in America. They met in the international business program their junior year and bonded over their shared continental roots. Spencer returned to London to follow in his father's footsteps by joining INTERPOL, while Alex remained in San Francisco.

"Why are you still here?"

Kaden smiled at the irritation in Alex's voice. "You think I believe the story you gave the *gendarmes?*"

"You heard Louise—there's a gang of thugs staking a patch in Lacoste." Alex kept his eyes closed, hoping to hide the truth.

"Alex, how tall are you? How much do you weigh?"

Alex opened his eyes and regarded his cousin, knew the game was up by the look on his face. At just over six feet, Alex had a build like most of the men in the family—broad shoulders with plenty of muscle on an otherwise lean frame. Not exactly an easy target for a random mugging. He sighed and hoped a piece of the full story would be enough.

"I joined a local poker game yesterday and won. There was a big mean bastard at the table who I should have stayed away from. Lou is right about the gang in the village. I'm pretty sure they're led by this guy, Etienne Matisse. He accused me of cheating in a crowded bar, no doubt to justify taking his winnings back. My conveniently recovered wallet still has all my credit cards and IDs. I think it's obvious who jumped me. But telling that to the *gendarmes* would only make it worse for me."

"And you were tempted to take him on why, exactly? Surely there are other games in the area that don't risk getting your neck broken."

Alex shrugged, avoiding his cousin's eyes. "I'd heard it was the best game around."

Kaden watched his cousin's reaction closely as he asked, "Did Spencer suggest you take that risk?"

The drugs must have been taking effect because Alex couldn't hide his alarm. Kaden closed his eyes and shook his head. "Bloody hell, Alex, what are you involved in? And don't bullshit me. This is bigger than a village poker game."

Alex sighed. "The game was my idea. I couldn't help myself—he really is the best player around. And it was the only way I could think of to get close to him. Spencer just wanted me to sniff around him." He glanced up at the door. If he was going to have this conversation, it needed to be private. Following his look, Kaden went to the door. He opened it wider and checked up and down the hall before closing it all the way.

When Kaden resumed his seat, Alex looked at him apologetically. "I didn't want to get you involved in this. I'm not even sure what 'this' is. Spence has some suspicions, well-considered suspicions, but nothing concrete."

"Let's hear it."

There was a moment's pause. "Spence says Matisse is involved in counterfeiting wine and transporting it out of the EU. There may be some outright theft of wine, too, but the majority of it is counterfeit labels from top houses. He thinks Matisse is a conduit for the fakes, and possibly the originator of the labels, and he asked me to see if I could identify any connection to the photo lab in Lacoste."

Kaden felt a measure of relief as he nodded thoughtfully. He had feared something far worse, but this he understood. His family had been in the wine business for generations, and he himself owned a small wine estate in Rasteau. The wines there were often compared to the high profile, much pricier wines of nearby Châteauneuf du Pape, and he suspected some in his village were not completely innocent in providing finished wine for mislabeling schemes. As serious as it was, people didn't generally get killed moving fake wine.

"Who else is involved in Lacoste? Spencer can't be so reckless as to send you in by yourself."

"Right now they've got a team in Lyon looking at fakes confiscated in raids and seizures over the last six months, analyzing everything from ink and paper and glue to dirt smudges on the bottles, trying to find some common thread. At this point, there is no official investigation in Lacoste, but Spencer says that can change if there's evidence."

Kaden looked skeptical. "This is something he knows or something he thinks he knows?"

"Spence is convinced that Matisse is involved, in the very least with the label production. Last fall INTERPOL busted a print shop in Bordeaux with stacks of counterfeit labels for several of the Premier Grand Cru châteaux, plus a couple of the big-name houses on the Right Bank. Matisse was circumstantially connected to the guy running that shop but nothing that could be proved beyond a legitimate business relationship."

"And there was a problem with that?"

Alex snorted. "Matisse was living with an aunt who farms a few hectares of vines in the Entres-Deux-Mers and the shop was printing her labels. Not too long after that operation was taken out, Matisse showed up here in the Luberon."

"So he's new to the area?"

"Yes and no. He's originally from here, but he's been away for a long time. His mother passed away some years ago, leaving him the family farm. As soon as the bust closed the Bordeaux print shop, he apparently decided it was time to come back home."

"Convenient. And a perfectly legitimate reason for him to return to the area."

"*Oui, oui, je sais.* This is why there's no investigation yet. Spence is checking on any other legitimate businesses besides the farm. Meanwhile, Matisse spends a lot of time at a crusty bar at the bottom of the village. That's where I played cards with him." Alex reached over and brought a cup of water to his lips, taking a small sip.

"It could mean nothing," he continued, "but last month a random customs inspection intercepted a shipment of empty bottles leaving Marseille, bound for Beijing. There was some problem with the manifest, apparently, which is what alerted the inspectors. The boxes contained Châteauneuf embossed bottles with Beaucastel labels dating back to the eighties. The bottles and labels were in pristine condition. They're being tested for authenticity now in Lyon."

Kaden whistled at that. "The *domaine* would never ship empty labeled bottles—no one would."

"The inspectors were smart enough to realize that and seized the shipment."

"Nice scam for someone, though. Fill the bottles with plonk for pennies, probably from one of those floating operations I've heard about, then sell them in upscale restaurants for hundreds of dollars each. It's all about the prestige of the label in China, not what's actually in the bottle."

Alex nodded. "The family is cooperating. Whatever paperwork was involved was faked, too. Unfortunately, there's nothing that ties back to Matisse or anyone in Lacoste. Just some circumstantial intel placing him near the Marseille docks. And therefore no authority to free up field agents at this point."

"What about the shipping agents?" Kaden asked the question but knew from experience that some agents looked the other way as long as the paperwork was in order and the fees were paid. It's what made smuggling such an easy crime to perpetrate.

"Dead end, according to Spence. The documents were in order, except for whatever irregularity on the manifest made them look twice. The fact they were forged doesn't make the agent liable."

"So you volunteered?" Kaden asked, steering them back to the real issue.

Alex looked his cousin straight in the eye, determination showing through the bruises. "Something like that." He paused, but his cousin remained silent. "Even if they had the manpower, it would be difficult to blend in here. It's too small of a village. My cover is perfect because it's legitimate. I'm enrolled in classes here, and I'm serious about photography." If Alex expected his cousin to protest that revelation, he was disappointed. Kaden simply nodded.

"Spence knew I was coming to see you, and he knew about my interest in the school here. He suggested I could make myself useful. So far, Matisse seems to have men in the village running errands for him but no legitimate business besides the farm, and he spends a lot of time playing poker. I have no idea what he does at night or where he goes, though."

"If this Matisse has you attacked for beating him at cards, what do you think he might do if he catches on that you're investigating him?"

"He won't catch on. I'm being very careful, and I suspect everyone."

The drugs were starting to take effect as Alex's last words were a bit slurred. Kaden didn't like the situation but elected to reserve judgment for now. "Get some rest," he said, leaving the topic. "I'll see if I can wrestle with your nurse to release you today."

Alex gave him a grateful nod as his eyes drooped. "Kaden …"

"Annie insisted you come back to stay at the house, at least for the short term. I have no intention of telling her what you're up to, but good luck keeping it from her." Kaden smiled at the thought of his perceptive and tenacious wife. "I'll head to Lacoste now and sort things out for you with the school. Do you need anything from your dorm room?"

As Alex sunk into oblivion after his cousin left, his last thought was of Annie. She was the only person who could read him better than Kaden, and no one had a bullshit meter as sensitive as hers. *Merde.*

Four

"This city stinks like last week's fish."

Philippe Lemans looked out the grimy window of his third-floor office to the vast shipyards of Marseille. He disliked the place, too, but that was irrelevant. "Perhaps you should have stayed in Bordeaux." Philippe despised weakness of any sort, and this worthless cretin, Jacques, was a study in it.

"But you pulled out! What was I to do?" The statement ended on a whine.

Philippe ignored the question more successfully than he could the stench of the man's body odor. *It's not the city that stinks,* he thought as he turned toward Jacques with a blank expression. "What do you hear from Matisse?"

Anxious to please, Jacques took a tentative step forward. "He says he has half a load already. He claims he'll have it completed in two weeks."

"So soon?"

"I didn't believe it myself, Monsieur Lemans, but this is what he said." Philippe was silent, so Jacques continued. "I don't know why you use him for this. He's slow and stupid, and I think he is lying."

Philippe looked at him sharply. "Do not make the mistake of underestimating Matisse." He pulled out his phone, his thoughts having already moved on. "That will be all, Jacques."

The man stood there a moment until his boss gave him a pointed look with a nod to the door. He scurried out like the rodent he resembled.

Philippe shuddered in disgust. *I've got to cut that sniveling idiot loose,* he thought. *This business with fakes is more hassle than it is worth.*

"If only I could trust Matisse," Philippe said out loud. "Why does the man allow others to think him dimwitted?" Matisse had been loyal when tested, and that's probably what bothered him the most. If anyone had reason to hate Philippe, Matisse certainly did. It could be simple laziness, but somehow that didn't fit.

Shaking his head at the mystery, he focused on his more immediate problem. He scrolled though the emails on his BlackBerry, cursing when he didn't see the one he was anxious for. He checked texts, too, but nothing there either. *Damn!*

He had excellent merchandise ready, and his usual buyer was ready to receive it. The timing of the thwarted bottle shipment had everyone spooked, but his primary trade route had not been disrupted. It was an inconvenience and nothing more, an irritant. Another reason to stop wasting time with that wine nonsense.

But now his agent in Beijing wasn't responding to him. The last message he'd received was that the buyer for the fakes was creating some local noise, demanded a refund of the deposit, against the explicit terms of the contract. Ying said he was working on damage control, but things in China were tricky. Things in China were *always* tricky. And the rules seemed to change regularly. Philippe was impatient, but his father had cautioned him to let the noise die down before he activated the next delivery, so he would wait.

With the near miss in Bordeaux—a shipment also headed for Beijing—and now this, Philippe's instincts were on alert. He considered that he may have a bigger problem than just bad luck. He'd been hoping to bring Ying into the main attraction, but now he wasn't so sure. It was time to do some fact-checking the old-fashioned way. The internet was only so reliable. His instincts had never failed him before.

Five

"Put him on the phone. *Merde, il est un idiot!*" Jean Claude Bouvier snarled into the phone.

"So you can beat him down a little more? Bloody hell, listen to yourself! Why do think he's here in the first place?" Kaden simply didn't understand his cousin on this.

"Someone has to knock some sense into him. You do nothing but coddle him."

Kaden struggled to keep his voice calm. "I talk to him like an adult, I listen to him, and I don't make assumptions. Perhaps if you gave him a little encouragement instead of criticizing everything he does, he'd actually *want* to tell you what happened."

"He's wasting his life. He should be well into a career now instead of playing with a fucking camera. What a joke, pissing away the afternoon playing cards. When I was his age—"

"When you were his age, you were shagging the chef's daughter in the walk-in. You'd have been lucky to escape with just a cracked limb if you'd been caught. Don't be such a self-righteous prick. And don't crucify the boy just because he hasn't found his calling yet."

"Mistakes along the way can be forgiven, but having no direction at all is unacceptable."

Kaden took a deep breath. Jean Claude was his best friend, but they flat-out disagreed where Alex was concerned. "You're losing him, you know. The more you push, the farther away he goes. He'd still be America if it were his choice."

"Yes, and it was his choice, wasn't it, and he fucked that up, too!"

"Perhaps that was a call for help."

"Well you certainly answered it."

Kaden heard the defensive tone in Jean Claude's voice. "Only because you wouldn't," he said quietly.

Alex sipped his wine and watched the sun go down over the vineyards from a chaise on the upstairs balcony of his cousin's house, the magazine in his lap forgotten as he soaked in the sight. Harvest was in full swing, but at this hour the fields were quiet. The heat absorbed by the fieldstones during the day was rising now, causing the last slanting rays of sun to waver, softening the landscape so that it resembled an impressionist painting. The air was warm and still, the rhythmic song of the *cigales* pulsed all around him, and Alex felt a peace in his soul the likes of which he could only ever remember feeling here in this place.

The sound of footsteps alerted him to company a moment before Annie Shaw Macallister emerged from the open door behind him. She laid a hand on his shoulder and leaned over to plant a soft kiss at his temple.

"It's beautiful, isn't it? I remember the first time I saw this view, I felt like I'd come home." She refilled his glass from the bottle she carried and then poured one for herself before stretching out in the chaise next to him. "I've been here more than twenty years, and I still feel the peace wash over me on nights like this."

"I've always felt it here," Alex said.

They were silent for a few minutes as the sun slipped below the horizon. "You can stay as long as you want, you know."

He nodded, not trusting his voice. Despite all the other doubts that rattled around in his brain, this he did know: her statement was unrelated to his convalescence. Annie and Kaden were so different from his own parents. With their unconditional love and acceptance, they gave him hope that he could someday find his own way. As bad as it got, they never gave up on him. They were not judgmental with their advice, only encouraging, and that motivated him to avoid disappointing them further. His father, on the other hand … well, there was a reason he was in Provence.

"Why do you do it, Annie?"

She shrugged, comprehending the question without looking at him. "We love you for who you are, Alex."

He sipped his wine and thought about that. "You know, I can't remember you ever not being in my life, but I remember so clearly my six-year-old self seeing you for the first time."

Annie laughed. "I'm not sure that makes much sense."

He grinned at her. "I remember thinking that you were pretty and Uncle Kaden looked like he wanted to kiss you."

"Nothing new there," came a deep voice from behind them. To prove his point, Kaden knelt beside Annie's chaise and gave her a loudly exaggerated smooch, then started tickling her. Annie screeched and batted him away. Grinning, Kaden turned to Alex. "And she's still the prettiest girl I know."

Alex couldn't help but laugh at their antics as Kaden lifted his squawking bride of twenty years off the chaise and plopped himself onto it, with Annie landing in his lap. He looked away as Annie snuggled up and kissed her husband on the cheek.

"All right, you two, try to keep it clean. There're kids around." His voice was light, but Alex felt a lump in his throat. What would it be like to have that kind of lasting love?

Engrossed in the document in front of her, Louise Marcel didn't notice the man limping toward her until his shadow fell over the page she was studying. Looking up, she didn't hide the startled look on her face. "Alex!" She scooted her chair back and stood to greet him, banging her knee on the table in the process and sending her papers flying in his direction. "Shoot!"

She stepped around the table, flustered, and bent to gather the scattered notes, but Alex gently took hold of her arm and pulled her up before she made it halfway down.

"*Bonjour, mademoiselle.*" With light dancing in his hazel-green eyes, he leaned in and kissed the air beside both her cheeks in that standard French greeting of friendly affection. "*Permettez-moi.*" He then bent down with surprising grace, given the clunky canvas boot on his right foot, and swiftly gathered the pages, glancing at them as he handed them over with a friendly smile.

"I hope I'm not disturbing you. I was coming in for a coffee and saw you occupying my favorite table." The café was nothing special, but the view was spectacular. Perched on the outer edge of the main road through Lacoste, the covered terrace offered a sweeping panorama of the valley below, the hilltop village of Bonnieux on the other side about six kilometers to the east, and the mountain range beyond. The tables along the ledge were almost always full with students, faculty, or tourists.

Lou let her fatigue show. "No, actually, you're a welcome distraction. I need a break from these crazy documents. It's bad enough struggling with French, but trying to decipher *old* French from handwritten documents is enough to make me insane." She shook her head with an exasperated sigh. "You'd think someone would have transcribed these by now. Please." She waived to the chair opposite. "How's the ankle?" She looked him over carefully, remembering the nasty bruises and the cuts and scrapes, and saw they were barely noticeable now. "The rest of you looks pretty darn good, considering."

Alex sank into the chair opposite her. "Better, after a week of mothering—more like smothering—from my cousin Annie. She wouldn't let me off my *derriere*. I finally escaped this morning." His fond expression as he voiced the complaint belied the words.

"It's nice you have family so close."

The server arrived and Alex ordered a coffee. Lou asked for another Coke Light. "*Avec de la glace, s'il vous plaît,*" she added, giving Alex a guilty look. "Some pleasures are hard to give up. Ice-cold Coke is practically comfort food where I come from."

Alex was delighted anew with her soft accent. "I never understood America's obsession with putting ice in everything. It must be a challenge for you here."

"You have no idea."

Their drinks arrived a moment later, a demitasse of espresso for Alex and a semi-chilled bottle of soda for Lou accompanied by a glass with two small ice cubes in it. Alex busied himself with stirring sugar into his coffee while Lou poured her soda over the ice, watching it melt into nothing. Sighing, she took a sip, eyeing him over the glass. She noticed his thick leather cuff, seeing now that it was actually a watchband, and remembered how blood from his cuts had seeped down under it.

"I see you managed to clean up your watchband," she said, nodding toward his wrist. "It's an unusual piece." She leaned in for a closer look at the intricate tooling on it, and he held out his arm to give her a better view.

"A souvenir from my time at university. The free spirits who make their living selling handcrafted trinkets to tourists in Berkeley used to fascinate me. I confess I spent as much time sitting in the street listening to reggae as studying."

Louise lifted her eyebrows at that.

"An essential part of college life. Along with the marijuana, of course."

"Not exactly conducive to studying," she observed.

"I managed." He finished off his coffee and set the small cup back on the saucer. "What brought you to Lacoste? Have you been here long?"

She stifled her automatic wariness, not wishing to appear rude. It was the middle of the day in a crowded café, and she'd met a member his family. She forced herself to relax, knew instinctively she was safe with Alex. "I'm here for the restoration of the Maison Basse." She nodded toward the sprawling complex of old buildings in the valley below. "I've been here for a few months."

"Are you here alone?"

It was an innocent question, but it sent her heart racing. *Oh, God, is this how it started?* She looked down into her glass for a minute, trying to settle her jitters, and forced her thoughts away from her sister. His beautiful eyes were so direct and open, he made her nervous, but she forced herself to meet them. She saw no calculation there, just friendly interest, yet still, she purposely misinterpreted his question. "Actually there are two of us here from my home university."

"No, I meant—"

"How about you?" She hoped her voice sounded steadier than it felt. "What brings you here?"

Alex held her gaze, tamping down his curiosity in the face of her overt deflection. Had he spooked her? The last thing he wanted was to scare her away. "I've been here since the middle of August, when the fall session started. I've always enjoyed photography and thought I'd see if I could make a go of it professionally. My expensive American education didn't have the desired effect."

"Oh?"

"Uh-huh," he confirmed. She stared at him, clearly expecting more. Alex only shrugged, ignoring the unspoken questions he could see in her eyes, grateful she gave him back the same respect and didn't push. He was done explaining and apologizing for his failures. "Chasing the American dream didn't work out for me. Living there was nice, but I missed home." He looked out across the valley and vaguely gestured. "I missed this."

There was much more to that story, and she was curious, but prying went both ways. Instead, she nodded, understanding the attraction to this place. This rural lifestyle, where the twenty-first century existed so seamlessly alongside the past, was going to be hard to give up. Especially since the thought of going home was so unappealing.

The silence between them was easy. Once she got over her initial jolt of fear from his question, she found herself relaxing with him. *Not everyone is a monster.* But still, she didn't want to encourage any questions about her past. Then she remembered something that had been nagging at her since the interview with the police in the hospital room. "There was nothing random about your attack, was there?"

That caught Alex off guard. "Why would you think otherwise?" His tone was cautious, but his expression made Lou think she'd been right.

"This is a small village of working-class people and college students. Tourists are long gone after the sun goes down. Why bother with a random mugging when the likelihood of netting more than a few euros is so … unlikely."

He shrugged. "Who can guess what goes on in the minds of desperate people?"

Lou regarded him steadily. She understood if he didn't want to talk about it, but she preferred him to say so rather than shutting her down so transparently. Not that she hadn't just done the same to him. "Whatever," she mumbled under her breath, taking a gulp of her soda.

Alex didn't care for her sarcastic dismissal, and he frowned. Hell, there were enough people in that bar to figure out what happened, it wasn't like he was letting out any great secret. "You're obviously more astute than the *gendarmes.*"

"So what happened?"

He didn't miss the tiny flash of satisfaction in her eyes. "There was a poker game at the bar that day, and I did quite well. I'm pretty sure that someone decided to relieve me of my winnings."

"Ah."

"Shit happens, as they say in America. I'll know better next time."

"Hopefully you'll know enough to avoid the next time."

"Hopefully." Alex toyed with the empty sugar packet in front of him. A subject change was needed, preferably to something that felt safe for both of them. "Tell me about your project. I've been down there for photo shoots, but I don't know anything about it." Besides just enjoying the sound of her voice, he truly did have an interest in the Maison Basse. A week ago, he'd seen Matisse there with another man and had thought it could be important.

Lou smiled widely and flashed perfect, white teeth. "It's a great property, isn't it? I fell in love with it long before I actually set eyes on it."

Enfin, Alex thought. Her entire face lit up at just the mention of the place, her lovely blue eyes glowing with excitement.

"It's owned by the school, but of course you know that. It'll be converted to student housing."

"Won't that diminish the historical importance of the place?"

"Not at all." She shook her head emphatically. "It's the best way to preserve it. In fact, we think that's how the property has survived this long—whoever owned it at any given time through the centuries modifying it to suit his needs, and so kept it from being completely abandoned and … demolished.

It's had a long and interesting life as a result. Have you been inside any of the buildings?"

"No, just the courtyard."

"Well, it's a hodgepodge of eras inside, that's for sure." She wrinkled her nose. "Some of it's just plain awful. It's been added on to and reconfigured on a regular basis for the last four hundred years at least."

She'd become animated, and Alex was enchanted, watching her face rather than listening to her words. He had to struggle to respond to what she'd just said. "But it was obviously a farmhouse at one time. Why not just bring it back to its original function?"

She gave him a don't-be-an-idiot look. "What would be the point in that? The school's got no use for a farmhouse. What they need is student housing. The exterior of the structure will be preserved as you see it today." She shrugged. "For the most part."

He appeared surprised by her answer.

"Look," she said patiently. "It's true that the property was most likely used as a family home at one time, probably by someone connected to the château here." She waived vaguely to the village behind them. "But by the seventeenth century, it had already been added on to in several sections, and we know it was being used as stables for the château. In the eighteenth century, it morphed into an inn, then an inn and gambling house, and there is evidence that was also a brothel at one point in time."

"*Vraiment?*" Alex had had no idea and was fascinated by her recitation.

"*Oui, vraiment.*" Her eyes sparkled. "It's actually pretty amazing that it's still standing at all, which is why it's so awesome to get involved in the restoration of it."

"What's so amazing about it?"

"The fact that there is absolutely nothing special about it." She enjoyed his bewildered look before continuing. "Typically, only the grand, important buildings were considered worthy of preserving. Structures like the *maison* were simply abandoned, and eventually they fell down or were taken apart, scavenged for building material. That's the beauty and value of Maison Basse.

27

It tells a story of the common man's everyday life over the span of centuries, not just the life of the nobility."

"I had no idea, but it makes sense," he said. "So what exactly is your role?"

"I'm helping to piece together and document the history of the property, and the physical structures themselves, to preserve what we know today." She paused for a moment. "It's unavoidable that the interior will change in order for the property to morph into its next role, and certain architectural elements will be lost or hidden. We recognize that and don't want to lose what history can be found there now, before we do anything more to change it."

Alex waived toward the stack of documents that he'd retrieved from the floor when he first walked in. "So this is part of the history?"

"Some of it. These are copies, of course, not the originals. Most of this stuff is just routine correspondence, receipts, bills of sale, that sort of thing. But clues can be found from notations in the most innocuous documents."

"May I?" He reached to pick up the stack.

"Sure, knock yourself out."

Alex smiled inwardly at the American expression as he looked at the first document, a copy of a faded handwritten page. He studied it for a moment then frowned, looking up at her. "I can't read it," he said with surprise.

"You're not originally from this part of France," she said, a little smugly.

"No, I'm from the southwest, near Bordeaux." He looked at her for a moment before understanding dawned. "Ah," he said and looked down at the document again. "Of course. It's written in the local patois."

"Now that you know what you're looking at, you should be able to make out most of it. The patois of your area is Gascon, right?"

He nodded, continuing to study the page.

"It's a major sub-dialect of the Occitan language, same as the local patois here, Provençal."

"How old are the original documents? I thought all records were supposed to be written in French after the revolution."

"Some date back as far as the early eighteenth century, but remember, we're a long way from Paris. It took awhile for that edict to make its way out into what was—still is—a very rural part of the country. And these"—she waived at the papers in his hands—"are not official documents, simply letters and receipts and such."

He was impressed and fascinated, but … "How is it that you lack confidence in speaking French, yet you can read these?"

"These documents aren't firing it at me at the speed of light," she said.

He chuckled at that, and she smiled, feeling her guard drop just a bit. "Seriously, though, I've been working on stuff like this for a while, and I recognize most of the words. In some respects this is closer to Latin than modern French. I have to take my time with it, of course. The biggest challenge is making out what the actual word is in the old handwriting, not translating it."

"So do you just study the documents, or do you work down there, too? I'd love to see the inside before it's renovated."

Six

Ellie tried not to flinch as the old woman slid a needle into the abused vein in her arm. Her back ached, she was bloated and hungry, but she knew better than to complain. Thankfully, this ordeal would soon be over and she'd be set free, if the bastard's promises were to be believed. At least this nurse was kind, unlike others she'd encountered, and she kept that creepy dark-haired guy who'd brought her here away. And she'd thought he was helping her! Christ, what a mess. She shivered at the burn rising in her vein as she welcomed the oblivion that descended down upon her.

Etienne Matisse reined in his impatience while he listened to the whining through the telephone connection. *Imbécile.* After another minute, he interrupted. "I don't care what you think you saw—it's too dangerous. When I have something, I will contact you. Until then, do as he says." Ignoring the sputtering protest from the other end, Matisse hung up.

"*Merde,*" he said to the empty room, thankful the *mec* didn't know his name. The cell phone was a prepaid unit, a useful throwaway, but now compromised thanks to the unschooled action of this amateur. Shoving it in his pocket, he made a mental note to follow up on the man's comments. If only to keep him out of the way.

The article he'd been reading on his laptop recaptured his attention, the technology it discussed fascinating to someone in his line of work. The use of spectrophotometry, the article prosed, had proved successful in identifying fraudulent wine without opening the bottle. As he reached for the now-cool bowl of soup he'd been eating before the interruption, a series of low beeps sounded from the direction of his television set.

He immediately activated an open program on the laptop that would erase any trace of his latest internet browsing before deactivating and hiding itself on his hard drive. Next he clicked on the poker game that he'd started earlier and watched as it opened across his screen. Exactly sixty seconds after the warning signal had been set off by the motion detectors hidden at the rear gate of his property, he heard a perfunctory knock as his back door opened. A distinguished-looking middle-aged man stepped into his kitchen.

"*Bonsoir, mon petit frère,*" Philippe Lemans's wide smile held the warmth of a shark. The endearment was as ridiculous as its sincerity was false, for although Philippe was twenty years his senior, Matisse was much taller and significantly outweighed him.

Matisse nodded, carefully arranging his features to present the appropriate amount of surprise. "Philippe."

Philippe stared at him for a moment before walking farther into the room to stand behind Matisse's chair, looking over his shoulder. He saw the poker game and scoffed. "If you spent half as much time working as you do playing games, you might actually amount to something." He turned, opened the refrigerator, and helped himself to a beer.

Matisse didn't react to the jibe, but said, "I get my work done. What are you doing here? I told Jacques I would have something for him in a couple of weeks."

"You don't sound happy to see me, brother." Philippe laughed cruelly. "I'll get my feelings hurt if you're not careful."

Matisse did not rise to the bait but sat there, waiting for Philippe to get to the point. He always did, once he finished with the insults.

Philippe sauntered into the adjacent room and sank into a large comfortable chair facing the television. "Jacques did tell me you would have a full shipment soon. I find it curious that you are so successful with collection while others seem to take much longer."

"There are still plenty of tourists in the area," Matisse replied evenly. "And I have a wide network of hungry students who know where to find what we want. They like the money."

Philippe took a long pull on his beer without further comment. Matisse rose from the kitchen table and took his bowl to the sink. He washed it then picked up the empty pot from the stove and washed that, too. Behind him, Philippe stood and returned to the kitchen. Matisse reached for the towel hanging above the sink and carefully dried the dishes, deliberately keeping his back to his stepbrother. When he had finished the cleanup, he turned around. Philippe had the browser up on the laptop, making no secret of checking the search history.

Matisse put his hands on his hips and let his irritation show. "What do you think you're doing?"

Philippe kept on for a moment, hoping to provoke a stronger reaction. When he didn't get one, he sighed and stood up. "I don't understand you, Etienne. Juliette was a smart woman. I didn't know your father, but I doubt he was simple in the head. Why are you content to be a low-level thief when you could be so much more?"

Matisse clenched his fists and struggled to contain the flash of pure hatred that spiked in his gut. How casually the monster in his kitchen talked of his mother, as if he had been fond of her. *Bâtard.* With a supreme effort, he kept his voice low and calm. "God did not see fit to grant me a handsome face like yours, Philippe." There was an understatement. Matisse had long since resigned himself to his own appearance, and he used it to serve his purpose as needed. "It's easier to take jobs where my face and size are assets and stay away from situations where I have to pretend to be nice."

When Philippe rolled his eyes, Matisse stepped closer to him, towering over the smaller man and narrowing his eyes. "You pay me for a job, and I do it well. What is it to you beyond that?"

A fair point, Philippe conceded to himself. There was no pretense of affection between them. Philippe had pushed Matisse's mother to an early grave and stolen a good part of his inheritance, yet his stepbrother seemed to accept their arrangement. Philippe had some small doubt in the back of his mind that Juliette had kept her promise of silence, but everything suggested that she had. Perhaps there was no more to Matisse's attitude than just a resigned acceptance. As a boy, Matisse had been painfully shy, and despite his size, had made a point to avoid conflict whenever possible.

Matisse thought this odd conversation might be the beginning of the trust he had been trying to develop, and he relaxed slightly. He nodded to his laptop, confessing what he suspected his stepbrother already knew. "I play online with low stakes. I win more than I lose, and in this way, I can supplement my income without having to be out in public. It's not much, but it's steady. Same with what you pay me. With the income from this property, it's enough." He paused. "My father was a simple man, as am I. I don't need luxuries. I do not have ambitions beyond my current comforts."

Philippe studied the poker face before him. "I could use a trustworthy, cautious man in my organization, Etienne. One who is discreet, does not overreact, and can think on his feet."

Matisse said nothing, just kept his eyes slightly downcast.

"I would like that man to be you."

The surprise in Etienne's expression was genuine as he searched Philippe's face for deceit, finding none.

"Think about it, little brother." Philippe stood. "But know this: there is more to my enterprise than peddling fake wine. It will require you to get dirt on your hands. Much more than you have now, but it will be worth it."

Philippe tossed his empty bottle into the trashcan and walked out without a glance back.

About that same time, Jonathan Spencer was lounging in his cubicle in London, headphones plugged into a video conference on the current wine fraud investigation. As an analyst, he didn't have anything to contribute; his role was to take in all the pieces of data and try to find a pattern in the noise. He could only hope that when he did, someone would take it seriously.

He longed to be in the field, regardless of its often tedious and boring nature, because he knew in his bones that he'd be good at it. He was only half listening to the call, as the reports were mostly repeats of what he'd heard previously. Government bureaucracy seldom changed. *Blah, blah, blah,* he was mimicking to himself, hoping he'd make it home before the end of the Manchester match, when the mention of Lacoste caught his attention.

"… picked up the decoys last week."

"Where are they now?" Spencer recognized the voice of the agent in charge, Commander Simon Purcell.

"We haven't activated the chip yet, sir. It has a sixteen-hour battery, and our source tells us the next shipment isn't expected to hit the launch point for another couple of weeks. We need intel in order to time it right."

Spencer cursed his wandering mind. He couldn't ask them to repeat the report. Now he'd have to wait for the written version to be delivered to his inbox. *What the bloody hell are they talking about?* This was the first he'd heard about a tracking chip—he assumed that's what it was. *And who the bloody hell is in the field down there?*

He took a chance and asked a question, thinking they must be talking about the pickup that Alex had witnessed Matisse making. "Who set up the decoys?"

"I'll get the intel," Purcell said, either missing Spencer's question or choosing to ignore it. "Macmillan, what do you have on the Beaucastel labels?"

Agent Macmillan reported that the labels matched the graphic details of the actual labels the family had provided for analysis, including some hidden details. Although they didn't have a chemical report yet, the preliminary conclusion was that the labels were authentic. Despite efforts to keep them safeguarded, labels were often used for marketing purposes, souvenirs at tastings, etc., making it virtually impossible to pinpoint whether a roll of labels had been stolen or had simply been used for another purpose.

When the call ended, Spencer stared dumbly at his computer. Clearly, he did not have all the facts. There was someone in the Luberon who had set up tagged decoys. But who? Was it a trap for Matisse, or did it have some other purpose? And why wasn't he in the loop? He was the analyst on the case. Something wasn't adding up here.

As he shut down his terminal and grabbed his coat from the hook behind his chair, he thought about how best to caution Alex. He'd already gone out on a limb by involving his friend. He'd probably get fired—no, scratch that, he'd definitely get fired—if Purcell found out he'd confided any of this case to an outsider. But he'd done it with honorable intentions, he reminded himself. The discovery of the shipment of empties had made the news, so it wasn't like that was any secret. And he was sure Matisse was involved. He had argued with Purcell that someone was needed in Lacoste to watch Matisse, and Purcell had shut him down. *Because he already has someone in place. Someone who is deep and wants to stay that way.*

⸻

Alex waited in the open courtyard of the Maison Basse the next day, admiring the old stone walls, when he caught sight of Lou walking down the path from the village. It was a bright day in the Luberon, typical for early October, with fat puffy clouds floating like cotton candy in the cerulean sky above. The air was brisk with the steady breeze, but the sun warmed his skin. His ankle hurt like a son of a bitch, but he refused to take anything stronger than ibuprofen for the pain. Even after just one night and day of OxyContin at the hospital, he'd experienced that familiar feeling of his skin being stretched too tight over his body. He got past it quickly, thanks to Kaden getting him the hell out of there, but it had scared him.

He was looking forward to this excursion in spite of the warning he'd received last night. Spencer had been vague about details but direct in telling Alex that he needed to watch his back. "There's more than just Matisse to worry about now. There's someone else sniffing around, and I'm not sure how safe it will be if anyone figures out what you're doing. Watch and listen, but don't do anything to interfere. No heroics, Alex, no breaking and entering, and no spying through windows. I mean it. It's not worth it."

He had assured his friend he would be careful. But that didn't mean he wouldn't keep his date with Lou to explore the old buildings. The property had intrigued him before he'd caught sight of Matisse down here the week before. Even with the distance from the village terrace where he'd been standing, he'd recognized Matisse by his size and by the big black SUV he drove. There had been another man with him. Spencer had speculated that it might be a drop spot, and Alex wanted to check it out.

All thoughts of Matisse melted away when the slim form of Louise Marcel appeared in the ancient archway of the courtyard. Backlit by the afternoon sun, she appeared as an angelic vision. He watched as she hesitated, searching the yard for him, then felt a surge of satisfaction when she smiled and waved. Her cheeks were rosy from the walk, and her eyes were bright with excitement. He'd thought her pretty before, but now, glowing with the exertion of her walk and the flattering light of the autumn afternoon, he found her to be nothing short of beautiful.

Without thinking, he lifted his camera and snapped off a few shots of her as she moved toward him. Surprise and something close to panic transformed her features, and she stopped short. She quickly looked back over her shoulder like she wanted to dash back in the direction she had just come.

Alex held up his hand. "Sorry. I should have asked, but you were such a vision coming through the archway, with the sun behind you, I couldn't help it." Thinking perhaps she didn't want her face in a photo, he added, "With the backlighting your face won't be recognizable. The photo will be more abstract that real, especially if I process it in sepia."

She hesitated, her internal struggle showing in her expression, and in that moment, Alex knew that something had happened in her past that made her nervous now. Although she hid it well, there was a fragility that didn't mesh with the confident historian. She managed to shake off whatever it was that made her panic and came toward him.

"I hope I haven't kept you waiting." Professional and polite, as if she hadn't just had a small panic attack, it was the academician, not the alluring woman, who addressed him.

"Not at all—I've only been here a few minutes myself." He held up his camera. "Listen, I'm really sorry about that. I didn't realize you were camera shy."

She took a deep breath. "No problem, you just took me by surprise. Are you ready?" She held up a ring of keys and jiggled them.

"*Après vous, mademoiselle.*" Alex gave her a mocking bow and gestured toward the small door to his right.

Whatever momentary tension there had been between them seemed to evaporate as she walked the short distance to the door and worked a key into the padlock. After a bit of jiggling, she pulled the lock off and pushed open the door. She hooked the open lock back onto its ring, then mirroring his previous bow, she gestured to the shadowed interior. *"Après vous, monsieur."* He arched his brow and hobbled past her into the building.

With a promise that he would focus on the building and not Lou, Alex trailed behind as she gave him a tour of the property, stopping every few steps to take shots. The interior was empty except for piles of rubble, but it was interesting in its random design and multitude of textures. The afternoon light slanted in through the small irregular windows, creating shadows that enhanced the rough texture of walls, windowpanes, ledges, and stairways. Forgetting his main purpose for wanting to explore the old property, Alex let the echoing silence of the interior penetrate his senses. It was a perfect palette for an abstract photographer, with just enough muted light to push the images. The rooms he wandered through faded away as he focused only on the patterns in the stones, window bracings, fireplaces, and floors.

They had been inside for perhaps thirty minutes and were standing in the upstairs loft when they heard movement and muted voices below. Lou retraced their steps back down to the main floor to see who it was. Alex finished shooting the roof tiles through a small window before shuffling after her.

As he rounded the corner at the bottom of the uneven stone steps, Alex looked up and almost toppled forward, he stopped so abruptly. Lou was facing the entrance with her back to him, hands on hips and slim shoulders squared tensely in a posture of aggression, staring up at none other than Etienne Matisse.

Seven

It would have been comical if it didn't make Alex's heart race like he'd just sprinted a mile. Matisse towered over Louise by at least a foot, and his bulk completely blocked the doorway. Ridiculously, an image from *Beauty and the Beast* flashed in Alex's mind. Matisse looked up at him over Lou's head, and their eyes met. Dark, penetrating eyes narrowed in recognition, but he said nothing. For his part, Alex didn't move, just stared. *What the fuck? Que fait il ici?*

Matisse looked back down at Lou, who hadn't moved. He nodded once to her, then turned, and with surprising grace for a man of his size, ducked out through the open doorway and disappeared.

Alex let out the breath he didn't know he was holding. Lou spun around with wide eyes then relaxed when she recognized him, as if she'd forgotten about him. Anger flared within him, along with suspicion, as the pounding in his chest faded.

"What the hell was he doing here?"

"You know who he is?" Her calm question stoked his anger higher.

"Of course I do—he's the one who sent his goons after me."

"You played poker with Etienne Matisse?" Her incredulous tone confused him even more.

"How the hell do you know him? How do you even know who he is?"

Lou cocked an eyebrow. "Come on, let's go, it's almost dark anyway." She crossed over the threshold of the doorway and stepped aside to let him pass.

He didn't move. "What was he doing here?"

She shrugged, seemingly unconcerned. "How should I know? Come on, let's go." She motioned to the exit.

Alex was dumbfounded but followed her direction anyway. She pulled the door shut and reset the padlock, then turned and started toward the archway.

"Lou, wait! What the hell just happened here? What did you say to him?" Something wasn't making sense. Why was she so calm?

She spun around on her heels and put her fists on her hips again, skewering him with an exasperated glare. "I told him Maison Basse wasn't open to the public and that we were just about to close up. I told him he had to leave." She looked at him with irritated confusion. "What has got you so agitated? People show up here all the time wanting to poke around. It's no big deal. We just tell them it's private property."

It was plausible and made perfect sense, but something just seemed off to him. Matisse had a specific purpose for coming to the property, and damn it, he wanted to know what it was. Could Lou be covering for him? The fact that she seemed more irritated with Alex than frightened of Matisse was just … odd. Everyone he knew was afraid of Matisse. Hell, *he* was afraid of Matisse. He couldn't think of a worse nightmare than running into the man in a deserted building at nightfall. Yet Louise wasn't rattled at all.

Realizing she was still waiting for an answer, he shook his head. "I don't know. It just seems a strange time to decide to go poking around a deserted building." They looked at each other for a moment. "Didn't he scare you? Even a little? *Merde,* the man scares the crap out of me."

She continued to stare at him, her posture unchanged. Then she burst out laughing. "God, I guess you're right. I didn't even think about that. I just treated him like I would any other looky-loo. It never occurred to me that he would actually hurt me."

Back in his own kitchen a few kilometers away, Etienne Matisse cursed his carelessness. He hadn't seen any vehicles at the *maison* and had mistakenly assumed it was vacant when he arrived to meet his contact. He'd been about to unlock the door when the guy pushed it open, commenting loudly that it was already unlocked, and then walked in before Matisse could stop him.

Matisse had grabbed him and shoved him back out with a terse *"Allez!"* before the girl saw him.

Never a man of many words, Matisse kept his mouth shut and let her assume what she would. He had to struggle to suppress a smile at her polite but direct dismissal. He hadn't intimidated her at all. Her irritation as she shooed him away had made her pretty face flush attractively.

They'd crossed paths in the village more than once, and he remembered her, not only because she was a pretty American. Unlike everyone else he encountered, she actually looked him in the eye and had a friendly smile for him when they passed in the narrow streets. Matisse normally frightened people just by looking at them. He was as ugly as he was big, and to make it worse, he had a nasty scar running down the side of his face, but he couldn't help his looks. It suited his purpose—people usually left him alone. When he wanted something, fear made people jump to do his bidding.

Matisse briefly wondered what it would be like to have a friend like the pretty girl, someone who would look past the rough exterior to the man inside. He shook his head in disgust. *Ne pas se passe.*

Seeing Alex Bouvier had been another surprise. The kid looked like he'd come through his beating well enough. Matisse regretted that necessity, but he'd needed to cover his tracks for getting trounced at the card table and also to confirm that Alex was actually attending his classes and not just pretending to be a student. It was unlikely that Alex was connected to Philippe, but he knew Philippe had someone watching him and, at this stage in the game, he could not afford to trust anyone.

The kid was smart, though. No doubt about it. And if he was afraid of Matisse, he hid it well. He had showed more anger than fear at the *maison,* despite the fact—or perhaps because of it—that he had to know it was Matisse who had set him up. He just hoped Alex stayed out of his way. He had nothing against the kid personally; even though he'd played at being cocky, he'd shown intelligence and maturity during their game. If circumstances were different, it would have been interesting to see if they could have become friends.

Merde! All this useless musing about friendship was giving him heartburn. He poured himself some wine and powered up his laptop. No sense in wasting the entire evening—he had plenty to work on.

Eight

"I'm capable of driving myself, you know," Alex grumbled as his cousin pulled shut the car door and started the engine.

"Trust me, you don't want to go there with Annie."

To stall the inevitable questions about his own situation, Alex asked about the harvest.

"The last of the Grenache will be coming in next week. Yields are down from the dry spring, but so far the quality of the fruit is very good."

"How's Henri doing?" Kaden's nineteen-year-old son had been involved with the vineyards and the winery since childhood, but this season marked a significant increase in his responsibilities. He loved the land like his father and was shaping up to be an excellent steward for the next generation.

"Having the time of his life on four hours of sleep a night." Winemaking was not for lightweights. "He's got the confidence to make good decisions without being cocky." Clearly proud of his son, Kaden talked of the harvest and crush for most of the drive to Rasteau. Alex was content to listen and watch the beautiful land pass by.

"So tell me about the lovely Louise." Kaden's swift change of topic caught Alex off guard.

"*Quoi?*"

"Surely you've seen her since you've been back."

Alex's rueful laugh had Kaden glancing over at him. "*Oui,* I've seen her. In fact, yesterday afternoon she showed me around the interior of the Maison Basse."

"And?"

"And … you're right, she is lovely, and smart and interesting, but … I'm afraid she's immune to my charm."

Kaden grinned. "No worries, mate. Annie was rather unimpressed with me when we first met. I acted like a horse's arse, and she called me on it. I think I fell in love with her at that moment."

Alex appreciated the humor—he knew the story—but he didn't see it applying to him quite like that. "I'm not really sure what's up with her, to be honest. I don't think I've offended her, but her mood seems to run from warm to cool pretty quickly. And she's jumpy, like she's afraid of something. She's very good at sidestepping anything personal."

"Ah, yes, I can relate completely."

Both men laughed at the incomprehensible entity that was a woman's mind.

"Seriously though, I get the feeling she's hiding something."

"We're all hiding something to some degree or another. The pleasure of building a relationship with someone includes taking the time to discover their secrets." Kaden paused. "That is, if you actually want a relationship. You seemed pretty interested at the hospital, but then again, you were pumped up on meds. Speaking of which, how are you doing with that?"

Alex wasn't certain what he wanted with Louise, beyond a desire to know more about her. There was attraction and chemistry on both sides, although she tried hard to ignore it. He found her interesting, but he found her equally frustrating. She didn't behave like the women he usually flirted with. She wasn't easily charmed. Actually, what he'd told his cousin was true—she didn't seem to be charmed by him at all.

"*Je vais bien,*" he said, answering his cousin's specific question. "You got me out of there in time." He unconsciously rubbed at the scars beneath his watchband. "I had a pinch of withdrawal symptoms, but … they passed. *Vraiment.*"

To Alex's relief, Kaden left it at that. But as they approached the village of Rasteau, he realized they had only a few more minutes of private conversation. "Etienne Matisse showed up at the Maison Basse while we were there yesterday."

Kaden lifted his eyebrows in question but remained silent.

"It was odd. You should have seen Louise. The top of her head barely reaches his armpits, and he outweighs her two times over, but he didn't scare her one bit. In fact, it was a little suspicious. I didn't hear what she said to him, but whatever it was, he took one look at me and left."

"Suspicious, how?"

"I got the feeling they knew each other, that something was going on that neither wanted me to know about."

Kaden laughed at that. "I think you have an active imagination. How could they possibly know one another?"

"I know it sounds crazy …" By the time Alex filled him in on the details of their exchange after Matisse had left the property, Kaden pulled the car up to his house. Fifteen-year-old Marie came out to greet them, and that was the end of the conversation.

Philippe Lemans crossed his right leg over his left with the grace of an aristocrat as he studied the man across the table. The small room at the back of his Marseille warehouse had no ventilation, and he did his best not to wrinkle his nose in disgust. *Does no one bathe anymore?* Unfortunately for the Chinese national bound tightly to the hard metal chair, personal hygiene was the least of his worries.

"Ying, this is getting tiresome."

"Know nothing! Not me!" The desperate man was in full panic.

Philippe considered the possibility that Ying was actually telling the truth, but at this point, he couldn't back down. The die had already been cast. *Mon Dieu,* he thought. *When did this turn into such a cluster fuck?* He disliked Americans but enjoyed their crass phrases on occasion. At least the men he'd sent to China had had the presence of mind to grab more than just Ying. He pulled out his phone, scrolled through his contacts, then tapped the screen.

Ying Lo, his formerly trustworthy Chinese broker for the counterfeit wine he shipped into Beijing, was now whimpering in a pool of his own piss. *Merde!*

Philippe discretely covered his nose with his handkerchief and willed his men to hurry.

The door to the room opened, and two men hauled in a squirming, struggling young girl. Bound hand and foot, gagged, and blindfolded, she nonetheless fought her captors fiercely.

Ying looked up in horror as his fourteen-year-old daughter was dragged into the room. "*No!*" he screamed, violently rocking in his chair. He would have overturned it had the man behind him not grabbed his shoulders. "Know nothing! Please! Know nothing!"

Philippe winced when one of his men smacked the girl across the cheek.

"Enough!" He was not opposed to necessary violence, but he disliked blatant cruelty, especially to women. Oblivious to the hypocrisy of his thoughts on this, he reached up and yanked the gag down.

"Papa!" the girl cried, tears smearing her cheeks despite the blindfold. "Papa, what do they want? Please, Papa! Help me!"

Philippe watched in satisfaction as the man's visage changed. In a heartbeat, he went from terrorized victim to agonized father, his anguish and defeat reflected in his voice. "Please, I beg you, do not harm my daughter. I will tell what I know."

Relieved and pleased that his instincts about Ying had been correct, Philippe suffered a moment of largess. "She will be on the next plane back to Beijing once I am satisfied."

"I pray you will let me ... know she is safe."

It's only fair if I learn what I need, Philippe thought as he nodded. Besides, she had no value to him beyond getting the truth from Ying, since she was Chinese. The girl was removed from the room, still struggling, and her father revealed all he had sworn to secrecy.

Philippe, with his warped sense of honor, kept his word, sending the girl home on the next available flight from Marseille. As Ying watched the flight take off across the harbor, he pretended not to notice the man approach from behind before the man's hands cupped his jaw.

Nine

The driving rain sluiced across the windshield of Lou's tiny car, barely held at bay by the fast-paced thumping of the wipers. Gusts of wind rocked the miniature vehicle as she drove as fast as she dared toward the Pont Julien. *Christ in a bucket!* She couldn't see two car lengths in front of her, and the smear that the wipers made on her windshield only made the glare of oncoming headlights worse.

She shouldn't have risked driving in this storm, but damn! She was so sick of cafeteria food. A craving for fresh greens had prompted the short trek to the supermarket in Apt. The bad weather had turned nasty while she was shopping, and now she was smack dab in the middle of it.

At last she came to the exit that would that would take her home to Lacoste, and she turned off the highway with relief. The rain still pounded her car, but she was able to slow down and improve her visibility.

Her relief was short-lived as another car with blinding headlights raced up behind her. Now on a narrow rural road, she refused to go faster. She'd been behind plenty of slow-moving vehicles on these small roads. The asshole behind her would just have to suck it up. The driver flashed his headlights, but she ignored it because there was no place to pull over. He hung dangerously close to her rear bumper, and she clutched the steering wheel tighter, trying to concentrate on the road in front of her.

The jackass hugging her rear suddenly swerved to the left and surged around her at the same time that lights appeared around the next bend, heading toward them. The passing car sped forward but cut back into the right lane too soon. With a jolt of fear, Lou yanked the wheel to the right and stomped on the brakes, but it wasn't enough. *Crap!* Her car skidded, then lurched headlong into the ditch and ground to a halt. The airbag opened with a *crack,* the force smacking her in the face and chest but preventing her head from bouncing into the steering wheel.

Her wits wandered for several pounding heartbeats as the hiss of the deflating airbag sounded over the pumping of blood in her ears. The rush of adrenaline seeped out of her system, leaving her trembling, and she felt a cold sweat break across her skin. Stomach churning, she fought back the rising bile, closing her eyes for a couple of quick, deep breaths. *Crap, crap, crap!*

Other than having the stuffing scared out of her and a bruising sting on her jaw from the airbag, Lou was unharmed. She released her seatbelt with shaky hands and struggled to push open the door. She crawled out of the car, sloshed through ankle-deep water, and hoisted herself up out of the ditch. Neither of the cars that caused her accident had stopped to see if she was okay, and no other vehicle had passed by since.

Terrific. She surveyed the pug-nosed car stuck at an angle in the ditch. At least it was out of the road. On the hill up ahead, she could just make out the top of the ruins in Lacoste—lit by spotlights—and figured she was about two kilometers away. It was still raining hard, and without a proper jacket, she was quickly becoming soaked. *Note to self: don't leave home in a rainstorm without a coat.*

Her brain stuck in stupid, trying to process what had just happened and what she needed to do, Lou flinched when a new pair of headlights came around the bend toward her. She instinctively ducked toward her car but stopped short of jumping back into the ditch. To her relief, the huge black SUV slowed to a stop beside her. She watched the passenger-side window slide down, then stood on her toes to look in and see the driver.

Etienne Matisse cursed his luck again as he recognized the drenched woman whose car was stuck in the ditch. "Get in," he croaked though the open window. She stared at him with wide eyes for what seemed like an eternity. Her hesitation fueled his perpetual frustration with the human race, not thinking to give her some slack for her shock-stricken state.

"Get in or walk!" His harsh bark penetrated her clouded brain, and without another thought, she yanked open the door and climbed in. She was shivering violently as she pulled the heavy door shut.

Wet to her skin and chilled to the bone, with her long hair plastered haphazardly over her face and neck, she looked like a drowned rat. Seeing her like this, stuck in the kind of shock that follows a life-threatening event, Etienne was pierced with an emotion he had never experienced before. He tried to ignore it as he put the car in gear and slowly pulled away, shaking his head in an attempt to clear the unfamiliar thoughts from his brain. But her shivering and the loud chattering of her teeth forced him to speak.

"I didn't mean to frighten you, but you could have been killed there in the dark."

"Th ... th ... thank you," was all she could manage. She was shaking harder now, whether from the chill or from shock or fear, he didn't know. He glanced at her in the dark, and in the illumination of the headlights of an oncoming car, he saw her eyes were wide, like an animal caught in the crosshairs. He knew only that he needed to get her warm and safe.

Without considering the consequences, Etienne reached over and touched her shoulder, surprised that she didn't flinch. "*Il sera bon, mademoiselle.* You've had a fright, but you're safe now. We'll get your car out of the ditch in the morning."

The comforting words coming from the huge beast of a man next to Lou were so incongruous that she could only stare at him. Seeing his expression of sympathy begin to close down, she quickly reached for his muscular forearm, grasping it lightly. "Monsieur, thank you. I was terrified out there on the road, but I'm not afraid of you."

"Perhaps you should be," he whispered as he turned left onto a small gravel road.

Lou said nothing as the SUV bounced along, slowing as they approached what looked like a sprawling farmhouse. He parked the car and jumped out. Before she could think what to do, he had her door open, offering his hand to help her down from the high step. The heavy rain continued to pound them, and she didn't resist as he led her toward the house.

What am I doing? Alex was right; I should be petrified of this man. She was in shock, she decided, to allow Etienne Matisse, the badass bully of Lacoste, to drag her toward an isolated farmhouse on a dark, rainy night. No one knew where she was—she'd left her purse, for God's sake, with her cell phone, in the car she'd abandoned in the ditch. But for some ridiculous reason, she wasn't worried. She didn't think he'd hurt her. She felt to her bones that he honestly wanted to help. Having no choice at this point, she gave in to her instincts and went along with him.

The interior of the house was dark, but he guided her through the foyer and into a large room, where he gently pushed her down onto a couch. "Sit here," he said. She did, trying not to think about the wet spot she'd leave on the cushion.

He crossed the dark room, to a fireplace, she thought, confirmed as he lit a match and touched it to a pre-laid pile of kindling. The room erupted in flickering light as the kindling flared, then dimmed as he patiently added small sticks, then larger ones, then a few logs.

As he bent to the task of stoking the fire, Lou studied him. He was one of the largest men she'd ever seen, but she would never call him fat. He was tall—six and a half feet, maybe more—and built like a linebacker, beefy but without any excess bulk. He had ridiculously broad shoulders that stretched the canvas of his coat and enormous biceps that threatened to pop the seams of his sleeves when he flexed his arms. Although wider than her shoulders, his hips were narrow in proportion to his own shoulders, and his muscular thighs, flexed and straining in his coarse jeans as he knelt to the fire, were like tree trunks.

She forced herself to look away from him, her eyes roaming over the room. It was simple but comfortable, clean and uncluttered yet … lived in—the main sitting room, she guessed. The house was dark except for the glow of the fire, but in the dim light, Lou could make out the kitchen across the foyer. Although grateful to be out of the wind and rain, she was still cold in her wet clothes, and her jaw was clamped tight to keep her teeth from chattering. She began to feel a hint of warmth in the room as Matisse finally rose and turned back to her.

He studied her a moment before gesturing to the stone hearth. "You will be warmer over here." He reached for a thick blanket that lay over the back of the couch and handed it to her. "Take off your fleece and wrap this around you. Would you like some hot tea? It will only take a minute to make."

She tried to smile around her clamped teeth, but it came across more as a grimace. "Yes, please, that would be … great."

She detected a hint of a smile on Etienne's rough face as he moved toward the kitchen. Lou stood and walked over to the raised hearth. Sitting down, she peeled off her wet fleece as instructed, then rubbed her hands up and down her arms to dispel the chill that had sunk into her, shivering anew. Her thin tee shirt clung to her skin, but the heat of the fire penetrated its dampness, warming her minutely. As she stared into the flames, it occurred to her that Etienne had been speaking English—quite well, in fact—since he rescued her. What an interesting and mysterious man he was turning out to be.

She held her hands close to the flames, enjoying the heat, and glanced around the room again. Who would have guessed the man lived in something so … cozy? From his reputation, she wouldn't have been surprised if he'd brought her to a cave. But other than the sharp reprimand to knock her out of her stupor at the side of the road, he'd been extremely considerate and … solicitous.

She heard his footsteps and swung the blanket about her shoulders as she turned to look. He had shed his coat, but that did nothing to diminish his size. He handed her a mug of steaming liquid then settled himself with his own mug in the overstuffed recliner next to her. She brought the cup to her lips and inhaled its fragrance before tentatively touching her lips to the rim for a sip. "Mmm, perfect, thank you."

Matisse watched her with fascination, busying himself with sipping from his own steaming mug. Either she was a very good actress or he did not intimidate her at all. Somehow he didn't think it was an act. *Incroyable!*

After a few sips, Lou turned and looked at him. Her eyes were filled with something he had never seen directed at him. Appreciation. Gratitude. Respect. There was no fear or revulsion in her gaze. "Monsieur Matisse …" she began, then paused.

"Etienne," he said gruffly, and she thought his ruddy cheeks actually turned a deeper shade of red as he said it.

"Etienne, then. Sir, I …" she hesitated again, as if not sure what to say.

He waited, curious to know how she would word her gratitude, but she went a different direction completely.

"Etienne, you're not the cruel and malicious man you lead people to believe you are."

It was a statement, not a question, and he had to cough into his hand to cover his smile. She was surprising and refreshing, and her presence lightened his spirit just a bit.

Doing his best to scowl, he growled as if in displeasure. "Do not mistake a single act of charity for a character trait, *mademoiselle*. I recognized you and did not wish to hear that you had been flattened on the road; that is all."

She smiled at him, and almost laughed. "Um hum, okay, well thanks for that." She continued to sip at her tea, turning away from him to stare into the flames.

With her back toward him, Etienne was able to stare at her without shame. His ears were still ringing from her use of his Christian name. God knows what possessed him to urge her to use it, and he hated to admit how good it sounded coming from her lips. She seemed perfectly comfortable in his home, as if she truly didn't mind that there was a large ugly brute sitting next to her. He was inordinately pleased to see her wrapped in his blanket, her wet fleece steaming on the hearthstones. Her hair was still dripping from the ends, but she was no longer shivering and seemed warm enough sitting in front of his fire. And she was either unaware or unconcerned about her bedraggled appearance.

"How long have you lived here, Etienne?" Her question startled him out of his musing.

For some unaccountable reason, he wanted her to know the truth about him. "I was born here, *mademoiselle*. This was my father's house before he married my mother, and we lived here happily until I was about six years old."

She looked at him with compassion—another look he was not used to seeing, and it shifted something inside him. "What happened when you were six?"

"My father died, and my mother was forced to remarry to a man she did not love in order to keep the property."

"How awful, I'm so sorry. Was her new husband cruel to you?"

Merde, he thought. She focused right into the heart of the matter. The answer to that question was so complex he didn't know how to answer it, and more importantly, he didn't want to. "I survived," he said coolly. She got the message and simply nodded, turning back to the fire. *A singular quality in a woman,* he thought, *to understand when to stop asking questions.*

They were quiet for a time, both seemingly absorbed in their own thoughts. Surprisingly, he did not feel compelled to fill the space with chatter, and she apparently didn't either. Then it suddenly occurred to him ...

"Excusez-moi, mademoiselle, but I do not know your name."

Again, she surprised him, spinning around and pinning him with blue eyes widened in dismay. "Oh my gosh, how could I be so rude? I'm so sorry! My name is Louise Marcel," she paused. "But please, my friends call me Lou."

Feeling like a schoolboy but unable to resist, Etienne asked what he thought may be a supremely stupid question. He prepared himself for a rebuff even though he couldn't help but ask. "Are you sure you wish to consider me a friend?"

"After what happened tonight? Of course I do." She seemed offended that he would think differently, and the ice that had encased his heart for most of his life thawed just a bit.

Aware of how dangerous it would be for him—and her—if anyone knew of their ... connection ... Etienne spoke more gruffly than he intended. "Well then, Lou, I suggest you keep our acquaintance to yourself. I am not the sort you want to be associated with."

Rather than looking worried, Lou narrowed her eyes at him. "Right, I get it. Being seen with such a good girl like me would ruin your badass reputation."

He coughed again to cover his laugh. *Mon Dieu,* she was priceless. Too bad he had no experience with women like her. His mind flickered to another woman, in another place and time, but he quickly tamped down the image. He gave Lou his best scowl, one that normally sent shivers of dread through the strongest men. She seemed unimpressed, but that didn't stop him from warning her off.

"It is dangerous to know me, *mademoiselle.* Certain men that I associate with would not hesitate to threaten you if they thought it would help them get something from me."

That got her attention. Her expression didn't change, but her shoulders stiffened. She said nothing, only nodded again, sipped her tea, and turned back to the fire.

As much as Etienne would have enjoyed keeping her in his home, cooking her dinner, and spending what would surely be an interesting evening, he was not joking about the danger to both of them. Bringing her to his home had not been terribly wise, no matter that he'd had little choice, and he couldn't keep her here. She was no longer pale—in fact her cheeks had a healthy glow to them. She still looked like a drowned rat with her hair plastered to her head, and some bruising was beginning to show on her jaw from where the airbag had smacked her, but the shock seemed to have worn off and he knew she would be fine.

He set his mug aside and stood abruptly. "Come," he said as he grabbed his coat and turned toward the door. "I'll take you back to the village."

She nodded and stood, then set her own mug next to his. Her fleece was still damp, but at least it held some warmth from the fire, and she tugged it on before following him.

Etienne drove Lou back to her car and helped her retrieve her purse and groceries—miraculously still there, as the car had been unlocked—then dropped her in a dark parking lot at the top of the village. He had been serious about not wanting to be seen with her. The rain had let up, and the moon shone down through a break in the clouds as she exited the vehicle. She waved as he drove off then headed down the narrow cobblestone lane toward her apartment. Neither of them saw the figure observing them from a high window at the top of the lane.

Ten

"Ying Lo is dead."

"What? Are you certain?" Simon Purcell looked up from the report he was reading to address the younger man standing in the doorway of his office.

"Yes, sir. His body was fished out of the Marseille marina this morning. Broken neck. Wallet was in his pocket with his ID, like the killer is sending us a message. We're running prints of course to verify, but they're positive it's him."

"Bloody hell." Simon pulled off his reading glasses and pinched the bridge of his nose, rubbing the corners of his eyes. "I didn't even know he was in France. He wasn't supposed to be."

"His wife reported both he and his daughter missing to the Beijing authorities two days ago. He picked the girl up from school but never went home."

"No one saw anything? Why are we just finding out about this now?"

"Nothing yet from China, sir, but ..."

Simon glared at his subordinate. "But, what?"

"Ying Li, the daughter, showed up at Charles de Gaulle airport last night on a flight from Marseille with a connecting ticket to Beijing. She tried to board the flight but was detained because she had no documents other than the ticket and a school ID. The gate agents said she was out of it. Confused and docile, not following what was happening around her, possibly drugged. It took immigration all night to figure out who she was."

"Jesus. She must have been taken to ensure Ying would talk."

"It looks that way, sir."

"Where's the girl now?" Too late, he realized he'd not even considered the danger to Ying's family, and for good reason. There shouldn't have been any. Would it have made a difference when Simon asked Ying to take on this assignment? And what would Ying have had to disclose, other than that INTERPOL was trying to nail Philippe? That was nothing new. Philippe didn't need to kill an agent to figure that out.

"She's in one of the holding rooms at the airport. Once they connected the dots to us, our people took over custody of her, but she's still at the airport detention center. Since Ying was your agent, they need your authorization to release her back to her mother."

"Of course we'll release her! Why didn't Ying's wife contact us when he went missing?" Why had it taken so long to get this information? They might have been able to save him, but they never got the chance. *Damn it!*

"I don't think she knew that Ying was one of us, sir."

Simon closed his eyes and dropped his head into his hands, rubbing his temples where a sudden headache was blooming. "You're bloody kidding me, right?"

"Evidently, he never told her. She thought he was still with Beijing municipal squad."

What a bloody waste, Simon thought. Then he took a deep breath and shook off the black shadow like he'd done so many times before, getting himself back in the game. "Okay, then, here's what you'll do. Get hold of Ying's wife and get her on the next flight to Paris. Say nothing about Ying. Then get yourself to Paris and make sure the girl is being taken care of—treated like a guest, not a prisoner. Make sure she gets decent food and sleep, and see to any other personal needs, clothes, whatever. Let her know her mother is on the way, but don't answer any questions about Ying. Once the mother arrives and the girl is released, escort them both here to London. Put them in a safe house, and let me know the minute they arrive."

"Yes, sir; thank you, sir." the young agent said, a tremor of excitement in his voice. As he turned to leave, Simon called him back.

"And, Spencer, ask the wife to look around for any unusual notes, documents, or envelopes—anything like that that Ying may have left behind. Tell her to bring anything she finds with her to London."

Spencer nodded. "I will, sir."

Alone again in his office, Simon thought over what he'd just learned. In his last report, Ying said that he had found something much bigger than fake wines, but he wanted to check his facts before he made any definitive statements. Simon had hoped that with his deep-cover agent in Lacoste and Ying in China, they'd be able to link something together that was significant enough to get the resources they needed to bring Philippe Lemans down. It was frustrating that they knew about the wine shipments but had nothing to pin on him; the legitimate shipments originating from his warehouse always checked out. And while the game he played with fake wine was lucrative, was it enough to commit murder? It didn't add up, but be that as it may, the stakes had just been raised. Significantly.

Etienne Matisse felt his phone vibrate against his hip but ignored it, intent on the cards in his hand. The men at the table were members of Philippe's tribe of thugs, and it gave him absurd satisfaction to defeat them in this simple way. He held a winning hand and wanted no distractions at the moment.

The betting went around the table again, upping the stakes. One man folded, the other two tossed money onto the pile in the middle of the table, and Etienne moved to do the same when he felt his phone vibrate again. *Merde!* He tossed in his wager and growled, *"Appel."*

Groans sounded from the two men when they realized they'd been beaten again. Matisse collected up his winnings, shoved it all in his pocket as he stood, and nodded to the table. *"J'ai fini ici."* Then he turned and left the bar. His cell phone vibrated again.

He had two missed calls and a text. The calls were from a number he knew well, and he cursed again. The text took him by surprise, and he almost laughed out loud but caught himself. Looking around, he kept the scowl on his face as he headed for the overlook behind the church where he knew he'd have privacy.

BA, thanks for the roadside service. My car arrived dented but intact. See you around, GG.

She's going to get us both killed, he thought grimly, at the same time struggling to keep the smile from his face. Last night on the way back to the village, she'd asked for his cell phone number. "In case I need another rescue," she'd teased. She'd actually teased him! He gave it to her but advised her to use another name in her contacts list. She laughingly told him his code name would be Bad Ass, and hers would be Good Girl.

He tapped the return call code for the other number, and Simon answered immediately, with no preamble. "Ying's body was found floating in the Marseille marina this morning."

"*Merde.*"

"Yeah, *merde* is right. And it's about to hit the fan. We're doing damage control up here, but you needed to know things have escalated. We can't wait much longer."

"Perhaps he really was onto something. He called me a few days ago, said he'd overheard a conversation between two government officials that had to do with the flesh trade."

"He mentioned it to me, too, but gave no specifics." Simon's voice was heavy with regret.

"He said the name Lemans was mentioned." Matisse took a deep breath. "I told him to do nothing, to be very careful, and to wait for instructions. It sounds like he ignored my advice. Fortunately, he didn't know who or where I was, only my code name. I dumped the phone in someone's trash bin."

Simon cursed. "His wife is on her way here now to collect the daughter. Hopefully she'll find something and bring it along." He quickly explained what they knew. It wasn't much.

"I've been offered a job," Matisse told him. "I didn't want to appear eager, but I think it's time to contact my dear brother and hear more about it."

"Perhaps he's finally decided to trust you—either that or he's onto you. Be careful, Etienne. Whatever he's into is bigger than we thought if he's willing to kill people. And if it's got anything to do with what Ying sus-pected ..."

Matisse nodded thoughtfully, but of course the man on the other end of the connection couldn't see that. "I have a request."

"What do you need?"

"Protection for someone if things go bad. A woman. An American."

"I thought you were working alone." There was accusation in the tone.

"I am," Matisse growled. "But I have a feeling she may end up in the middle somehow. Don't ask me to explain. Just do it."

"What's her name? Who is she?"

"Louise Marcel. She works at the school. She's on the Maison Basse project."

"Jesus."

"No more rendezvous there, either. We need to move all contact to the alternate site."

Simon paused then let out a sigh. "Okay, done. We'll do our best to take care of her, but for God's sake, do what you can there to keep her out of it. I don't like the smell of what's coming at us."

Matisse ended the call and stared out across the valley, hoping he hadn't just put Louise in more danger. He couldn't shake the feeling that he'd set something in motion with her last night that couldn't be reversed. Ensuring her protection when the end game arrived was simply smart planning. *It's done now,* he thought as he headed back to the bar.

Eleven

The rain beat a soft tattoo against the thick stone walls of the cozy reading room, but Louise barely heard it. The room had been created from the remains of the original village bakery: a few comfortable chairs, an area rug, and halogen reading lamps had been arranged inside what had once been an enormous oven. It was an ingenious and creative way to both preserve and utilize the old building, and it appealed to her sense of history at the same time the warm space soothed her.

She had spent the better part of the afternoon paging through a stack of old ledgers from the village archives. The one in her lap at the moment was from the church, and she was meticulously tracing the lives of the old families through births, marriages, and deaths. If she could decipher the spidery handwriting, it was then a straightforward exercise to trace the lives of the people who inhabited the Maison Basse, and she duly recorded each entry for further cross-referencing in other documents.

The surname Matisse, she discovered, first appeared in the village ledgers in 1875, with the baptism of Hubert Etienne Matisse of La Ferme du Vieux Pont. She had searched back through the ledger but couldn't find any earlier reference to the family, so she guessed the Old Bridge Farm had come to the Matisse family through purchase shortly prior to 1875. Flipping to the next ledger, she traced the family through several generations until she came to 1935 when Ricard Etienne Matisse was baptized. Etienne's father, she was sure.

The next entry concerning the Matisse family was not until 1946, the official beginning of the baby boom, when another baptism was recorded—a daughter, presumably a baby sister to Ricard. She was named Regina Matisse.

Lou chuckled to herself. *Etienne's grandfather obviously made it home from the war.* He was recorded to have died in 1960, followed closely by his wife. That left Ricard, then twenty-five years old, with a fourteen-year-old sister to look after. Lou wondered how much of this, if any, Etienne knew.

In the last ledger, she found the details for Etienne. His father, Ricard, had married a local girl, Juliette Moreau of Les Prés—The Meadows—in 1973. Etienne was born in 1975, which made him thirty-five years old—so much younger than she had imagined! She thought back to his admission the other night about having "survived" his childhood under his stepfather, and her heart filled with compassion. It may have been wishful thinking because he'd been kind to her, but she was convinced the gruff bully was an act. *Perhaps it was an act of self-preservation dating back to his childhood,* she thought, and her heart broke a little for the awkwardly large boy who had been mistreated.

Continuing her perusal of the ledger, Lou found the entry for the funeral of Ricard Matisse in 1980 as she'd been told, then the marriage of Juliette Moreau Matisse to Jean Luc Lemans in 1981. So soon! But then, Etienne had said his mother needed to remarry to keep the property.

Lou flipped to a new page in her notepad to record the Matisse family timeline. Not wishing to examine her motives too closely, she told herself Etienne would appreciate knowing a bit of his own history. When she reached the entry for Regina, who was presumably his aunt, she wondered if she was still alive and if he knew her.

Studying the entries more closely as she copied them into her notebook, she found an entry for the double funeral of M. and Mme. Moreau of Les Prés. It was closely followed by Ricard's marriage to Juliette in 1973. They must have been Juliette's parents, she decided and considered whether their death could have precipitated the marriage. Looking at her notes and calculating dates, she realized that Ricard had been almost forty years old at the time. She flipped back through the ledger and, after some searching, came across the baptism of Juliette Moreau in 1955. She had been just nineteen when she married Etienne's father. *Huh.* What had become of her home, Les Prés? If Etienne was her sole heir, shouldn't it have gone to him? Unless Juliette was forced to sell it. Did Lou dare ask him about it?

The next ledger was a copy of a property tax register from the eighteenth century. The original was too fragile to handle, but the village authorities had allowed the school to have it duplicated for research purposes. And it contained a wealth of information relating to the château and its ancillary properties.

More than just a tax record, the ledger was a fantastic history of property transactions in the area, revealing a great deal about what was happening at the time. She saw annual entries for La Ferme du Vieux Pont as far back as the beginning of the eighteenth century, but nothing for Les Prés. It was entirely possible that property hadn't come into existence yet.

Mention of Maison Basse first appeared in 1716, when the château and its ancillary properties were sold to a Gaspard François de Sade, the grandfather of the château's most notorious inhabitant. The record of the transaction took up an entire page, as each individual property included in the sale was listed and detailed, including size and location. The details for Maison Basse coincided with her knowledge of the property at the time. She jotted down the specifics to cross-check against other records. Another property included in the accounting caught her eye—Les Presons. It was not a property she was familiar with, and she recorded its particulars to follow up on later. Without a map she couldn't be sure, but the coordinates seemed to place it quite close to the Matisse property.

The next transaction of interest was the sale of the château by the infamous Marquis de Sade in 1796. She knew from other accounts she had read that the château had been looted and destroyed when rioters had sacked the village during the French Revolution. This time, the transaction did not include the ancillary properties.

Turning to the next ledger in the series, this one covering transactions of the nineteenth century, Lou found the entry that noted the sale of the Maison Basse to a local family. And just following that entry was a transaction for the sale of Les Presons to François Moreau. *How interesting.* Could Les Prés and Les Presons be one and the same?

Preson was not a French word that Lou was familiar with, and it wasn't in her dictionary either. She pulled up the Occitan-English translator on her phone and entered in the word. Processing the request took only an instant. *Huh.*

——————————◆◆——————————

Ellie was sweating and shivering as she writhed in agony on the bed. *What's wrong! This isn't supposed to be happening!* The kind nurse was with her, speaking soothing words Ellie didn't understand and wiping her brow with a cool cloth. Another torturous pain hit, and she gritted her teeth to keep from screaming.

"*Quel est le problème avec elle?*" The gruff voice was almost—almost—a relief. At least it gave her something to think about other than the hell her body was putting her through.

"*Elle est en difficulté, c'est ce que!*" The nurse snapped out the words. "Make yourself useful and call a doctor!"

"*Ce n'est pas une option,*" the man said, as if they were discussing the dinner menu.

The nurse cursed and turned back to her charge as Ellie tensed against another wave of intense pain.

——————————◆◆——————————

It was early evening and almost dark by the time Louise hauled her box of ledgers back to the archives, housed in the school's administrative building. As she pushed open the door, she saw Alex Bouvier leaning against the reception counter, looking entirely too gorgeous, and speaking with Pierre D'Arcy, the dorm RA who had helped her the night she'd found Alex unconscious. Both men turned to look at her at the same time, and their conversation abruptly stopped.

"*Bonsoir,*" she said to them. They each nodded and returned the greeting.

Alex smiled warmly as he limped forward on his awkward boot, arms outstretched. "Here, let me help you with that."

She gratefully allowed him to take it and shook her arms at her sides to ease the cramping that had started. "Thanks, it's heavy. Are you sure you can manage?"

"No, but Pierre can." He winked at her, then pivoted, took two steps back to where he'd been standing, and set the box on the counter.

"It's full of ledgers from the archives. I need to sign them back in." She looked at Pierre. "Do you mind carrying it downstairs for me?"

"Don't worry about it." He waved dismissively. "I'll take it down later, when I'm off the desk here."

Lou didn't get to where she was in her career by being careless with reference materials, especially those whose access was limited like the records she'd been using. In addition, something about Pierre's too-casual tone struck her as a bit off.

"Uh, actually, never mind. I'll take them down." She said. "No offense, but you should know I'm responsible for this stuff until it's signed back in by the archivist. There'd be hell to pay if something went missing."

Pierre stiffened slightly but shrugged. He was about to say something when Alex leaned in and knocked her shoulder playfully with his. "I'll help you."

She turned to him with a grateful look. "Thanks. If you can carry a couple of the heavier ones I'll be able to manage the box easier." She pulled off the lid and grabbed two ledgers—the copies of property tax registers—and handed them to him. Pierre was peering into the box as she replaced the lid.

"What were you researching?"

"Just doing some routine cross-referencing," she said. *What's it to him?* She picked up the box and nodded to Alex. "Much better."

Alex followed her around the corner and down the stairs to the archives, handing her the two volumes he'd carried after she set the box down on the check-in counter. She laid them next to the box then pulled a two-part carbonless form out of her bag and handed it over to the attendant. They stood silently while he looked carefully at each ledger, compared its title and document number to the form she'd given him, and methodically ticked each volume off after examining it. He signed the form in two places, turned it around for her to sign, too, then separated the second sheet and handed it to her. "*Merci, madame.*"

"*Je vous en prie, bonne soirée,*" she replied then turned to Alex and gestured up the stairs. "*Allons-y.*"

He chuckled, amused as always by her accent and pleased that she seemed to be in a friendly mood tonight. *No time like the present,* he thought as he held out his hand to her, holding her gaze until she reached out to take it.

At the top of the stairs, he tugged her to a halt, out of sight of Pierre at the front desk. They were standing very close, still hand in hand. He leaned closer and whispered in her ear. "Will you have dinner with me?"

She looked at him in surprise. "Tonight?" she whispered back.

He raised one eyebrow and let the corner of his lips curve up slightly. "*Bien sûr mademoiselle, ce soir.*"

She hesitated. Part of her wanted to say yes, wanted to know him better. A deep feminine urge inside her wanted to explore a friendship with a beautiful young man, but another part—the emotionally scarred part—was afraid of encouraging any sort of intimacy.

"Say yes," he prompted, still whispering. "Think of it as a thank-you for showing me the Maison Basse, and … and also as an apology."

"An apology for what?" She was having a hard time focusing with him so close—his warmth invaded her senses, and his beautiful eyes were mesmerizing.

He tilted his head slightly without breaking eye contact. "For what I said after Matisse left. For getting angry for no reason."

"I already forgave you for that, no apology necessary."

"Good. Have dinner with me anyway."

"Um, okay," she let her feminine senses override her caution before she could reconsider. "Why are we whispering?"

He smiled his sexy smile, dimples and all, and winked at her. Then he brought the hand he still held to his lips and planted a soft kiss on her knuckles.

Her eyes widened, her mouth opened slightly, but she made no sound.

He gently turned her around, and they walked back toward the front desk. Pierre appeared to be watching for them. Alex let go of her hand, and she briefly mourned the loss of his touch. Neither paused on their way out the door but simply bade Pierre *bonsoir* and stepped out together into the night.

Twelve

Etienne Matisse regarded his stepbrother from across the shabby desk in the office above the Marseille docks. He had driven down to deliver the palette of older vintage wine bottles he'd collected over the past several weeks and, as he'd hoped, Philippe was there to meet him. Once the delivery was inspected and secured in the warehouse, Matisse had been invited to the office for payment and a drink.

After the usual insincere small talk, Philippe got to the point. "Have you considered my offer?"

Matisse hesitated. "You didn't give me anything to consider, Philippe. Do you expect me to agree to something before I know what it is?"

"Don't you trust me?"

"No." No hesitation there.

Philippe chuckled and sipped his Cognac. "Understandable, *mon frère,* but consider, if you do this, all that should have been yours could be returned."

"I told you I have no ambitions for wealth."

"All men have ambitions for wealth. You came to me a year ago looking for work. I gave it to you. You've done your job well. I'm simply offering you a higher-level position."

"Doing what?"

"There is more to my enterprise than simply moving wine around. My father did not build this business to accommodate the world's lust for unattainable bottles of wine. That is merely a distraction. There is something much more lucrative, and much more … challenging."

Matisse lifted one brow slightly and purposely looked around the small, dingy office. "Lucrative?"

Philippe shrugged unapologetically. "This image serves." When Matisse said nothing, Philippe tossed out a tidbit he'd just picked up. "I hear you have a new acquaintance."

Matisse's black eyes narrowed, and his scowl deepened. He prayed his features did not betray his suddenly racing heart. *Merde, did someone see me with Lou?* He said nothing.

"A pretty blonde, I hear." With a lecherous smile Philippe added, "You surprise me, Etienne."

"Don't get yourself excited, Philippe. I pulled her from a ditch on the side of the road in a downpour and dropped her in the village."

"How chivalrous."

"Would you have let her drown in the ditch?"

"Probably not," Philippe conceded. "But if she's as pretty as I hear, I may not have taken her home right away." He tossed back the rest of his Cognac and set the glass down. "I'm leaving for Bordeaux tonight. I'll be back at the end of the week. Come to Les Prés Saturday night at ten o'clock, and I'll tell you more about your new job."

Matisse rose from his chair and turned to leave. His ability to mask his hatred was slipping, and he could not yet give himself away.

"Come to the back door, Etienne."

Matisse hesitated for just a moment then disappeared through the doorway without a backward glance.

Seven kilometers from Lacoste in the neighboring village of Menerbes, Alex and Louise sat at a corner table in a nearly deserted restaurant. They sipped *kirs* while studying the menu.

Alex was pleased that the conspiratorial mood he'd created in the school office had remained with them. She had even taken his arm as they walked from his car to the restaurant. Watching her now, she seemed relaxed. She glanced up and caught him looking at her.

"It all sounds delicious. What do you recommend?"

"This time of year, anything with truffles." At her blank expression, he asked, "You don't like truffles?"

"I have no idea—I haven't tried any. What are they like?"

He closed his eyes in an exaggerated expression of ecstasy. "Mmm ... earthy, pungent and delicious. Another culinary dimension. Like nothing you've ever experienced."

She looked unconvinced. "Trust me, you'll love it." He reached over and pointed at the handwritten note pinned to the inside of her menu. "Try this"— indicating the special. "Duck breast with mushrooms and black truffle sauce."

His enthusiasm for the dish, coupled with the fact that she loved duck no matter how it was dressed, made the decision easy. She smiled and nodded. "Okay, I'm game."

When the server returned, Alex ordered salads and the duck special for both of them, and a bottle of wine. When they were alone again, he asked about her project, and they talked comfortably for a few minutes.

At a lull in the conversation, Alex took a sip of his *kir* then asked softly, "It is true that Etienne Matisse gave you a ride home the other night?"

Lou was so startled by the question that she almost spit out the sip she'd just taken. "Who told you that?"

He narrowed his eyes a bit. "Pierre claimed he saw you getting out of his SUV not too long after that big storm. That you waved to him like an old friend. He asked me if I knew anything about your relationship. I thought you said you didn't know him."

She stiffened. Gone was the charming gentleman who'd invited her to dinner. The man across the table from her had accusation in his eyes. Or was it hurt? "Is that why you asked me to dinner? So you could interrogate me?" Before Alex could answer, Lou shook her head in exasperation. "Why are you so obsessed with that man? And what business is it of yours if I know him or not? Why do you care?"

At that moment their salads arrived. Alex conversed briefly with the server about the wine, and then he was gone.

Lou watched him with a mixture of disappointment and hurt, her lips pressed firmly together, and it affected him more than he wanted to admit.

He'd let down enough people in his life. He was only concerned about her safety, not judging her, but she didn't see it that way. With a deep breath, he reached for her hand, gripping it tightly when she tried to pull away. "Listen, I know it's none of my business who you call friend, but he's dangerous. I don't want to see anything happen to you."

She studied him carefully, detecting not insincerity so much as confusion as he let her pull her hand away. She took a slow bite of her salad, thinking about what she could tell him. The truth was the best option and no doubt easier, and she had a feeling she could trust him, but first ...

"How well do you know Pierre?"

He frowned, not liking the change of subject but going with it. "I have a room in his dorm, been there for a couple months now. He works in the photo lab, too, so we chat a bit. He seems to have taken more interest in me since my, ah, accident. I wouldn't necessarily call him friend—more an acquaintance. Why?"

"What do you know about him?"

He sat back and thought for a minute. Pierre had asked a lot of questions lately about everything Alex was doing. He'd been asking about Lou when she'd walked in on them earlier that evening. "Nothing beyond the surface. Why?"

"Because there's something about him ... I don't trust him." She thought about his behavior with the ledgers. "He had to know about the strict controls on reference materials. I wouldn't leave that sort of thing with my best friend, much less someone I barely know. Why was he so curious about my research? He has nothing to do with my project."

She had a good point, but ... "Was he lying about seeing you with Matisse?"

The server came back to the table with the wine, forestalling her answer. He presented the bottle to Alex, who nodded curtly, frustrated with the interruption. The bottle was ceremoniously opened, tasted, and poured, and their salad plates cleared, before they were alone again at the table.

Alex picked up his glass and, biting back his impatience, tipped it toward her in a small toasting motion, gazing straight into her eyes. She returned the gesture, and then they both took a sip. She savored it on her tongue for a moment before swallowing. "Mmm," she murmured. "This is really delicious. Rich and spicy, lots of layers, but so smooth." She turned the bottle toward her to study it. Her wine knowledge was limited, but she wanted to remember this one. "Wow! This is more than twenty years old!" She looked up at him in surprise.

Alex smiled but didn't want to talk about the wine right now. "I'm glad you like it. 1989 was a fantastic vintage in the Rhône Valley. Was Pierre lying about seeing you with Matisse?"

"No," she admitted, "but I didn't think anyone saw us." She gave him the short version of what had happened the other night with her car, leaving out the visit to his home. "I agree he's probably dangerous, but honestly, Alex, I don't think he would hurt me. His manner was gruff, but otherwise he was very considerate. No nefarious intentions in evidence." She smiled. "He even arranged for my car to be towed out of the ditch and returned to the village."

Alex had to laugh. "You must be the only one in the village—in the valley probably—who isn't scared to death of him." Then he sobered. "But I know for a fact that he's dangerous, and not just because of what he did to me."

"You don't know for sure it was him," she defended. She hated to think that Etienne really was the mean bastard he wanted everyone to think he was.

"Lou, he's involved in illegal activities."

"Oh, really?" She arched her eyebrow. "What kind of activities?"

"He's a key suspect in a major wine-fraud investigation." Okay, he hadn't meant to blurt that out.

"And you know this how, exactly? Are you some kind of cop?" A punch of fear hit her, and she was suddenly horrified that she'd been fooled by him.

Merde. "No, I'm just trying to help out a friend."

She took a breath to calm herself, reached for her water, and took a long sip. *I met his uncle, or cousin … whoever. He was beat up, hurt. That was real.* She was concentrating so hard on pushing the panic attack away that she flinched when Alex gently touched the hand she had wrapped around her water glass.

"Louise, what is it?" Her face had turned pale, and it looked like she was trembling.

She shook her head and forced herself to look at him. "Ah, nothing, sorry. But it just occurred to me that I really don't know much about you at all. I thought you were, uh … you felt … trustworthy, and I guess I let my guard down."

It was Alex's turn to take a deep breath. "I am trustworthy. I'm not going to hurt you, and I won't lie to you. I definitely have skeletons in my closet, but I'm trying my best to get past them." He paused and watched her reaction. "But this has nothing to do with any of that."

She studied him carefully, looking for any sign of deception. But she simply saw the truth in what he said, and then felt a little foolish. She tried to pick up the thread of their conversation. "So, you're trying to help out a friend by watching Matisse—a friend as in, a detective friend?"

He nodded and to his surprise, she laughed at him, incredulous. "Are you serious? If you think he's so dangerous and involved in some big fraud ring, what the hell are you doing getting involved here? Do you have any investigative training at all?"

The way she said it, it sounded so absurd, he suddenly realized. *She's right; what the hell am I doing?* He squirmed in discomfort. "Uh, no, not exactly. Listen, I know this sounds crazy but what he's doing—what he's suspected of doing—it's incredibly damaging to the French wine industry. We … ah, my friend's organization, has reason to believe his activities could involve much more than just wine fraud. Since I'm here attending classes, I offered to keep my eyes open, try to get close to him if I could, and see what I could find out."

"Well, you certainly found out he doesn't like to lose at poker." She took the sting out of her words with obvious compassion in her tone. She'd seen how hurt he'd been, and that was no laughing matter.

Alex said nothing. He busied himself with his food and regrouped his scattered thoughts.

"Look," she said. This time she was the one who reached across the table to take his hand. "I have no idea what the deal was with you getting beat up.

But I've got to tell you, Alex, Etienne is not what he seems. I'm good at reading people—"

"Lou—"

"No, listen to me." She held up her hand. "I've always had this ability. It's why I'm sitting here with you—I know you're safe, even if you did make me panic a little."

His lips quirked at that, and he quickly looked down at his plate.

"Etienne is not the bad guy here, although for some reason he wants everyone to think he is. He's big and scary looking, no question, and he may be involved in something on the wrong side of the law, but there's something else going on. If anyone in town gives me the creeps, it's those other losers who hang out with him. Or Pierre. Now there's one who scores high on my creep meter."

"That reminds me"—Alex looked up—"I've been meaning to ask you something since we first met."

She looked at him expectantly.

"When I was in the hospital, why did you get so angry at the *gendarme* when he asked if those men had bothered you before?"

Eyes narrowing, Lou leaned back in her chair and crossed her arms over her chest. "What an ass he was. Did you actually listen to his question?" She could tell Alex wasn't following. With a deep sigh, she shook her head. "'Why were you so afraid of them, *mademoiselle*,'" she mimicked. "'Had they harassed you before?' For God's sake, do I have to have a better reason to be scared than being a petite woman on a dark night with no one else around? With a handful of big obnoxious creeps in my path, who leer at every female in town? Don't tell me you've never heard the stories about Lacoste."

At his confused look, Lou drew back in surprise. "Seriously? Do you mean to tell me that you've never heard about the missing women from this village?"

"No, I haven't."

With a faraway look, almost as if she was reciting something she'd read, she said, "For the past several decades, a young woman has gone missing from the village of Lacoste each year, almost without fail. Some say the village is cursed, some say it's a bitter coincidence that Cardin contrarians have turned into something sinister—which is ridiculous, since he hasn't been here long enough—and others say it's the work of some weird cult that sacrifices virgins."

"*What?*" Alex appeared genuinely stunned.

"Right, I don't believe the cult theory." *At least that's what I keep telling myself.* "But honestly, even without that troubling statistic, why did I need any other reason to be frightened of those creeps? What *wasn't* there to be scared about?"

"But why didn't you just say that?"

"Because the way he asked made it sound like he had some reason to be suspicious of *me!* Jesus, Alex, you believe the worst about Matisse but don't think anyone else can be a mean brute? You must not have any sisters."

"You're right, I don't. I guess I never thought about it from a female perspective. It wasn't until you confronted Matisse at the Maison Basse that I thought you should be afraid. But you weren't. You weren't afraid of Matisse when he was right in your face, but you *were* afraid of the others when they couldn't even see you—that just doesn't make sense to me."

She shook her head. "I don't know how else to explain it. I've been here long enough to have seen them all around town. My creep meter goes off with the others, but not Matisse. Besides, it wasn't in the middle of the night, and you were right behind me."

They ate in silence for a few minutes, enjoying the delicious meal, both lost in their own thoughts. "He agrees with you, by the way," she said softly.

"What? Who agrees with me?"

"Etienne. He said it was dangerous to know him. He didn't want me to tell anyone he'd helped me. Didn't want anyone to see us together. He's not gonna be happy that someone did."

"And that doesn't make you suspicious?"

"I have no facts, no knowledge of what's going on, but I can tell you this. His mean bastard act is just that: an act. Things are not as they appear where he's concerned."

Alex scowled, not ready to think differently about Matisse.

"He's trying to protect me from someone," Lou insisted. "I have no idea who. But here's my concern. What I told the *gendarmes* is true—there is something going on in that village. I think you know that, too. So if Matisse isn't the real bad guy, who is?"

Thirteen

Matisse read the text that just came in and swore. *Learned something important that concerns you, need to meet ASAP. Tonight! GG*

Incroyable! The lady has no sense of self-preservation, he thought, even as he tamped down the excitement at the prospect of seeing her again. It was just past ten o'clock, and the night was dark but clear. Where could they possibly meet? He couldn't chance being seen with her in the village. Could he risk having her come to his house? With Philippe in Bordeaux, they would not be interrupted. But he couldn't be sure his house wasn't watched. He replied: *Where are you?*

My apartment in Lacoste.

He scooped up his keys and shrugged into his coat, texting his reply as he left the house. *Drive the back road toward Menerbes. I'll be waiting at the fork. Flash your lights when you see my car then follow me. Do you know the road?* He was heading down the gravel drive toward the main road when her reply chimed.

Yes. Leaving now.

Heart pounding, Lou tugged on her heavy coat and a knit cap, shoved her notepad and a flashlight into her bag, and quietly left her apartment. She had expected Matisse to refuse to meet her and couldn't quell the shiver of doubt that maybe this wasn't such a good idea. But as she walked as casually as possible toward her car, she reminded herself of what she'd said to Alex earlier—Etienne would not hurt her.

If anyone observed her driving away, she wasn't aware of it. She was beginning to think the village had eyes, and she tried hard not to look suspicious. It was unprecedented for her to be leaving at this time of night, but who would notice? Who cared what a mid-level temporary staffer did to amuse herself at night?

When Lou approached the fork in the road and saw Etienne's black SUV, she flashed her lights and slowed, allowing him to ease onto the road ahead of her. They drove the speed limit and stuck to the back roads, traveling up into the forest that formed the south side of the valley. After about ten minutes of driving, he led her into a deserted trailhead parking lot.

Etienne shut down his engine, got out of his car and locked it then marched over to her. She did the same, grabbing up her bag as she turned to meet him. The waning gibbous of a third-quarter moon was just beginning to rise across the valley, casting them in a pale, shadowed light as it filtered through the trees around them. He loomed over her wearing his customary frown. She simply smiled up at him and said, "Thank you for meeting me."

He held out his hand to her. "Come." He was surprised that she did not hesitate at all but placed her small hand in his much larger one. He turned and pulled her up a wide, well-marked path through the trees. His stride was long, and she had to practically run to keep up or risk being dragged, taking two steps for each of his. She finally tugged hard on his hand and whispered, "Slow down!"

She thought she heard him chuckle, but he did as she bid, slowing his pace but not letting go of her hand. They had gone perhaps a quarter mile up the path when they reached a plateau where the trees thinned out. She'd been concentrating on trying not to trip on the rocky path, looking down at her feet rather than where they were going. When Etienne stopped abruptly, she knocked into him but he steadied her. She looked up and gasped.

Nestled in the cliffs across a deep ravine were the ruins of an old village, complete with ramparts, its ancient stones glowing eerily in the pale moonlight. A soft breeze rustled the leaves on the trees above them, and the swaying shadows made the place seem otherworldly. He pulled her more gently toward the edge of the plateau, where a rustic log bench was placed for a perfect view of the ruins.

He finally let go of her hand after guiding her to sit on the bench. He straddled the opposite end of the bench, facing her, and leaned forward, resting his thick forearms on his knees. "Now tell me what is so urgent, *mademoiselle*."

She ignored his intimidating tone. "Do you know Pierre D'Arcy? He's an RA in the dorms in Lacoste and works in the college administration office."

Etienne's eyes narrowed dangerously. "I know who he is. Why?"

"Apparently, he saw us the night you dropped me off. This evening I learned he'd asked a friend of mine what he knew about our relationship." When Etienne said nothing, she continued. "I walked in on their conversation. I didn't hear anything because they stopped talking when I opened the door, but Alex told me later. Just a little while ago, at dinner."

"Alex? The same man you were with at the Maison Basse?" He struggled to keep the jealousy out of his voice. Comparing himself to a handsome young man like Alex Bouvier was beyond ridiculous.

She nodded, watching him carefully in the moonlight. "Etienne, did you really have him mugged?"

He looked at her closely, trying to see her expression in the shadows. "Is that what he told you?"

She nodded again.

"*Merde,*" he muttered, then bowed his head and pinched the bridge of his nose, rubbing to ease the tension he was feeling. "Lou …" He hesitated, not sure what he should say. What he *could* say. Normally he would scoff such questions off, but he found he could not—did not *want* to—lie to her. "He left me little choice," he said in an unexpectedly gentle voice. "It was for his protection. I did not intend for him to be hurt so badly; I regret that he was."

She said nothing. She seemed to be watching him as carefully as he was watching her. He hadn't felt so powerless since he was a boy, and he feared he would make a serious blunder if he wasn't careful.

"Things are not always as they seem, *petite*. He would have been in much worse danger if the wrong people thought there was something more between us than a poker game. Not unlike you and me. I told you before that this is exceedingly dangerous." He waived a hand between them.

The tender endearment, unconsciously spoken on his part, sealed the deal for her—she believed in her heart he was one of the good guys. "I don't trust Pierre. I don't know him, really—I just see him around. He was the first person I could find to help me that night that Alex was beaten up. Did you know that I was the one who found him unconscious beneath the stairs?" The look on Etienne's face indicated that he had not.

"Yeah, well, that's a whole 'nother story in itself. Anyway, Pierre's just got a creepy presence. He's always watching people. Lately he's been watching Alex. Alex told me tonight that ever since his, uh, accident, Pierre's been asking him all sorts of questions about what he's doing and where he's going. Then today he told him that he'd seen us—you dropping me off—and started asking Alex what he knew about us. What's up with that?"

Matisse took a deep breath. "I think you may have stumbled onto something very interesting." Perhaps the weasel Pierre was Philippe's snitch in the village, the one who'd told his stepbrother about Lou. That had interesting implications. "How well do you know Alex Bouvier?"

"Not real well. We only just became friends recently. I'd never seen him before I found him that night. I went to his hospital room the next morning to make sure he'd be all right. He has family nearby, an older cousin he's close with. He spent a week there after he was released. Since he came back to the village, we've seen each other a few times."

"Are you dating him?"

She frowned. "No."

"But you had dinner with him tonight?"

"Yes, but—"

"What were you doing at the *maison* with him?"

She clenched her jaw. "He asked me to show it to him. He's a photography student and had been to the site for photo shoots. When he learned what my job was there, he asked if I could take him inside. What were *you* doing there?"

He ignored the question. "What is your job there?"

She laughed, and that made him frown. "Do you want to know about me or Alex?"

"Both," he said truthfully.

Feeling strangely pleased with his answer, she gave him the short version of her job at Lacoste, but she left out the real reason she was in France. "Actually I came across some information in my research today that I thought you might be interested in. It was another reason I wanted to see you."

"What information?"

"I'll get to that in a minute, but there's something else you should know about Alex." Etienne scowled but nodded, and she laughed. "No wonder everyone is so afraid of you—that look is positively fierce!"

"Then why, *mademoiselle,* does it not work on you?"

She gave such a well-executed Gallic shrug that he almost laughed. "Who knows? Maybe I just see through it. Anyway, I need to tell you something, but Etienne, you have to promise me that you won't hurt him again. Alex may be in over his head, but he's not one of the bad guys."

He stayed silent. "I mean it," she persisted. "I don't know what you're up to, but I'm beginning to suspect it's some sort of undercover work. You don't need to tell me one way or the other because, honestly, I don't want to know"—*unless it has to do with missing women*—"but I don't want Alex to get caught up in whatever is about to go down."

"What makes you think something is about to go down?" *Mon Dieu,* she was the most perceptive person he'd ever met.

"Etienne, promise me."

He couldn't resist her, had no defense against her, not when she used his name like he was her trusted friend. He found himself yearning to be that person. "I promise, *petite,* I'll do my best to protect him."

She frowned.

"Without hurting him," he added.

She hesitated only slightly. "Alex told me, accidentally—it just slipped out and then he was stuck—that you are the primary suspect in a major wine fraud investigation."

"Did he now?" *And where would he have come by that information?*

"Uh-huh, he did. When I asked him if he was some sort of cop, he said no, that he was only helping out a friend. He said the organization his friend works for thinks that in addition to this major wine fraud operation, there's something even more sinister going on."

"*Merde.*" Etienne shook his head. "He has no idea what he's stepped into."

"That was sort of my read on it, too. I think he's truly trying to help his friend, but I can't believe his friend has any idea what's going on here."

He looked at her sharply. "Do you?"

She shook her head. "No clue, but I'm not stupid. There're a handful of creeps hanging out in the village—sometimes with *you*—and then there's you playing the town mean bastard, having people beat up and all, and then there's Pierre skulking around asking questions and spying on people, and now there's Alex trying to sniff around. I have a real fine-honed creep meter. You don't register on it at all—how about that? But the rest of them sure do. Except Alex, of course."

He laughed. He couldn't remember the last time he'd truly laughed. It wasn't even funny, but she was just too much. "*Désolé, ma petite,*" he said when he caught her irritated look. "This is no laughing matter. But tell me, are you sure you are not a detective yourself? You seem to have a keen power of observation."

His genuine smile softened his ravaged features, and even in the moon-lit shadows, she could see a sparkle in those dark eyes. Without conscious thought she reached up and lightly touched the scar on his face. He flinched and jerked away, and she yanked her hand back as if scorched.

He cleared his throat. "You said you found something in your research."

She swallowed back the sudden lump in her throat and nodded. *How long has it been since he's been touched in friendship?* To hide the unwanted emotion bubbling inside her, and the tears that threatened to spill, she burrowed into her bag for her notepad and the flashlight. "I spent most of the afternoon today slogging through church ledgers. My purpose was to track the births, marriages, and deaths of the residents of the Maison Basse." She chanced a look up at him. "As it happens, I found the history of the residents of *La Ferme du Vieux Pont* as well."

He stiffened but remained silent, so she continued. "The first mention of the Matisse name appeared in 1875, with the baptism of Hubert Etienne

Matisse—your great-grandfather." Still no reaction, so she turned on the flashlight and recited the chronology of events—the baptisms, marriages, and funerals, up until the last one mentioned: Juliette Moreau Matisse Lemans was buried in 2001.

Lou flicked off the flashlight and waited for a response. Still he said nothing. "Etienne," she said softly, "did you know your aunt Regina? Is she still alive?"

Matisse abruptly stood and took a few steps toward the edge of the plateau. The moon had risen higher now, and its light shone directly down on him. He faced away from her, but she could see his strong profile, his fierce expression. Standing there, silhouetted against the glowing stones of the ancient ruins across the ravine, he looked like a formidable warrior—his posture tall and erect with his wide shoulders held back, feet spread, fists at his hips.

Although he kept his expression rigidly controlled, the emotions roiled inside him. How is it that this tiny woman had so easily discovered his family! What could she possibly hope to accomplish by dragging the tragedy out of the past and worse—confront him with it! He'd had a lifetime of controlling his emotions and his reactions, and it had served him well until now. She could have no idea how quickly her factual recitations had opened old wounds. His anger bubbled inside, and he wanted to rage at her for her audacity, but he couldn't. He had heard her voice as she recounted the history. She had spoken as a friend, her tone innocent of malice or judgment. He heard true compassion in her question about his aunt.

He took a deep breath then spoke without turning. "You remind me of her, *petite*. She was fiercely protective of me after my father passed. She was older than my mother and even more innocent of the world, yet she had your uncanny 'creep meter' as you call it. She was not afraid to speak her mind. She begged my mother not to marry Jean Luc, and they fought. But in the end, my mother acted as she believed she should, not comprehending what a terrible mistake she was making."

He turned to her then, gesturing to the notepad in her hand. "Why did you do this? What possible relevance can this have to you or your research?"

His voice was gruff with accusation, and Lou was suddenly unsure of herself. "I, ah, it's not relevant to my research—at least, I don't think it is." She fidgeted, fingering the curled edges of the pad. She glanced up at him to see he was watching her, waiting for a better answer.

"I was curious, I guess, and when I saw the first entry, I just couldn't help follow it. You told me your father had died when you were young and your mother had to remarry to hang on to the property, so I guess I just wanted to see if I could collaborate that with facts." She tried to shrug off the sting of his rebuff. "It's what I do. I'm sorry if I intruded. For some stupid reason, I thought you might like to know what the ledgers said about your family."

"Is that all?"

She swallowed and cleared her throat. "I, um, I guess I also wanted to learn more about you." She said it so quietly, he barely heard the words.

"Why?"

She looked at him, some of her fire coming back, and she snapped at him. "Where I come from, that's what friends do—they learn about each other and they try to help."

"How could you possibly think that I need your help?" he snapped back.

"Fine, I'm sorry. I should have known better than to … Oh, never mind." She turned away from him, but she couldn't hide the hurt in her voice.

Stunned by the emotion behind her words, Etienne found himself moving back to the bench to sit down. "I've never met anyone like you."

Fourteen

They sat at opposite ends of the log bench, silent for long minutes in the eerie moonlight. Finally, Etienne reached out his hand. "*Je peux?*" Lou tore off the pages and handed them to him, along with the flashlight.

He flicked on the light and scanned the entries that she'd recorded on the page. "You are very thorough, *mademoiselle,*" he said, not unkindly. "You have showed this to no one else?"

She shook her head. "Of course not."

"I knew most of it, not exact dates, but the general chronology. Regina lives near Bordeaux now. She has a small vineyard and makes a passable wine that is popular in the local markets."

"Do you ever see her?"

"Not recently, not since I moved back here six months ago. But before that, I lived with her. She took me in when I, ah, when it became no longer possible for me to live in my mother's home. *Depuis l'âge de seize ans.*"

"What happened, Etienne?" Lou's voice held such compassion that he could feel it wrapping around him, comforting him. It was a feeling he'd never had before.

He turned off the flashlight and set it down on the bench, then folded the papers and put them in a pocket inside his jacket. He glanced at her to see if she would protest, but she only pulled her legs up and wrapped her arms around her knees, waiting for him to continue.

"Are you sure you want to hear this, *petite?* It's not a pretty story. I'm not sure why I am compelled to tell it now—I've never done before." He gave her a small smile. "I think perhaps you have bewitched me."

She nodded. "If you're willing, I'd like to hear it."

"Why?"

"Because I want to know you better."

He regarded her a moment then shook his head as if he thought she was nuts. But instead of talking, he pulled out his phone and scrolled through the contacts then rapidly tapping out a text to someone. It was a long message, and Lou had a brief flash of concern that he was giving away their location. But she'd already decided to trust him, and there was no backing out now.

Dropping the phone back in his pocket, he turned to her. "Regina lived with us when I was small. Before my parents were married, she ran the house while my father tended the land. Most of what I know of the past, I learned from her, after I left Lacoste. Apparently my father never intended to marry. Accordingly to my aunt, he was extremely shy and uncomfortable around women. I inherited his size and … *visage,* so I understand the feeling."

He was sitting on the bench facing the gorge, leaning on his thighs, looking relaxed. The moon was bright now, but his features were mostly obscured from her view by his thick, dark hair. It fell in a straight curtain to just below his chin, but when he glanced at her, it shifted slightly and she could see that his expression had softened.

"My mother was the only child of his closest neighbor. She was just nineteen years old when her parents were killed in an automobile accident. Their property was not as large as my father's, but it was adjacent—"

Lou gasped. "Adjacent?"

"Yes." His eyes narrowed slightly. "Why does this surprise you?"

"You're familiar with the property then?"

He shook his head. "Not really. When I was small, the house was leased out to tenants. After my mother's second marriage, her stepson took over the property, and I was not allowed beyond the gate that separated it from ours. Why do you ask?"

"I found something else in my research—something strange that I think has to do with that property." She quickly explained her discovery that the old château prison may in fact be one and the same as the current Les Prés.

Matisse thought about that for a moment. Something stirred in his memory, but he couldn't quite latch on to it. Perhaps dredging up the memories of that horrible time would trigger something. If it would help nail Philippe, it was worth it. He became less ambivalent about what felt like a confession and continued with his story.

"As a girl, my mother, Juliette, was a friend to the brother and sister next door, although they were many years older. There was a man—a business associate of her father, I believe—who had been pushing for her hand in marriage, but according to my aunt, Juliette didn't like him. My mother was no beauty and had very little experience with men. She assumed Jean Luc pursued her only for the land she would one day inherit, although it appeared he had plenty of wealth himself."

"Jean Luc? Is that the same man she eventually married after your father passed?"

"*Oui.* He became quite persistent after Juliette's parents were killed, and he frightened her. She came to my father and begged him to help her. They had always been fond of each other, as I said, they had been friends since she was a child. She somehow convinced my father that she would take care of him, would bear his children and would be a good wife, if he would marry her."

"Your father was twice her age, wasn't he?"

He nodded. "Regina told me that he agreed out of friendship for her parents. He knew she was not ready to manage the farm and Jean Luc was pressing her hard, cruelly almost. My father couldn't bear to see her fall victim to such a man. So he married her. Later, it surprised them all when Juliette and Ricard actually fell in love."

"What a sweet story," Lou whispered, not expecting him to hear her.

"It was what you would call a happy accident," he agreed. "And then I came along and, according to my aunt, we were the perfect little family. My aunt and my mother conspired to run the house and take care of me. My father continued to manage and work his land as well as my mother's. I ran free through the vineyards and orchards when I wasn't in school. I played alongside my father while he worked, thinking I was helping, of course. Most likely I was a pest, but he didn't seem to mind."

He fell silent, gazing off into the distance as if remembering those days. Lou remained quiet, watching him.

"When he died we were all devastated. I was not too young to understand I would never see my papa again. My mother withdrew, locked in her grief. Regina tried to console us both while dealing with her own grief. I had no friends to speak of. I was very shy and with my mother buried in her own grief ..."

"But your mother remarried so quickly! She must have snapped out of her grief."

"Oh, yes," he replied bitterly. "Jean Luc started coming around almost immediately. The first time he had tried to court my mother, he had been aggressive and demanding in his pursuit. But after my father's death, he was gentle and consoling, and my mother, in her grieving state, could not see the falseness of his feigned sincerity. My aunt tried to keep him away, but he managed to work around her. He wooed my mother gently, in part by pretending to be my friend. I am ashamed to say we both believed him."

"But you said she was forced to marry to keep the property," Lou reminded him.

He nodded. "You have to remember the time—it was the early 1980s and inflation was out of control. Interest rates were impossibly high, and credit was scarce. Neither my mother nor my aunt knew the first thing about running a farm. While my father had some trusted men working with him, he had kept the finances and the general running of both properties to himself. Regina tried to step in, but routine farm activities went unfinished because the men either had no direction or hadn't been paid, which resulted in an inferior harvest and lower prices, and mortgage payments were missed."

"So Jean Luc took advantage of this and convinced her that he could salvage it all?"

Etienne nodded again, still gazing out into the night.

After a few moments of silence, Lou ventured her next question. "And then the really bad stuff started happening?"

He laughed without humor. "*Tu n'a aucune idée.*" *You have no idea.*

Simon Purcell reread the text three times until it finally penetrated that he had a serious problem. *Who the fuck is Alexander Bouvier, and who in bloody hell got him involved?* Swiveling his desk chair around, he quickly accessed the INTERPOL database, and in less than five minutes, he had facts. Now what he needed were answers.

Unlike his boss, Jonathan Spencer was not still in his office. He'd left a couple of hours earlier and stopped off at the pub in his neighborhood to catch the rerun of tonight's soccer match. One pint of beer turned into three as he and his buddies rehashed their team's win. At eleven o'clock the pub was still crowded and noisy, and his friends were making no moves to call it quits. Peering into his empty glass, he was about to signal for another when he felt the vibration of his phone in his pocket. He pulled it out, saw who it was, and cursed.

"Gotta go, mate," he said to the man next to him over the din in the pub. He held up the phone in explanation at his friend's questioning expression. The guy nodded, waved a farewell, and turned back to his conversation.

Spencer tossed money on the bar and stepped out into the street to answer the call.

"Where are you?" No polite chit-chat from the boss.

"Just finished up dinner with friends and heading home. What's up?"

"I need you back here. Now. Something's come up."

Spencer's blood suddenly ran cold. "The Yings?" Since escorting the widow of their Beijing agent and her teenage daughter from Paris, he'd taken a personal interest in their welfare.

"No, no, they're fine. We have a, ah, situation in Lacoste."

Another sensation seized Spencer at that moment. A chill knifed down his spine, and he had to bite his lip to keep from asking more questions. "I'm twenty minutes away by tube."

"Take a cab and get here in ten," was the response before the connection went dead.

Alex stared at the ceiling above his bed, hands behind his head, replaying his evening with Louise in his mind. He didn't know what to make of her, but he was drawn to her as he'd never been drawn to a woman before. She was lovely, with a sensuous smile and a compact, curvy body, but for the first time in memory, the surface beauty was just that—the surface. It was what lay beneath that intrigued him. The heart of her, the essence of what made her uniquely Louise. It was her spirit, her nature, her ... substance ... that ensnared him.

She didn't like to talk about herself—was adept at steering the topic elsewhere—and she didn't pry into his past either. Normally that's how people learned about each other, relating stories of the past. Not Louise. Through their conversations he felt that she'd probed him, took the measure of his character, and somehow learned all she needed to know about him. And he was unclear whether he'd left a favorable impression. She seemed to value honesty, honor, and conviction ... was more interested in what he thought and felt about something than what he had accomplished. *Good thing, because there isn't much there but a spectacular crash and burn.*

Women usually pursued him, not the other way around. He knew women found him attractive. He didn't consider himself vain, but after years of hearing it from beautiful and desirable women, he accepted it and had never thought about it beyond that. Had the women in his life ever looked beneath the surface? Had they cared? And if they had, would they have liked what they would have seen? Did Lou?

It would seem that she looked at Matisse in the same way—with a scope below the surface. It was obvious she'd found those admirable traits in him— the honor and conviction that she seemed to value so highly. What if she was right?

Louise stared at Matisse in horror, not sure she'd heard him correctly. "Your stepbrother raped your mother? Where the hell was her husband?"

"I warned you the story was unpleasant." Matisse was regretting his momentary lapse of sanity that had him relaying the sordid details of his past to this woman. How could she not be repulsed by him now?

"But why didn't she get the police involved? Why didn't she leave? What about your aunt?" The outrage in her voice was unmistakable.

Matisse just looked at her, unwilling to continue. "Oh, God," Lou whispered. "Your aunt, too? Jesus Christ."

"My mother was a strong woman in many ways, but in this she was not. Philippe was only six years older than she was, and he was very strong. He threatened to hurt me and Regina both if she didn't cooperate with him. Regina tried to intervene, and he made good on his threats—Regina took several beatings, usually due to her efforts to protect me."

"But why didn't she go to the police?"

It was a question he'd often asked his aunt, and he now repeated her words, even though they still burned in his gut. "Domestic violence is tricky. It was her word against Philippe's, and if my mother refused to cooperate, there was nothing to be done. She could have left. She quickly learned her efforts to stop it only made things worse."

"Oh God," Lou whispered, imagining the helplessness the women must have felt.

"But what about you?"

"Philippe never missed an opportunity to goad me. I was a big lad, and strong, but unsure of myself and confused about what was happening. Once when I saw him strike my mother, I jumped on him, trying to get him to stop." He looked out into the darkness, watching the scene unfold. "It was a mistake I learned not to make again. He was much stronger than me, of course. He tied me to a chair and told me he would teach me to not interfere again."

Tears streamed down Lou's face now, the unimaginable horrors that this little boy had faced twisting her stomach in knots. She wanted to cover her ears, make him stop, but she couldn't.

"He raped her, right there in front of me. My mother screamed at him, begged him not to make me watch. He only slapped her harder and told her to shut up or he'd rape me, too."

"Holy Christ," she whispered.

"Once," he continued as if he hadn't heard her, "I was late coming home from school, and he took his belt to me. My aunt tried to stop him, but she only made him angrier. He hurt her very badly, so badly that my mother was allowed to tend her."

"Allowed?"

"He kept them apart. Regina lived in our house with me but he kept my mother in the house on the other property—the house she grew up in. I presume he lived there, too, because he never stayed in our house. I never knew what she did there, and I was never allowed to go see her there. If I behaved, if she behaved, she was allowed to spend an hour with us in the evening. But never alone. There was always someone guarding us, making sure she didn't whisper anything to me that I was not supposed to know."

"What do you think was going on?"

He hung his head. "I never knew. Something that frightened her, but … I never tried to find out, because anything other than perfect behavior was punished. Not just me, but my mother, too. For every one of my transgressions, we were both punished. It was easier to pretend our life was normal than to rebel against the injustice."

Lou could sense his shame and felt the outrage rise in her. She leaned over and gently touched his arm. He stiffened but did not pull away. "Etienne," she said softly. "You were a child. It wasn't your fault. It wasn't up to you to save her."

It was a truth he had eventually learned to accept, although it hadn't been easy—still wasn't after all these years. "My aunt finally got out. After that last beating, she was severely weakened, and there was nothing she could do for either of us. My mother refused to fight him, and I was afraid to do anything that would cause her more punishment, so in the end, Regina decided to save herself."

"Where did she go? How did she escape?"

"Only my mother was restricted to the property, so it was easy." He shrugged. "She went out to the market as usual and simply never returned."

"She abandoned you?"

"I would have done the same thing. In fact, a few years later, I did."

"You abandoned your mother?" Lou was incredulous.

He nodded. "She insisted that I leave, and she was right. Regina left us when I was ten years old. She had put up with it for three years, trying to make a normal life for me, but she just didn't have the strength for more abuse. After she left, I found an envelope under my pillow with some cash, a telephone number, and some instructions. I kept it hidden for six years before I used it."

"And your mother?"

"Once I made it to Regina, we contacted the police, of course, but my mother refused to press charges, insisting it was a misunderstanding." He closed his eyes briefly. "We never spoke to her again. Philippe didn't come after me, not until …" He cleared his throat. "I think he just wanted me gone. Whatever it was that was going on in that other house, neither of us had any knowledge of it."

He was silent, as if the story was over, but Lou just waited. Doing the math in her head, she knew many years passed between his leaving his mother and her death. And many years more before he returned to Lacoste. But there was another piece of the puzzle that didn't make any sense.

"Etienne, whatever happened to Jean Luc?"

The question seemed to jolt him out of his own thoughts. "*Quoi?*"

"Jean Luc—your mother's second husband. You talked about Philippe like he was the husband."

"I never saw him after the wedding."

"But isn't that a little strange?"

He shrugged. "What one might consider strange in that situation is relative. It's possible that he came and went at the other house—I was never allowed over there. But my mother never mentioned him."

Well, that's certainly true, she thought. "What about Philippe?"

"What about him?" Etienne was already regretting this conversation, and the reliving of his miserable childhood had given him a pounding headache.

"What happened to him?"

"Nothing happened to him. He owns the house—he managed to get the title to it before my mother died, so it was not part of her estate. He stays there occasionally."

"What? He lives next door to you? And you haven't killed him?"

He chuckled. "Not yet, *petite*. Not yet."

"Do you think it could be the old château prison? Do you think that had something to do with Jean Luc's obsession with the property and the strange behavior of his son?"

He snapped his head toward her. He was staring at her, but in his mind he saw something else: his mother's fear, Jean Luc's absence, the guards, the locked gate, the cruelty, the secrecy. His eyes narrowed dangerously as they focused on her. "Tell me again what you found."

She swallowed, then picked up her notepad again and reached for the flashlight. She flipped to the page where she'd recorded the property transactions. "I didn't have time to find collaborating evidence yet, but according to an old property tax register, that same property used to be referred to as Les Presons. In the early eighteenth century, it was part of the château property, like the Maison Basse."

He said nothing, just continued to focus his sharp eyes on her, so she cleared her throat and continued.

"In the Occitan language, *preson* translates to "prison." I guess it makes sense that the château would have someplace to hold criminals, but usually those old castles had some sort of dungeon. By the time the property was sold to …" She consulted her notes. "By the time the property was sold to a François Moreau, the name had been shortened and the accent added, changing the meaning. But look," she pointed to the coordinates she'd copied from the old records. "It's got to be the same property." She looked up at Etienne, but he had stopped paying attention.

"Etienne?" Between the light of the moon and the flashlight illumination, she could see his face clearly. "Whoa," she said and almost scooted back. He looked downright deadly. "Are you okay?"

He turned those cold eyes on her, and she actually shivered, but then they softened ever so slightly as he cocked his head and stared at her. "Twenty years ago I swore I would bring that bastard to justice. For the past two years, it has been my mission—my job, in fact—to make it so, but he has covered his tracks well. You may have just given me the means."

———————————

"Why does Alexander Bouvier believe that Etienne Matisse is a suspect in a wine fraud operation?"

Spencer flinched at the direct question. He held up his hands as if to protect himself from the tightly controlled fury that was rolling off his boss. "I can explain."

"I should hope so." Simon Purcell picked up a page sitting on his desk and started reading from it. *"Alexander Bouvier, born 1984 in Sarlat to Jean Claude and Nicole Bouvier of Les Eyzies. Attended primary through high school at Les Eyzies public schools. Graduated University of California in 2006 with a baccalaureate degree in International Finance. Recruited out of school by Goldman Sachs in San Francisco but was released in 2009, then voluntarily admitted himself to an inpatient drug rehab program at Mercy Hospital where he stayed for the full 30 days of the program. No known employment since. Returned to France via London June 2010 with an expired visa. August 2010 enrolled SCAD Art College, Lacoste campus. Address on college record is a Rasteau address belonging to a Kaden Macallister."*

He put the page down and glared at Spencer. "A friend of yours, I presume?"

Spencer sucked in a deep breath but refused to cower in front of his boss, nor make excuses. He knew he'd breached security by confiding in Alex, and God only knew how many prickly regulations he'd violated by asking him to snoop around Matisse, but he was too frustrated with the apparent lack of interest in the goings-on in Lacoste to feel any remorse. "Yes, he's a college chum. He's in Lacoste for photography classes. Listen, sir," he blundered on before Simon could stop him. "I realize what I did is a breach of protocol, but since we seem to have inadequate resources to put someone in that village, we'll never get anything on Matisse. I saw an opportunity and took it."

Simon regarded his agent calmly over steepled fingers. "What led you to believe Matisse needed investigating?"

Spencer stared at his boss. "Ah, sir … sir, it's obvious he's involved. He was in Bordeaux, involved in that print shop that we raided. Then he moved to Provence, and not too long after that, the fake Beaucastel shipment was discovered. He's installed himself as some mafioso wannabe in Lacoste and runs a gang of thugs collecting empty wine bottles. You've mentioned him yourself!"

"And if I thought he would provide us one iota of information, why have I not put agents on him? Why, do you suppose, if I had a concern about this man, that I wouldn't have had someone reporting on him?"

"That's just it, sir—it makes no sense!" The frustration of the past few months and his superiors' continued denial of what Spencer thought was obvious overcame his usual reticence to push his opinion beyond the written reports. His career was toast at this point, so holding back wasn't going to do him any good. "I'm the analyst assigned to this case, and I've repeatedly put in my reports my suspicions about this bloke, but my conclusions have been ignored."

Simon sighed heavily and twisted his head back and forth quickly to get the kinks out of his neck. *What a bloody cluster.* The passionate commitment to discovering the truth interlaid with the reckless enthusiasm of his best analyst had him questioning his own judgment. Deep undercover agents could be such a bloody pain. It was his own damn fault for keeping the kid in the dark, and now it had come back to bite him in the arse big time. Matisse was going to be furious, but there was nothing to be done for it. "Spencer, Matisse is one of ours."

If the young man's jaw had not been attached to his head, it would have dropped to the ground. He stared at his boss, his mentor, the man he trusted and respected, and couldn't find the muscles to work his mouth or brain waves to form a coherent sentence. But his expression screamed, *What the fuck!*

Fifteen

By the time Louise stumbled into the commissary the next morning, the little village was abuzz. A young woman had been found dead in the grass behind the church. The grizzly news sent a whisper of foreboding up her spine. She listened with dismay to the American student who rang up her purchase as the sordid details—true or fabricated, Lou had no idea—were relayed with morbid excitement.

"No one knows who she is, but they say there was a lot of blood. Some sort of stomach wound." The girl shivered and put her hands to her own belly. "And," she added in an even lower tone, "They say she had bruises on her wrists, like she'd been tied up!"

Lou was horrified. "And there's no idea at all who she is or how she got there? Are there any suspects?"

The cashier shook her head. "That's all I know. I got here at six this morning, and there were lights flashing everywhere down there. I tried to see what was going on, but they were keeping everyone away. I think the church groundskeeper found her. I've only gotten snippets myself from people coming in."

Lou took her coffee and croissant and found an empty table in a corner away from the door. It had been a long night, and she was exhausted. Her calendar was clear of meetings today, thank the stars, because she needed time to process everything she'd learned. And she had to get to Alex first thing, before he did something crazy, like point the finger at Matisse for the girl's death. She had convinced Etienne to let her give Alex some basic information to get him to back off. Before they'd left the plateau last night—early this morning, actually—Matisse had received an answer back that the connection with

Alex had been determined, and that he checked out. Everyone agreed that he needed to be warned away and keep his distance from Matisse.

But now, the appearance of a dead girl frightened her. Etienne had not confided his suspicions about what might be going on with Philippe, but it was clear he had pieced something together in his head. Whatever it was, it had made him furious. Other than telling her that the thugs in the village who appeared to be controlled by Etienne were, in fact, Philippe's men, he refused to say more. They returned to their cars, and he cautioned her again to stay as far away from him as possible. She drove the direct route back to the village while Etienne went a different direction.

She had to warn him, despite his directive that she not contact him. *Did you hear the news? Please be careful, GG.*

Next she texted Alex, not sure if he would be awake yet. *Thanks again for dinner. Meet me for coffee this morning? Lou*

Not surprisingly, the answer from Etienne came almost immediately. *Yes, you too. BA.*

She couldn't help but smile as she felt a surge of warm affection for that big gruff man. Maybe when this was all over—whatever *this* was—he could drop the act and they could actually be friends. She hoped it happened before she was finished in France. Not that she'd made any progress at all on her true purpose for being here. She shoved that dismal thought aside.

She'd finished her croissant and was contemplating another when Alex finally texted her back. *Would love to. Where?*

Fifteen minutes later, Alex met Lou at the bottom of the cobblestone lane across the parking lot from the church. The emergency vehicles were gone, but the yellow crime-scene tape was still blocking the small park behind the building, and there were plenty of curious spectators milling around in front. She took his hand as she leaned in to kiss his cheeks. "Don't say anything," she whispered. "Just come with me." They walked together, hand in hand, down to the lower lot where she'd left her car.

He stayed silent as she maneuvered onto the road, waiting for her to explain. After a few minutes, she glanced over at him and smiled. "Sorry to be so mysterious, but from now on, we have to be real careful about what we say around anyone in Lacoste."

He raised his eyebrows. "Where are we going?"

"I'm not sure—somewhere we can be private in public and inconspicuous on a Tuesday morning. Any ideas?"

He thought for a minute. "Have you been to the market in Gordes? I'm pretty sure it's today, and it's not too far away."

"Perfect! I haven't been to it yet, but I've heard about it."

They made the short drive, and as they rounded the curve at the bottom entrance to the village, cars were stacked up waiting to turn into the parking lot. Alex directed her past the traffic jam and up into the center of town. She laughed as they drove straight through the market itself, with vendors situated all around the main roundabout, then farther up the road to a less-crowded parking lot above the town. She parked and grabbed her shopping bag as they headed down the short hill back to the market.

Alex didn't press her to talk about what was on her mind but simply enjoyed being with her. It was a beautiful fall morning—crisp and clear—cool enough to need a coat but not so cold as to be frigid. He had no idea what she was up to but suspected it had something to do with the phone call he'd received from Spencer this morning. She obviously knew more about Matisse than she was letting on, since Spencer had confirmed her assertion that he was "one of the good guys," apologized for getting him involved, and told him to keep his distance.

Hand in hand, they meandered through the vendor stalls, taking in the unique creations of local fashion designers, the brightly colored tablecloths with motifs of sunflowers, lavender, and fleur-des-lys; handcrafted leather purses of all shapes, sizes, and textures; basketfuls of Marseille soap made from the many fragrances of Provence; and ceramic pitchers, platters, and bowls glazed with the deep yellow of mustard and the distinctive red of the poppies that covered the fields and hillsides in the spring. Lou pulled him to a stop when she discovered a stall with a large awning draped with colorful scarves in a multitude of designs and textures. She boldly bargained with the little white-haired lady while Alex cheered her on, and she ended up with three fashionable scarves, one of which she wrapped around her neck to wear immediately.

"I can't believe so many people really shop at these markets," she commented as they made their way to where the food vendors were doing a brisk business, realizing that the crowd was not all tourists. The scent in the air shifted from the delicate scent of lavender and perfume to the earthy pungency of cheese and the mouthwatering decadence of roasting chickens. The display of goods shifted too—now it was all glossy olives, nuts and spices, rounds of cheese and baskets of salamis of all description, fresh fish shining with the luminosity seen only when pulled from the sea that morning, steroid-free meat and poultry, and incredible-looking fruits and vegetables, including seasonal delicacies such as mushrooms and truffles—and every purveyor seemed to have a line of people waiting to buy.

Alex looked at her in surprise. "Why not?"

"I don't know, it just seems so … impractical."

Alex smiled down at her and squeezed her hand. His father was a chef, and he knew only too well how picky the French could be about what they bought and who they bought it from. "It's very practical. These markets offer a far better quality of product than what the villagers can find at a supermarket. Besides, it's a long-standing tradition for the French, going back centuries, and much more satisfying than pushing a cart through a supermarket."

She looked at him with raised eyebrows, clearly surprised.

He nodded to the crowd in front of a large table covered with plump red tomatoes, fluffy heads of lettuce, and neatly arranged shining apples. "It's a social event for the locals, a chance to catch up on gossip. For some, it's the highlight of their week."

"I had no idea." Looking at the people with a new eye, she realized many had rolling net-canvas carts that were filled with bags of produce and butcher paper–wrapped packages. If they weren't chatting and laughing with neighbors, they were haggling with the vendors. All looked to be thoroughly enjoying themselves. She found it fascinating.

After they'd exhausted the market, Alex led her down a side street away from the fray and into a small café. Even though it was market day, the café was mostly empty. Once their order had been delivered, Alex leaned back, sipped his coffee, and waited.

Lou took a deep breath and blurted out her news. "They found a dead woman behind the church this morning."

Alex choked on his coffee.

"I don't have any details," she clarified, looking grim. "I just heard about it from a student this morning. They took the body away before I came down. That's what the yellow tape was all about by the church. Apparently the groundskeeper found her."

"*Jésus Christ,*" Alex muttered, shaking his head.

Reaching over to cover his hand with hers, she held his gaze, her voice low and serious when she said, "Alex, Matisse had nothing to do with this. Don't even go there."

He yanked back his hand and ran it roughly through his hair, trying to rein in his exasperation. "How can you know that?" Despite what Spencer had told him, he was having a hard time changing his opinion of Matisse, and it only pissed him off more that Lou seemed to be on the inside of whatever was going on.

"Because he was with me."

Incredulous, Alex stood, shoving back his chair so that it banged into the wall behind him. Not caring who might hear, he practically barked at her. "You spent the night with him?"

"Oh, for God's sake, Alex." She was more amused than angry. "Sit down and shut up for a minute. No, I did not spend the night with …" She glanced over her shoulder and caught the café owner watching them from behind his counter. She turned back and lowered her voice. "Sit down," she hissed.

Stunned, he sat.

"Now you listen to me. Whatever's going on is way over your head and mine. Etienne is a friend, and I won't have you sputtering around making accusations you can't back up." Her pale blue eyes were gleaming with sparks of ire, and she brought to his mind the image of an avenging Valkyrie, all but snarling at him.

"After what you told me last night, I had no choice but to contact him. He is *not* what you think, and he is *not* the bad guy, and if you don't stop snooping around him, you'll get him and yourself in deep shit."

He knew this now but couldn't understand how she did. They stared at each other for a long moment. To his surprise, she blinked first. "Sorry, I'm not angry with you. Well, maybe just a little." She took a sip of her coffee and then, resting her elbows on the small table, massaged her temples. "It was a long night."

Very softly, he said, "He's undercover with INTERPOL."

Her head snapped up.

"My friend called me this morning. Turns out he was out of the loop. Whatever you told Matisse last night apparently got everyone's attention."

Lou nodded in satisfaction. "Good to know."

"You have good instincts, *mademoiselle*."

The corner of her mouth lifted slightly at his admission, not in triumph but with understanding, and she reached across the table again for his hand. He took hers firmly and interlaced their fingers. "He said to tell you he was sorry for your injuries. He felt he had no choice, given the people who witnessed your game. He'll return your money."

"I probably deserved it. I made it impossible for him to ignore me."

Coffees finished, Alex dropped some coins onto the tray with the check, and a short time later they were walking back through the market. With her arm tucked into his, Lou acquiesced to his request and told him the full truth about her encounters with Matisse, including the part about going to his house that night of the storm. She kept the details of her research to herself, as well as the story of Etienne's childhood, having no wish to break his confidence. But she did say that his investigation centered on his own stepbrother.

"Do you think the appearance of the dead woman in the village has anything to do with what might be going on?"

She shook her head. "I have no idea. Etienne didn't give me any details about what he was doing or what he thought was going on, other than it involved Philippe. Clearly, it's more than just wine fraud. I don't even get what the point is with the wine fraud, unless it's supposed to be a distraction to put suspicion off what the real play is. Did your friend have any more information for you?"

"No." He motioned to a table that was overflowing with delectable fruits and vegetables. "You should pick out some stuff so we don't come back empty handed. I think from now on, we both need to be careful about appearances."

When they returned to the village, she parked in the upper lot. As they walked down the steep cobblestones toward her apartment, they encountered Pierre coming out of the front door of his dormitory. When he saw them, he waved his hands excitedly. "Did you hear?"

"You mean about the dead woman?" Lou asked. "Yeah, we heard."

Pierre nodded vigorously, almost gleefully. "They just arrested Etienne Matisse for the murder!"

Sixteen

Simon Purcell was just pulling into the underground car park below INTERPOL's London headquarters when his cell phone buzzed. He listened to the brief report then cursed. "I'm on my way up now." He'd had only three hours of sleep, which was about three hours too few, and he was in a foul mood.

He headed straight for the conference room, tossed his coat and briefcase into the only empty chair at the table, and poured a cup of strong black coffee from the sideboard. His staff remained silent as he took his first few sips.

He squared his shoulders and faced his team. "This case has just gone straight into the shitter. How the bloody hell did we manage to blow a deep cover agent *and* let him get arrested for murder, all before breakfast?"

Thirty minutes after that dismal briefing in London wrapped up, the telephone in Kaden Macallister's home office rang.

"Macallister."

"Bloody hell, mate, are you getting soft? Why aren't you out picking grapes?"

"Since when are you interested in grapes? I thought your poison was whisky."

"So it is, so it is. I could use some right about now, as a matter of fact."

Kaden glanced at the clock: 10:45 a.m. Leaning back in his chair, he sighed. "Spit it out, Simon. I get the feeling this isn't a social call. Somehow, I think I've been expecting to hear from you."

"Who is Alexander Bouvier?" Direct as ever, Simon knew Kaden well enough to know when to cut the bullshit and get to the point.

"He's my cousin—Jean Claude's younger boy. But we're close, Simon. Very close." There was a hint of warning in Kaden's voice.

"Sounds like you may have a better idea than I do about just what he's been up to while he's been snapping pics down there."

Kaden hesitated before replying. He and Simon went way back, as far back as Cambridge, almost forty years now. Fresh out of graduate school, while Kaden was climbing into the upper echelons of London's investment bank community, Simon had taken his international business degree to INTERPOL. His climb took longer within the government bureaucracy, but he'd stuck with it, unlike Kaden, who'd crashed and burned after a little more than a decade of brilliant success, complete with the humiliation of a society-page divorce.

Kaden had left his London chums behind without a second look; most of them had ducked for cover when he'd been unjustly fried in the gossip rags. He would have lost touch with Simon, too, had it not been for a couple of situations that had required the assistance of the international cops. In the high-stakes world of international finance, the temptation to cheat was often hard to resist. Whether it was patent infringement, corporate sabotage, illegal bribes, or forged contracts, Kaden had uncovered plenty of anomalies in his pursuit of companies with innovative ideas.

With a gift for spotting potential and an expertise in emerging technologies, Kaden had remained active in the investment game, albeit on a much smaller scale. His home office amidst the vineyards of rural France was a far cry from the London financial district. But the game didn't change much—careful due diligence was still needed and anomalies were still noted. In one recent transaction, he'd detected some carefully disguised discrepancies in the movement of funds across borders. He'd called in Simon, and together they'd collected enough evidence to prove the company had engaged in illegal sales of sensitive software to prohibited nations. The principals went to jail, and Kaden was able to step in and sweep up the assets—valuable patents and designs for cutting-edge security technology—at pennies on the pound. Kaden not only trusted Simon, but he owed him.

"While he was recovering from getting the crap beat out of him in Lacoste a few weeks ago, he may have mentioned something about the counterfeiting of wine labels. Since when do you stoop to minor infractions like wine fraud?"

"Is this phone secure?"

Kaden laughed. "Not at all. We don't get much terrorist activity down here in Rasteau."

"Look, old chum, your boy is flirting with some dangerous people, and now there's been an unfortunate development down there. I could use his help, and possibly yours, too. How quickly could you meet me in Paris?"

"Lucky for you it's been a particularly routine harvest and Henri has been a little possessive of my lab. Annie and I could sneak a quick evening away."

"Think you could come up with a reason for Alex to tag along?"

"So much for a romantic getaway with my bride."

"How about an impromptu family holiday?"

Smiling to himself, Kaden said, "Actually, Simon, that's not such a bad idea. Alex has recently met a girl in Lacoste—an American—who he seems to be fond of, but she apparently hasn't fallen for his charms. Perhaps a whirlwind trip to Paris compliments of his eccentric cousin might be in order."

That got Simon's attention. "An American, you say? Do you recall her name?"

"Louise Marcel—I met her briefly, seems like a nice enough young woman. She's on staff at the college in Lacoste for a special project."

Simon whistled. "Must be my lucky day," he said cryptically. "By all means, see if you can bring them both."

Etienne Matisse kept his trademark scowl planted on his face as he cooled his heels in the holding cell at the Bonnieux *gendarmerie*. They'd confiscated his phone when he'd been picked up at his home earlier that morning, and last night's text messages from Lou gnawed at him. Had he remembered to delete them? No matter what happened to him, he didn't want to drag her into it. Even if she was his alibi.

As per French protocol, he'd been allowed a telephone call, and he'd contacted the safe intermediary that Simon Purcell had set up for him. He'd briefly explained the situation and had been told to sit tight. He hoped that the chain of events to set him free had begun.

Now that he had a suspicion of what was going on at Les Prés—and the appearance of the dead girl practically confirmed it—his time was running out. If Philippe was to be believed, he had until Saturday, but with this latest development, he wondered if Philippe would return sooner. Somehow, he had to get into the basement of that house before his stepbrother returned.

For the umpteenth time, he sifted through the possibilities of who could have been watching him. Whoever it was had reported to the *gendarmes* that he'd left his house late in the evening, not returning until after midnight. The time in which he was absent from his home fit the preliminary time of death of the victim. Coincidence? He had no way of knowing. And what proof did they have? Could that same person have planted evidence in his vehicle?

A door slammed somewhere in the building, followed by heavy footsteps and muffled conversation. Then his door opened and four uniformed men walked in, all looking serious and stern. He recognized only one of them—the *capitaine* who had been on duty when he'd been brought in earlier in the day.

"Monsieur Matisse," the *capitaine* said. "You are being transferred to Cavaillon, where you will be arraigned in the morning. I suggest you go willingly. Any trouble on your part will only make things worse for you." He held up a pair of handcuffs and motioned for Matisse to turn around.

Matisse narrowed his eyes at the *capitaine* but did not move immediately. "What about my lawyer?" he asked gruffly. "He was to meet me here. I expect him any time."

"Ah yes, Monsieur Favre telephoned not long ago, shortly after I received word from my superiors that you would be transferred. I relayed this information to the *avocat,* and he said to tell you he would meet you at the Cavaillon station. Please turn around." He again motioned and held out the handcuffs.

Matisse grunted and did as he was told. *This better be Simon's doing.* He thought it likely that the *capitaine* or others in the employ of the local *gendarmerie* might be taking contributions from Philippe, and letting a murder suspect go, regardless of any lack of evidence, would be viewed as suspicious, especially if it required intervention from a more powerful law enforcement agency to step in.

It was a quiet ride. The three *gendarmes* who had come to fetch him in Bonnieux were silent—not even a murmur, which was odd, wasn't it? One drove, one sat shotgun, and the third sat on the bench in the back of the van across from their prisoner. His handcuffs were attached to a bar behind the low bench on which he sat, preventing him from seeing out the front window.

Well short of the time it would have taken to reach their destination, the van pulled off the main road. The vehicle bumped over what had to be a dirt road for a few minutes before coming to a stop, and Matisse's senses kicked into high alert when the two men in front jumped out. When the back doors opened, he could see they were at some sort of old equipment barn. The third man released him from the bar, but his hands were still cuffed behind his back as he was escorted out of the van. None of them appeared overly cautious, but they all remained silent.

Matisse stayed alert but cooperated as he was led through the open door of the barn. Compared to the bright light of day outside, the interior of the barn was shadowed, and it took his eyes a moment to adjust. But then his eyes widened in surprise, not because he recognized the short, thin man who appeared before him, but because the large man standing just off to the left could have been his own double.

"Release him," snapped the short man, and the *gendarme* who had sat with him in the back of the van stepped up behind him to unlock the cuffs. To Etienne he said, "*Désolé pour le retard, mon ami.* It took us a while to get Jérôme here." He turned and indicated the man behind him.

At Etienne's look of confusion, Reynaud, the short man who was obviously in charge here, grinned broadly to show a row of uneven teeth. "A happy coincidence, no? Jérôme hails from the Jura—good mountain farm stock. I wouldn't be surprised to find a common ancestor if we studied your genealogies. I'll explain later, but now, we don't have much time."

He turned to the driver of the van and motioned impatiently. He was handed a plastic evidence bag that contained Etienne's cell phone and wallet.

He retrieved the phone and handed it to Etienne, then turned to Jérôme, who dropped his own phone into the bag. "We'll have to keep your wallet, I'm afraid, but we won't leave you hanging." After handing the bag back to the driver, he reached into his own coat pocket and extracted an envelope, which he presented to Matisse. "Some euros, Jérôme's ID, and a prepaid credit card that should get you through the next few days before we can get you released from jail." Reynaud laughed at his own joke.

Turning to Jérôme, he became serious again. "Keep your mouth shut and your head down. Refuse to talk to anyone but your attorney, Monsieur Favre. He will be there to meet you. Do not allow any other visitors to see you, and do not speak with any other prisoners. We can fool the *gendarmes,* but anyone who knows Matisse will not be fooled."

Jérôme nodded. "*Bonne chance,*" he said to Matisse then went with the others, allowing them to cuff his hands before they left the barn.

"*Viens, nous allons sortir d'ici.*" Reynaud motioned for Etienne to follow as he made his way through the barn, around a few ancient tractors, and out a back door. Outside was another delivery van, this one unmarked. "Get in the back—we don't want anyone to see you. There is a plane waiting for you in Avignon. You're going to Paris."

Seventeen

"*Paris?*" Louise wasn't sure she'd heard him correctly.

Alex shrugged, smiling at her reaction. "Kaden is what you might call a serious foodie, and trust me, this is no strain on his budget. I haven't told you much about him, but he's probably one of the wealthiest men in France. He doesn't look it, nor does he live anywhere close to that lifestyle, but it's true. He does this sort of thing occasionally, and I've learned to just go with the flow and enjoy it." He reached for her hand. "Please say you'll come with us. You will love Annie, and she'll love you, too. I promise."

She shook her head in amazement, not sure whether it was the outrageous invitation or the temptation to accept it that shocked her more. She looked at her watch. "It's already three o'clock."

"We've got time. The train leaves Avignon at 5:00 p.m., and it's only a two-hour ride to Paris. We'll go straight to the hotel to change clothes before heading for the restaurant. We'll have a fantastic meal, spend the night, and return in the morning. You can be back here by noon tomorrow."

"Alex, I can't spend the night with you!"

He chuckled. "To my regret, *chérie*, he's booked us separate rooms."

"But I don't have anything to wear!"

He only grinned. "No little black dress hiding in the back of your closet?"

She couldn't help a small smile. "Well, I guess I have something that might work. How cold will it be? I don't have a dressy coat with me, but I do have a warm shawl."

"Kaden will have a car organized to take us door to door, so you won't be outside for long. A shawl for the evening should be fine." He saw her mind working and squeezed her hand. "Can you be ready to go in thirty minutes?"

She nodded. "I must be crazy." *And hopefully it will take my mind off of Etienne. I just wish I knew how to help him.*

———— ••• ————

Philippe Lemans cursed a foul streak through the phone connection as Pierre D'Arcy relayed all he knew. "Whose fucking idea was it to implicate Matisse?"

"I don't know," he said.

Philippe didn't believe him, but now was not the time to get into it. "Forget about Matisse for now. There's nothing you can do anyway. I need to speak with Bernard."

Philippe had not gone to Bordeaux, as he'd told his stepbrother, but had flown to Hong Kong where he was to smooth over ruffled feathers and finalize the terms for his next delivery—or what was supposed to have been his next delivery. And now he was half a world away from where he needed to be, standing impotently in a hotel room overlooking Hong Kong harbor.

"*C'est moi.*" Bernard's rough voice could be heard loudly over the receiver.

"*Dis-moi,*" Philippe growled. He did not have to specify what he wanted to be told.

"She went into labor early. Mathilde was here and at first thought it was false labor, but it went on and on. Her water broke, but apparently there was not enough dilation, and the girl was weakening. Mathilde said she either had to attempt a C-section herself or we had to get her to the clinic. I approved the procedure."

Philippe closed his eyes in frustration. "The child?"

"A girl. She lives, seems healthy, but she's small. She took to the breast fine, and Mathilde was able to stitch the girl up and sedate her. Everything was under control at the end. Mother and child were sleeping and the worse was over."

"But?"

"*Monsieur,* the girl was exhausted and sedated, and had just had major surgery. When Mathilde suggested it would be better to leave her unbound so that she could nurse the child, I didn't think there was a risk."

"You left her alone unbound?" Philippe's voice dipped dangerously low.

"All the interior and exterior doors were locked and alarms were active. The monitors were on. I did not think it was a risk."

"Yet she managed to escape, and now she is dead."

The silence stretched out—no answer was expected. Philippe gazed out at the harbor below him where the lights sparkled like jewels as they reflected off the water and the glass of the high-rise buildings downtown. He had spent twelve long hours in the air and then had gone straight into a grueling negotiation. His cell phone had run out of power somewhere between Paris and Hong Kong, and he hadn't had a chance to recharge it until he reached his hotel room, rendering him unable to receive the message that he was negotiating a sale for damaged goods. Severely damaged.

Philippe let his employee hang in suspense as he contemplated his next move. Finally he spoke. "Do not let Mathilde out of the house. Lock her up with the babe if you must. Tell her if the infant dies, she will be next."

"*Oui, monsieur.*"

"This complicates things significantly. I won't be leaving as soon as I had hoped. Get to Matisse and tell him that I will arrange an attorney for him. Do not, under any circumstances, talk to anyone else. *Est-ce que tu comprends?*"

"*Oui, monsieur.*"

"I want a full report on how the girl escaped, how she ended up in the village, why she died, and how the hell Matisse was implicated. And Bernard, put someone on Pierre. I smell a rat."

Simon Purcell took the high-speed train from London rather than fly into Paris—even with his security clearance, it took less time and was simply more comfortable, especially when carrying a weapon. A driver awaited to deliver him to the company's private hangar at Orly.

In that morning's briefing, Simon had ordered his staff to get every detail available on the dead girl and to start working on her identity. While he waited for Matisse to arrive, he accessed a secure server and read the file that had been compiled so far. He was just finishing reviewing the data when he heard the whirr of a jet engine taxiing toward the building.

He stood in the doorway as the plane's hatch opened and the stairs dropped down. Matisse moved with remarkable agility down the steps, and before he reached Simon's location a few steps away, the hatch was already being closed and the plane taxiing off. Simon knew that Orly's air traffic control supervisor was advising his staff that the plane had not actually stopped. They all knew the drill and went on about their business.

The two men stepped into the building before shaking hands, and Simon used the contact to pull Matisse into a quick embrace and pound his back. He then led his guest to a small conference room where a screen had been pulled down along one wall and a small projector was hooked up to Simon's laptop.

Simon gestured to an array of liquid refreshments set out on a table. "Have you eaten at all today?"

Matisse grimaced as he helped himself to a cup of coffee. "Just a stale sandwich from the *distributeur automatique* in Avignon."

"Let me see what I can find in the pantry here." He returned a few minutes later with a tin of mixed nuts and a bottle of wine, which he held up with a grin.

Not much made Matisse smile, but that sight did the trick. "After the night and day I've had, I think it is not too early for a sip of wine," he said.

Simon pulled the cork from the bottle and poured them each a glass while Matisse devoured a handful of nuts. They sat at the table and clinked glasses. "*A votre santé,* and also to your narrow escape from the clutches of the local *gendarmes.*"

Matisse nodded and took a sip. "My thanks to you, old friend. The last place I need to be right now is locked up by *imbécile* bureaucrats. I believe our opportunity to nail Philippe for good is finally here. I have much to tell you."

"How about start with last night—and tell me more about this Louise Marcel."

Taking another sip of wine, Matisse thought for a minute. "She's difficult to explain."

"How did you meet her?"

"She appeared in the village a few months ago. At first I thought she was a student—she looks young enough." He nodded at his friend's laptop. "I'm surprised you haven't looked her up yet."

Simon smiled. "Only just this morning," he said as he typed some commands on the keyboard. On the screen in front of them, a head shot of Lou appeared. "Pretty girl. What do you actually know about her?"

Matisse studied the image. It was the kind of photo that would be used on a résumé. Her blond hair was loose around her face with wispy bangs falling softly from a side part, and her pale blue eyes were staring straight into the camera. She had a ghost of a smile, as if she was enjoying some private joke. It was one his favorite expressions. "*Oui,* she is very pretty. And she has never been the least bit afraid of me." He smiled at that.

"The hell you say?" Simon knew how most people reacted to Matisse.

Still studying the photograph displayed on the screen, Matisse nodded thoughtfully. "I first noticed her because she was open and friendly; she actually said hello as she walked by me in the parking lot one morning. Not a hint of reserve or fear. It was remarkable in its singularity.

"A couple of weeks ago, I ran into her at the Maison Basse. I was meeting Reynaud there, and since there were no cars parked in front, I assumed the place was empty. But the padlock was off the door, meaning someone was inside of course, and Reynaud pushed it open before I could stop him. I shoved him out the door and told him to disappear before anyone saw him. Louise came down the stairs just as he was out of sight." He smiled at the memory. "She was very direct and very bossy. Told me the building was not open to the public and that I needed to leave. The top of her head is barely level with my chest, but she stood her ground with hands on hips, glaring at me. I almost laughed out loud."

"Sounds fierce, indeed," Simon chuckled.

"Yes, but she wasn't alone. Alex Bouvier came down the stairs right behind her. He did not look quite so fearless, especially with his right foot in a therapeutic boot, but to his credit, he didn't flinch." He shrugged. "I thought it best to just leave without argument."

By the time they'd finished the bottle of wine, Simon had been briefed on all that had transpired that night of the storm. Matisse also reported the details of yesterday's meeting with Philippe and last night's rendezvous with Louise, including her research into his family and her startling discovery about Les Prés. Fortunately, he had burned the pages he'd taken from her in his fireplace when he'd returned home.

Simon was not as quick to make the connection with a prison, but when Matisse explained a few things he remembered from his childhood, he couldn't help but agree that it fit.

"Is it truly possible that Philippe has been running a human trafficking operation from that old farmhouse for two decades? *Bloody hell.* We've been sniffing around him for years, but nothing has ever indicated something like this. And now ..." He paused as he fished a rumpled envelope out of his satchel. "This photo suddenly make sense." He opened the envelope and pulled out a grainy black-and-white of an elderly Caucasian gentleman with a beautiful young, nubile blonde girl on his arm. The photo was taken in some ritzy place, possibly a club. There were several others caught in the image, all Chinese men, and all were watching the girl. Even with the poor quality, the resigned expression worn by the girl was evident.

"Ying's widow found it in his safe. She just arrived in London a few days ago."

"*Jésus,*" Matisse breathed. "It's been more than twenty years, but I would swear that's my elusive stepfather Jean Luc." He and Simon shared an alarmed look. "I had assumed he was dead. Speaking of which, what do you have on the dead girl?"

In Simon's fascination with the story of Louise Marcel and the interesting triangle that had formed between her, Matisse, and Alex, he had momentarily forgotten the main reason they were there. He cleared his throat and quickly pulled up a different file, switching the image on the screen from the lovely Louise to a grim crime-scene photo of the dead woman. Her skin was white as paste, and her eyes looked like sunken purple smudges. Her blond hair was matted and tangled around her head. She was wearing what looked like a threadbare bathrobe and filthy, bloody socks, no shoes. She was curled on her side in a fetal position that didn't hide the dark stains on her bathrobe where it was wrapped around her hips.

The image was sobering, and Matisse muttered a soft curse. Simon advanced to the next slide. For this photo she'd been rolled onto her back, and the edges of the robe were opened to show the naked body beneath. There was a horizontal gash just above her pubic bone. It looked like it had been stitched together, but most of the stitches had ripped open, and a large amount of blood had escaped the wound, painting long trails down her legs and matting in her pubic hair, as if most of the bleeding had occurred while she was upright.

"*Mon Dieu,*" Matisse breathed. "Is that what I think it is?"

Simon nodded gravely. "According to the preliminary autopsy report, the girl had given birth by C-section less than twenty-four hours earlier. We were able to take control of the body and the autopsy, although we are reliant on the local *gendarmerie* for crime-scene data. Her fingerprints are being run through all EU member databases as we speak, as well as our own, but it's too soon for an ID."

"The baby?"

"No sign of it, but teams have been searching the surrounding area, from ditches to fields. If it was left somewhere out in the open, it's possible a wild animal got to it first. We may never know."

Matisse grimaced at that possibility. "But how did she end up in the village? Did someone dump her there?"

"It's not clear. What is obvious is that she walked—or ran—for some distance. Her feet were badly torn up and bloody, and the flow of blood from the wound suggests the same thing. The incision is practically ripped open, consistent with the constant jarring of ambulatory motion, and the large quantity of blood on the front of the robe at her abdomen and smeared on her hands suggests she was trying to hold the wound closed. Cause of death is no surprise—she bled out."

Matisse had always thought his stepbrother a monster, but he had difficulty understanding how anyone could let such a thing happen. Of course,

Philippe was not there at present. Perhaps something went terribly wrong while he was attending business elsewhere and his tribe of goons couldn't handle it. He spoke his thoughts to Simon.

"I wouldn't be so quick to attribute any sort of compassion to Philippe," Simon said carefully. "But here's another piece of information we discovered. Philippe is not in Bordeaux. He boarded a flight to Hong Kong at midnight last night."

They finished the wine and the nuts over speculation of when Philippe might return to the scene and what sort of time that might leave them. Simon's email pinged. Glancing at it, he frowned.

"Did Ms. Marcel ever disclose anything of her past, or did she just dig into your own history?"

Etienne snorted. "It never occurred to me to ask."

"Then this may interest you, although I doubt it's relevant to our current situation. Her sister, one Elena Marcel, disappeared off the streets of Paris four years ago. She was twenty-one." Simon looked at his friend and shook his head. "The girl is still listed as missing."

Eighteen

Annie Macallister hadn't known what to expect when her husband told her she'd finally get a chance to meet the young lady that Alex seemed so smitten with. She'd heard about her, of course, since Kaden rarely kept anything from her, and she'd agreed to go along with this last-minute boondoggle to Paris, determined to play her part with good humor and support the people she loved. The truth was that she rather enjoyed this sort of thing and in the twenty years she'd been married to Kaden, he never ceased to surprise her.

Despite their simple life in the country, Kaden had financial interests everywhere. His passions were many—Annie, their two children, the land, good food and good wine, cutting-edge technology, and the thrill of the deal, to name just a few. It was the latter two that had made his fortune—and continued to build it, in fact—but he was good at keeping that part of his life in balance with the rest. Annie had never been able to figure out how it came so easily to him.

Kaden's first cousin and best friend since childhood, Jean Claude Bouvier, had become a chef and had taught Kaden to understand and appreciate fine cuisine. Jean Claude also had many contacts in the restaurant business throughout France and the world, and Kaden enjoyed backing the promising young chefs that Jean Claude brought to his attention when they were ready to go out on their own. Thus it was that Kaden was a silent partner in a number of successful restaurants in Paris, Lyon, and elsewhere. As such, he was an honored guest at just about any restaurant in the country. When he called for a table, the *maîtres des maisons* tripped over themselves to accommodate him.

Therefore, the ostensible reason for this trip was to visit one of his newer investments. Rather than attending opening night, Kaden preferred to wait a few months until the media hype had calmed down, the kinks in the kitchen and dining room were worked out, and the nerves of the staff had settled. His presence alone often put everyone on edge, despite his efforts to remain positive, supportive, and low-key. It was just the nature of the things.

So here they all were, ensconced in the forward section of a first-class car on a high-speed train, barreling their way toward Paris.

Annie was delighted with Louise Marcel. She was a beautiful woman—no surprise there, but she was also poised and mature without appearing stiff or arrogant. Her smile was easy, her manner relaxed, her conversation genuine. There was a wholesomeness to her that made Annie feel glad to be near her. If this crazy scheme of Kaden's fazed her at all, she didn't let it show. She laughed along with them as Annie and Alex regaled her with stories of their past adventures doing this same sort of thing, while Kaden pretended to read a journal. Annie almost—almost—felt guilty that the whole thing was a setup.

What Annie found most remarkable about Louise—or Lou, as she preferred to be called—was her affect on Alex. Like Kaden, Annie loved Alex like a son and knew him almost as well. Up until today, she had always recognized the restlessness of his nature. She'd seen him around plenty of girlfriends in the past. Alex was a tall, handsome young man and was rarely without a girl. Some he'd been hot for, some not so much, but none of them affected him like Lou seemed to do. She appeared to calm him, or make him more serious or perhaps respectful, but in a fun-loving way or something like that that she couldn't quite put her finger on. Annie didn't know if they'd been intimate yet, but if she had to guess, she'd say no. As friendly and affectionate as Lou seemed to be, Annie detected a hint of wariness, or perhaps a deep-seated sadness—a barely perceived shadow of some sort in her interaction with Alex. She wondered what had caused it.

A sleek black towncar awaited the group as they emerged from the train station. Their meager baggage was stowed in the back, and within minutes the driver had maneuvered the vehicle into the busy evening traffic of central Paris.

For Lou, the first part of the evening passed as though she was watching herself in a movie. Their hotel was a beautiful old building from the early eighteenth century that had been converted from a private residence and still retained much of that quiet old-world charm. Kaden had booked three rooms that all adjoined a spacious private sitting area with comfortable couches and chairs, a few low tables, and a bar.

After a brief stop so they could freshen up and change clothes, the same driver took them to a very trendy restaurant that Lou had read about, where they were given the royal treatment. Seated at the back of the main dining room on a raised section that was separated from other tables by a low railing, they could see the entire room, and be seen, of course. They were fussed and fawned over, the chef came out immediately upon their arrival to shake hands and welcome them, and Champagne appeared as if by magic.

Lou never saw a menu and didn't think anyone else had, either, but that didn't prevent the flow of course after course of exquisite dishes. Each course consisted of just two or three bites of whatever delectable fare was presented. The pacing of the food was perfect, and with each new dish a new wine was delivered—just a small amount each time—that seemed to enhance whatever was presented on the plate, but by the eighth remove, she prayed the gooey chocolate truffles she was looking at were the last dish. Three and a half hours after they'd stepped into the restaurant, they were saying their farewells to the chef and dining room staff.

Kaden had suggested that they finish the evening with coffee in the sitting room, but there was another reason he wanted them to remain together. He opened the door to the suite and held it while his guests entered, unsurprised by the gasp inside.

"Etienne!" Louise wasted no time in crossing the room and throwing her arms around the very large man who stood warily against the far wall. "I was so worried about you!" She seemed to catch herself and stepped back from him. "But, what …?" She glanced behind her and took in the startled expressions of all her companions except Kaden, who wore a slight scowl.

"I don't understand," she said as she looked back at Etienne, who hadn't moved or spoken yet, nor had he taken his eyes off of her. He looked different, she realized as she tilted her head slightly to study him. His thick hair was neatly pulled back and tied at his nape and he was clean shaven, the scar giving him an almost distinguished look. Rather than the rough jeans, work boots, and canvas jacket she was used to seeing him in, he wore a neatly creased pair of dark slacks that broke just so over the top of polished boots, an equally dark button-down shirt, and a beautiful black leather jacket that fit his large frame well. He could never be called handsome, but his current appearance was a far cry from the local thug he'd previously portrayed.

Without acknowledging anyone else in the room, he reached out and gently touched her cheek. "I'm sorry you were worried, *petite.* You should have known I would take care of myself."

Behind them one of the men cleared his throat, and it seemed to break the spell between them. Lou turned around again and faced her companions, feeling more than a little bewildered, and noticed for the first time another man standing near Kaden. She looked at Alex, who was regarding her with a small smile. Annie was watching Alex.

Kaden cleared his throat again. "Forgive me for the subterfuge," he began. "But it seemed to be the best way to get us all here without raising suspicion." He smiled slightly and shrugged his shoulders. "And we had to eat anyway, yes?"

Annie snorted her laughter and moved to a chair, setting her purse and wrap on a nearby table before turning to Kaden's friend. She touched his arm as she leaned into him to give him a quick double kiss. "*Bonsoir,* Simon. It's good to see you again."

Simon returned the gesture with a smile. "You too, my dear."

Kaden introduced Simon to Alex and Lou, then looked over at Simon's companion.

Matisse stepped forward and held out his hand. "Etienne Matisse," he said in his deep voice as Kaden shook his hand.

"Kaden Macallister," he said. "And this is my wife, Annie."

Matisse held out his large hand to Annie, who took it with a warm smile. Turning back to Kaden, he continued in French, not sure how much of the language the ladies understood. "Please forgive me for involving your family in this. It was not my intention for anyone to be hurt. I would keep them from taking any more risks." He glanced quickly at Louise.

Kaden's expression remained neutral as he studied the man. "I'm not the one to apologize to," he replied in French. "But as to keeping them out of it, I don't think that is Simon's intention." He looked over at Simon, then turned to his wife and smiled. "I think we'll be needing some coffee."

Annie's eyes twinkled as she nodded, then moved to an elegant sideboard where a service had been set up with a large urn of fresh coffee. Kaden turned back to the assembled group.

Alex and Lou were standing side-by-side, waiting to be clued in, so Kaden addressed them directly. "Simon asked me to bring you here because it seems that you both have inadvertently become involved in something quite serious down in Lacoste. At this point it's not important how that came about. What is important is that we keep you both safe," he shot a glance at Matisse, who nodded in agreement. "But Simon has a request to make. I'm sure I'm not going to like it, but I agreed to get you here so he could talk to you both directly without being observed."

Kaden gestured to the furniture arranged around them. "I suggest we get comfortable."

Alex took Lou's hand and guided her to the couch, Simon settled in one large overstuffed chair while Kaden took the other. Matisse reached for a wide straight-backed armchair that stood against the wall and pulled it toward the group, sitting gingerly at first, as if to test its strength before leaning back and crossing one ankle over the opposite knee. Annie served out the coffee, set the urn and accoutrements on the table in the middle, then scooted Kaden over in his chair, curling herself into the wide cushion next to him.

"Well then," Simon began. "This is a bit of a muddle, but perhaps we should give some background. A story, if you will." He looked to Matisse, who nodded. Simon cleared his throat.

"Etienne and I have known each other for many years. We met quite by accident when he was just a lad and I an idealistic agent assigned to Bordeaux." He looked at Kaden. "I was stationed there, as you know, for some years, and witnessed the first real surge in international wine fraud—the creation of counterfeits to be shipped around the world and passed off as bottles from the great houses."

"The late eighties," Kaden supplied.

Simon nodded. "My post was to act as liaison between INTERPOL and the Police Nationale in Bordeaux. I quite liked the position, getting back fluency with the French language and all that, but I despised Bordeaux. It's better now, but back then it was dirty and noisy, with a crime-infested, grubby waterfront. After a month in the company-provided intercity apartment, I opted to rent my own place. I found a small town nearby in the midst of vineyards that allowed an easy commute to headquarters. There was a youth rugby league in town, so I volunteered to help coach."

"I had just arrived there, having left Lacoste to search for my aunt." Matisse looked at Lou as he spoke. "I'm not sure what Regina thought she would do with me when I finally found her, but she had the good sense to enroll me in the local youth sports club. Rugby suited my size and temperament."

Thus it was that Simon and Etienne met. In the oversized young man, Simon recognized a deep shyness, a severe lack of confidence, and a quiet agony. He was attentive on the field, but off field he interacted as little as possible with his teammates and they, in turn, gave him a wide berth. He was exceedingly uncomfortable with the whole team-sports thing, but Etienne was loath to let his aunt down, so he showed up every day for practice and made an effort to improve his skills.

Within the structure of the club, Etienne soon learned how to control his strength and gained the flexibility necessary to move quickly and gracefully on the field. Simon noticed that his increased confidence on the field began to show in his posture off the field. Before, he had slumped his shoulders as if trying to disguise his height, but now he stood tall with shoulders back. Where before there would be no eye contact, Etienne lost his fear and learned to stand his ground and look people in the eye. But his eyes were always shadowed.

"I eventually learned that Etienne lived with his aunt who owned a vineyard on the outskirts of town. I also discovered that we attended the same church. Regina was sharp, very protective of Etienne, and naturally suspicious of anyone who gave notice to him."

"She insisted on an introduction," Etienne said. "I remember one Sunday after the service when she all but trapped Simon, and we stood on the steps of the old church for what seemed like hours while Regina grilled him." The two men made eye contact as if sharing a private joke. "Regina ended up inviting him to supper that day, and from then on, he was a regular fixture at our Sunday table."

"It was not all social, though," Simon continued. "Etienne and I spent the time between church service and supper working on his English lessons, and we became close. From Regina, I eventually learned of his childhood." Simon paused to glance at his friend.

"I watched him grow into a strong, intelligent young man. Regina and I grew close as well, and the three of us became a family of sorts. I thank God for her tenacity and for offering Etienne a way out of hell and then keeping him out of it. She did not let him wallow, she did not let him relax, but she gave him plenty of love and support. When he wasn't in school or at the sports club, he was studying or working in her vineyards. I began joining them on the weekends during pruning and harvest. I think together we managed to make a decent little wine." He winked at Etienne then, and to Lou's surprise, Etienne smiled.

Lou listened intently, watching the men as they spoke. She found the story fascinating, the miracle of a lost and battered boy finding a home. After the devastating tale she'd heard the night before, it warmed her to know that Etienne had not been so alone as she had feared.

"INTERPOL extended my assignment in Bordeaux for another three-year term," Simon continued. "Wine fraud had gone from a nuisance to a major problem. With the world demand for top wine growing and prices keeping pace, the trend for fraud had risen sharply. As the fakes began making their way out of the country in larger quantities, Bordeaux seemed to be the main point of exit. With my insider's knowledge of the local wine business, it made sense for me to stay on."

"I'd wondered why you stayed so long down there," Kaden said to his old friend.

"Yes, and I'm glad I did because it was during that second term that I came across Philippe Lemans. A very dangerous man, one who was not, it turned out, content to leave the past alone."

Lou shifted in her seat. She knew who Philippe was, and just the mention of him gave her shivers. She had been watching Etienne for most of Simon's narration, and at the mention of his stepbrother, he glanced over at her then quickly looked away. Who knew what he was thinking? This couldn't be easy for him to listen to.

"You see," Simon addressed Kaden directly, "it was Philippe's father, Jean Luc, who had seduced Etienne's widowed mother into marrying him, then abandoned her and Etienne to the sadistic whims of his own monster of a son. Neither Regina nor Etienne knew the full extent of the abuse Juliette endured, and she refused their help. But he obviously had some power over her that they never understood.

"Philippe told Regina that Juliette had died of a stroke and that he was looking for Etienne to settle some paperwork. In his arrogance, Philippe assumed he could bully his way back into Etienne's life and use him just like he had used his mother. Fortunately, he hadn't taken the time to find out anything about him beyond the address of his aunt, and it was that mistake that allowed us to keep him safe."

"What do you mean?" Lou had the impression that Etienne had gone looking for Philippe, not the other way around. Etienne had left this bit of the story out last night.

Simon looked at Etienne with a father's pride. "By this time, Etienne had earned a full scholarship to the Sorbonne in Paris and was completing a degree in linguistics. Thankfully, he was in Paris when Philippe made himself known."

"If you had not been there," Etienne interjected, "who knows what he would have done to Regina."

Simon shrugged. "I may have prevented any physical harm coming to her, but it was your aunt with the quick wit." Turning back to the group, he explained with a chuckle. "Regina turned into a hellcat when Philippe showed up. We were in the vegetable garden, and she kept waiving her arms and poking at him with her clippers. He had to jump back more than once. It was a delight to see." Then he sobered. "But she was smart. She railed on him about how he had ruined her nephew, said Etienne had turned into a mean, angry young man. She told Philippe that he had been conscripted for military service straight out of secondary school and she hadn't heard from him since. She was so convincing that I began to wonder if there had been two nephews."

Etienne chuckled at that and stole a glance at Lou, which she noticed because she was still watching him. He'd said she reminded him of his aunt Regina, and she felt a swell in her heart that he could see her as being even close to that kind of fearless.

"After he left, I got on the phone to the General Secretariat in Lyon. It was clear than Philippe meant to drag Etienne into whatever he was involved with, and since Regina had set it up so perfectly that he was roaming somewhere under the radar screen, INTERPOL simply adjusted records to reflect the story she'd told. Under the guise of entering a witness protection program of sorts, the sports club records were eliminated, as were his records at the Sorbonne. We also created an unremarkable military service history."

"But had you finished your degree?" Lou wanted to know, asking the question directly to Etienne.

"No, and unfortunately that was no longer possible at the Sorbonne," Etienne answered with a tinge of regret. "But Simon was able to get my school records altered to match another person, Emile Moreau, a name that I have carried for many years. I was able to finish my degree at Oxford under that name."

"But when did you take back your real name?"

"I never actually stopped using it. I have papers for both names. I used Matisse when I was back visiting my aunt, and to secure the transfer of the Lacoste property that was mine by inheritance from my father, but I used Moreau to continue my studies, and for employment and travel to and from the UK."

Simon picked up the story again. "Etienne came to work at INTERPOL, but he's a hard fellow to hide." That got smiles from the group. "In addition to very useful language skills, he had an aptitude for computers and expressed an interest in learning more, so we assigned him to the IT department at the company. Up until about two years ago, he spent most of his time in the basements of the General Secretariat complex in Lyon, working under the name of Emile Moreau. But then Philippe came to our attention again with some suspicious wine shipment activity in Bordeaux, and we decided it was time for Etienne Matisse to reappear." Something they had planned for all along.

"Philippe is extremely careful, but he is also arrogant," Etienne said. "At INTERPOL we monitored what we could. His financial holdings are inconsistent with the profits from his legitimate wine export business, but without infiltrating his operations, we were unable to connect him to anything else. No one in the field had been successful in getting close to him."

"Couldn't you get him for tax evasion?" Lou asked. "It worked for Al Capone."

Simon did his best not to laugh. "We actually thought about it, but the French are not quite as … unforgiving as the Americans. He would have been slapped with a penalty, with little or no jail time, and it would have done nothing but put him on notice that we were watching."

"Oh," Lou mumbled, embarrassed. But when she glanced at Etienne, he was regarding her with something that looked suspiciously like admiration, and when she met his gaze, she saw his lips quirk up slightly.

"We decided to play to his arrogance, and it worked." Simon continued. "With carefully planted criminal records, including several stints in jail and other tidbits of information, to anyone watching it appeared as if Etienne Matisse returned to his aunt as a paroled ex-con. We guessed that Philippe had someone in Regina's town as an informant because it wasn't long before Philippe found Etienne in a local bar."

Etienne actually smiled as he recalled that first meeting after so many years. "My stepbrother was shocked at my appearance, and when he surmised that I'd been cut in a jailhouse fight, I didn't correct him." He traced the scar that ran diagonally across his cheek. "But I refused his offer of employment. Instead, I worked with Regina in her vineyards, laid low, and appeared as if I was simply trying to stay out of trouble. He came often to that same bar, but I continued to turn him down. We played this game for a while before he eventually left me alone. The goal was for him to think I wanted nothing to do with him."

"How *did* you get that scar, Etienne?" Lou had always been curious about it.

"In a training accident. I was able to defer my military service but not avoid it completely. After joining INTERPOL I was conscripted under my assumed name. Simon was able to get me posted to a remote base in the Alps so I could stay hidden." He fingered the scar. "We were doing back-country search-and-rescue drills in the snow, and my team got caught in an avalanche." He paused. "I was one of the lucky ones."

Simon cleared his throat in a way that only a stiff Brit can do. "So to get back to our purpose here, Etienne eventually went to Philippe and asked for work. That was a year ago in Bordeaux. Philippe didn't trust him, but as we suspected, in his arrogance he couldn't resist having Etienne under his thumb. But he never used him for anything significant, and we know now that Philippe was testing him."

Alex finally spoke up with a question. "The raid on the print shop?"

Simon nodded. "Philippe hadn't paid close enough attention and was exposed there. Etienne managed to wipe out the electronic records of his involvement just before the raid. It didn't serve our goal to have Philippe caught up in something that small. It flushed a few minor players out—the printer, for instance—but fortuitously, it proved Etienne's loyalty. We knew there was something bigger going on. I think Philippe was getting greedy, and with his contacts, peddling fakes was just a sideline for easy money, not the main business."

"What *is* the main business?" Kaden had stayed silent, listening to the admittedly interesting story, but he was impatient for them to get to the point.

"It turns out, it wasn't in Bordeaux." Simon gave Alex a pointed look. "Very few people in INTERPOL know who Etienne Matisse really is. They know Emile Moreau, of course, but due to the nature of his role in IT, only a handful of people in the company have actually seen him. And none of those are people in the field. It's the sad truth that there is plenty of corruption in local law enforcement. His cover is perfect because it's real, and I couldn't risk anyone knowing the truth."

Alex nodded his understanding. "So what Spencer assumed was exactly what you wanted everyone else to assume."

"Yes, that's correct. But even so, he should never have involved you. It wasn't his call, and as you found out, it put you at significant risk."

Isn't that the truth? Alex thought.

"But I take the blame for that," Simon admitted with some regret in his voice. "He is the analyst on the Lemans case, and I should have given him the facts. He took initiative because he thought I had chosen to ignore his concerns about Matisse."

The room was silent for a moment as everyone absorbed the fascinating story of the double life that Etienne had lived. Kaden was the first to speak up, losing his resolve to remain patient. "Simon, this is all fascinating, but what the hell are we all doing here? Surely you didn't gather us together to tell stories?"

Etienne frowned, but Simon laughed out loud. "Bloody hell, mate, you never did have an ounce of patience." Kaden glared at him and pointedly looked at his watch. It was almost midnight.

Simon held up his hands and got serious again. "All right, but the next part will make more sense now that you have the background." He looked straight at Louise. "I understand, young lady, that you've been doing some research and have come up with some very interesting facts indeed."

Startled, Lou looked at Etienne. She had not shared her discoveries with anyone but him.

"It turns out, *petite*," Etienne said softly, "that the very discovery you made about Les Prés was the final piece to the puzzle we've been working on for many years. And it may help us tie Philippe directly to the dead girl found in the village this morning."

"What discovery?" Alex turned in confusion to Lou. "What haven't you told me?"

"I'm sorry, Alex, but it wasn't my story to tell." She glanced at Etienne, gratified to see approval in his eyes.

"What we never understood, Regina and I, was what was so important to Jean Luc about marrying my mother. While her property was valuable, it wasn't any more valuable than those around it. It had vineyards and orchards like all the rest. Neither of us had been inside the house—it was rented out when I was small, and then after Philippe took over the property, I was not allowed beyond the back gate of our own property."

Etienne nodded to Lou. "Can you summarize what you found?"

She swallowed, cleared her throat, and then proceeded to describe the trail her research had taken her the day before, and her discovery that Les Prés may have been originally used as a prison for the château in Lacoste. "But nothing has been collaborated yet," she hedged.

"When I heard this, certain memories started coming back to me—snatches of conversations that I wasn't supposed to hear, cryptic comments my mother made, the guards, and the odd living arrangement that Philippe forced on us." Etienne looked directly at Kaden. "The main business, I believe, is human trafficking."

Neither Annie nor Lou could stifle their gasps, but Lou was quick to make the connection. "Do you think the girl in the village was one of their ... captives?"

Simon and Etienne both nodded. "It's very possible," Simon added, "that if she was, then it's a whole lot worse than just women." He reached into his satchel and pulled out a manila folder. Laying it on the table, he hesitated. "This is not for the faint of heart."

He flipped open the cover of the folder to reveal the photo of the dead girl with the bloody bathrobe open to expose her ripped incision. Those who had not seen the photo before leaned forward to get a closer looked. Only Etienne was not looking at the photo—he was watching Louise. He saw the normal reaction of someone looking at a truly horrendous photo, but then he saw something else.

Lou looked at the photo and grimaced, feeling a wave of sadness. *So young,* she thought. *No one deserves to die like that.* Then she looked closer at the face, and her eyes widened at the same time her blood ran cold. She brought a shaking hand to her mouth. "*Oh, God. Ellie ...*" she whispered.

Nineteen

Alex heard the barely audible whisper and turned to Louise. She had gone pale as a ghost and was shaking badly. He wrapped his arm around her and held her against him as tears welled up in her eyes. They fell unhindered down her cheeks as she closed her eyes tightly. When she opened them again, Etienne was kneeling in front of her and reaching for her hand.

"What is it, *petite?* Do you think you know who this girl is?" He glanced at Simon, who had turned a shade paler. *Please, no,* he prayed, but feared it was too late.

She could barely breathe. She curled into Alex at the same time she gripped tightly on Etienne's hand, but she looked at Simon, who was regarding her carefully.

"I think …" She hiccupped and coughed. "I, um …" She took a gulp of air and closed her eyes, pushing more tears down her cheeks. She took one more fortifying breath and opened her eyes, looking straight at Etienne. "I think she's my sister."

Even with her reaction to the photo warning him, Simon was as stunned as the rest of them to hear the words. She curled into a tighter ball against Alex but kept her grip on Etienne's hand and used her other hand to cover her face. Alex wrapped both arms around her as she sobbed into his chest. He brought his gaze to Etienne, and they shared a look of helpless bewilderment.

"Shh, baby, we've got you." He rocked her slightly as he murmured into her ear. "Take your time." The entire room was silent as she let the emotions pour out. Eventually Lou calmed, sniffed, and wiped her face with her free hand. Annie had come around to kneel on the other side of Alex and put a handkerchief into her hand.

"Thanks." Lou sniffed and used it to wipe her eyes and blow her nose. She looked up at Alex with pure misery in her eyes. "I'm sorry," she whispered.

"Shh, no, don't say that, don't even think it." He rubbed her back as she moved to sit up. She looked into Etienne's eyes and saw concern and compassion. She squeezed his hand before letting it go. "Thank you," she whispered to him.

Etienne moved away from his position at her knee but only as far as the couch cushion next to her. She blew her nose again and looked at the table where the photograph had been, noticing that the folder had been closed. She looked at Simon, then back down at the table. "God," was all she could say. A few heartbeats passed, everyone waiting for her.

Lou's emotions were in turmoil, equal parts shock, relief at finally knowing the fate of her baby sister, and horror at how her life had ended. She'd always assumed it was bad. She was more floored to know she was only just now dead, rather than years ago. *We were so close to each other, and neither of us knew it.*

She took a deep breath, cleared her throat, then looked at Simon again. "Is there a close-up of her face?"

Simon nodded, picked up the folder and shuffled quickly through the photos. He extracted one and placed it close to her on the table. She picked it up and studied it, tears falling again from her own eyes as she looked at the lifeless ones staring out at her. She put the photo back down and pointed to a dark patch of skin about the size of a dime beside the woman's left ear. "It's a birthmark," she said.

When Simon took out a notebook, Lou cleared her throat and focused on what she needed to do. "Her name ... is Elena Marie Marcel. American, obviously. She'd be ... twenty-five now. She was ... she should be ... in your Missing Persons database." Turning to Kaden, she asked, "Is there any whisky? I could sure use a drink about now."

"I'm thinking we all could," he replied as he stood and moved toward the bar. "This just gets stranger and stranger," he muttered to himself.

Settling back against the cushions, Lou felt comfort from the two large men who flanked her. Their presence calmed her rioting emotions and gave her the strength to keep talking. "Ellie is my baby sister. The carefree wild child. She used to think I was boring as hell." She smiled to herself at that memory. "While I was sifting through old stones, she was ... chasing her dream at ... at the New York Design Institute."

Kaden handed her a glass with a two fingers of amber liquid. She thanked him gratefully and took a small sip, closing her eyes to the burn in her throat.

"Ellie was good. Real good. She had serious prospects. She begged my parents to let her go to Paris for her twenty-first birthday. It was ... it was for the Paris Fashion Week. A group of her friends were going. There were chaperones—instructors, I think, so it was ... it was supposed to be safe. My parents gave in." She took another sip of the whisky as she remembered how excited her sister had been to be able to go on that trip.

"They were there for ... a week, I guess. They had a packed itinerary. Barely enough time to sleep, much less get in trouble." Lou snorted at that. "Except no one knew how to find trouble like Ellie. Later, we found out she'd met a guy. At one of the shows. He wasn't French or American. Eastern European, maybe. Anyway, they said she went out with him on the last night. Instead of going with the group." Her voice broke. "That was the last anyone saw of her."

She drained her glass, wincing at the burn, set it on the table, then leaned back and curled her legs up, wrapping her arms around her knees. "Starry-eyed pretty girl goes missing on a school trip. Some guy involved. No trace of either of them." She took a labored breath and stared across the room at nothing. "No closure."

She recited the reality of missing persons so coldly that Etienne had to clinch his jaw to keep from cringing. He could only imagine the helpless agony Louise and her family had gone through. Very few people who went missing like that were ever discovered, and if they were, it was usually because they turned up dead. Like Elena.

Without thought, Etienne reached over and took hold of her hand. "I'm so sorry, *petite*."

She looked at him, and her eyes filled with tears. She blinked, and they fell down her face. "Thank you," she whispered.

He reached up and cupped her face in his large hand, using his thumb to wipe away the tears.

His touch was so gentle that Lou couldn't help but smile through her pain.

He released her hand and nodded, glancing at Alex as if he knew he was treading on thin ice. But Alex only looked at him thoughtfully, and the men shared a long look over Lou's head that communicated an understanding of caring that surprised them both.

Simon had been scribbling notes, but now he set his notebook aside and regarded Lou soberly. "I'm so very sorry for your loss, my dear. If I'd had any notion—"

"You couldn't have." Lou said sadly. "But Simon, this changes things for me. I know it's personal, but … I'll do anything to help catch that bastard. I'll shed more tears, but I want to be involved. I need to."

Simon exchanged glances with Etienne then looked at Alex. "Well," he said, and cleared his throat. "There's more. It seems the … that is, your sister, had given birth just prior to her, ah, just prior to her death. So far the infant has not turned up."

"What?" She looked between Etienne and Simon.

"According to the autopsy, a baby was delivered by cesarean. We have no idea how she ended up in the village, but it's clear from, ah, the trauma to the incision and the condition of her feet that she either walked or ran for some distance."

"Good God," whispered Annie. She was curled up against Kaden in their chair with his arms wrapped around her.

Alex spoke up, echoing everyone's thoughts. "So if Les Prés really does have some sort of underground prison that's being used to confine women moving along a human trafficking pipeline, and Ellie was there when she gave birth, then there's a possibility that the baby, if it lived, is still there?"

Simon nodded. "Yes that's quite possible, and there might be other women there as well."

"Then why can't you just bust into the place?" Lou practically shouted her outrage.

"Calm down, *petite*. It's not that simple." Etienne reached for her hand while Alex stroked her back.

"Why the hell not?"

Despite the gravity of the situation, Etienne wanted to smile. She was a spitfire. "They've already lost one woman, and if I understand how this disgraceful business works, the child will be valuable. They won't risk losing a second life."

"And moving an infant child across borders is hard enough with the mother. Without her, it's extremely difficult," Annie added. "I can't imagine they'd risk moving a newborn."

At Lou's frustrated look, Simon reminded her that it had all just taken place in the last twenty-four hours. "Actually, this is precisely why we needed to speak with you tonight. We have an idea on how to proceed, and catch everyone in the net. We were going to ask for your help anyway, before we knew … before we knew your connection to the … to Ellie. But if you're to help us, we need to get you back down to Lacoste first thing in the morning."

Alone in her room later that night, Lou tried to shut out the ghastly image of her sister. Annie had given her an Ambien and offered to stay with her. She'd taken the pill but refused the company. *God, Ellie. How am I ever gonna tell Mom and Dad?* Lou tried to envision that moment as the sedative took hold.

"Désolé, mademoiselle. *I wish I could help you, but I don't remember anything else.*" Louise blinked back her tears before turning away. Back out on the street, she drew a line through the name and headed toward the next address.

"Désolé, mademoiselle, *but I don't know anything else.*" She felt her shoulders slump as she turned away, wiping the tear off her cheek. She crossed off the next name and took a deep breath before heading across the street to find the next address.

"Désolé, mademoiselle, *I have not seen this young man.*" She took back the sketch and turned away. She couldn't keep the tears from coming.

"Désolé, mademoiselle … désolé, mademoiselle … désolé … désolé … désolé …"

Louise closed her eyes and saw the faces of the frazzled fashion people swirling around her like a sick collage. Someone had to have seen him! Someone had to have known him! She felt the metro car slow and glanced up to see they had reached her stop. The last name on her list. She stumbled out of the car with the crowd and climbed the stairs to the street.

"Yes, he worked here, but it was only temporary, just for the show. He's gone now." The man began to turn away.

"Wait, please, monsieur. *He's the last person who was seen with my sister. What is his name?"*

"Désolé, mademoiselle—"

"No! Please, I beg you … just a name, and … an address?" Louise felt the tears on her face again, and perhaps that did the trick. No man is comfortable with a woman's tears.

The man hesitated, then shrugged. "Attendez." He left her standing in the open doorway of the design studio for an eternity, but finally he returned with a scrap of paper. "Bonne chance," he said gently as he handed it over to her.

She took it with shaking hands … Petre Valeriu …

Lou woke with a start. Petre Valeriu, a Romanian national who had likely been in the country illegally, since the authorities seemed to not have any record of him coming or going. It had been the last dead end before her money ran out and she was forced to return home empty-handed.

She looked around, momentarily confused. Why was she dreaming about him? Then it all came slamming back to her. *Oh, God, Ellie. I'm so sorry.*

As she lay in her bed in the dark, now wide awake, she thought about everything she'd learned in the last two days. Simon seemed to have resources beyond anything the local police forces had. Perhaps he could find something on the name. It was too late for Ellie, but not for those who were still vulnerable.

Twenty

"The consortium will not be pleased."

Philippe watched his father pour himself a glass of Champagne, admiring the way he filled the flute in one long stream without allowing it to bubble over. It was a skill that took practice, but he imagined Jean Luc had plenty of that. Though he had not stepped foot in France in almost thirty years, the old man had not gone without his favorite native luxuries.

"Then you need to remind them that this is the first time in decades that there has been any sort of problem. With such high-risk merchandise, they should be pleased we've done so well for so long."

"They have zero tolerance for failure. And this one was anticipated to bring a very high price." Jean Luc raised his flute in salute as if they were discussing the weather.

"They also knew the timeline yet insisted on my presence here for the negotiations. Why could this not have waited? Things would have been different had I been there." Philippe struggled to keep his voice calm and his frustration from showing. His father had lived for so long in China that he had become an expert at masking his emotions, and he expected nothing less of his protégé.

"Do you really think so?" Jean Luc raised one eyebrow and studied his son, sighing inwardly at the other man's losing battle to hide his feelings. The frustration was understandable yet unacceptable to display. He had hoped this trip would be proof to his rather demanding colleagues that Philippe was capable of taking over, but it was now clear that would not be the case.

"I've followed the medical reports, just as I suspect you and all the members have. We knew this one was at higher risk, and I should have been there to monitor it. I could not have prevented the circumstances of the birth, but the girl would certainly not have escaped."

"How exactly do you suppose that happened?"

Philippe was not deceived by the calm manner in which the question was asked. Jean Luc knew as well as Philippe that the cellar at Les Prés was rock solid and impenetrable. It was what made it so valuable to their business. He narrowed his eyes at his father, knowing he was trapped. "That's rather obvious, father. She had help. Not very reliable help as it turns out, so it can't have been for her sake. Someone seeks to discredit me."

"Someone within your organization." The statement was like a whip and Philippe barely caught himself from flinching.

"I can assure you that I will find out who it is and deal with him personally."

"You don't suspect the midwife?" "A figure of speech. At the moment no one is above suspicion, but the sooner you release me, the sooner I can identify the problem and resolve it." Philippe knew his impatience was showing but didn't care. What he did care about was getting back to Lacoste before things got any worse. They still had the child, a female of considerable value.

Jean Luc sipped his Champagne, evaluating the options. He certainly could not bring Philippe in front of the consortium now; they'd eat him alive. But his son was right—their track record was impeccable, and even the Chinese understood that fate sometimes intervened no matter how well each step was planned. The immediate problem was to find and deal with the traitor.

Making a decision, Jean Luc nodded. "Yes, *mon fils,* I agree you should get back immediately. Leave the consortium to me. I will tell them the girl died of complications after the delivery, which is the truth. Implicate the midwife as incompetent if necessary." He thought for a moment. "She's expendable, I presume?"

Philippe nodded his agreement without hesitation. *Whatever it takes,* he told himself. *Whatever it takes.*

Alex and Lou sat together on the crowded train, Kaden and Annie a few rows in front of them. A storm had moved in, and the French countryside was obscured in a heavy gray fog as they sped south. They hadn't spoken much, but Lou held on to his hand and seemed to welcome the comfort of leaning against his chest as she gazed out the window.

Alex was content to hold her, stroke her arm, and occasionally drop a kiss onto the top of her head. He wanted more, but for now he leashed his desire. After her shock last night, the last thing he wanted to do was come on too strong. "You miss her," he said softly.

She turned to look up at him with her big luminous eyes. "I do." She turned back to the window. "She's the reason I jumped on the Lacoste project. I thought if I was here in France, I'd have the chance ..." She sighed out a deep breath and shook her head. "I've missed her so all this time, but now it feels like I just lost her all over again."

He dropped another kiss just above her ear. "You were incredibly brave last night."

She took a deep breath, feeling unworthy of the comment. "She was so beautiful, so full of life."

"Just like her sister."

She shook her head. "Not hardly."

"I've admired you from the first, *chérie*. You have the most remarkable strength, yet you are passionate, intelligent, loyal, and brave." He ran his knuckle gently along her cheek.

Lou squirmed, uncomfortable with the praise, but she appreciated his words. She squeezed his fingers.

"You make me want to be those things, too," Alex confessed.

"I think you hide the same qualities behind a façade of carefree recklessness."

Alex wished it were true. "Your wariness of men ... of me ... it's because of Ellie, isn't it?"

She held very still, and Alex waited. Finally, she nodded.

"Not everyone is a monster," he whispered in her ear.

Suddenly she turned in his arms and looked up at him. "Alex, what do you think will happen to her baby?"

Surprised at the question, he just stared at her for a moment, not sure what she was really asking. "I don't know—do you mean before or after … assuming we succeed with Simon's plan, do you mean after we rescue it?"

"We have to succeed. There is no other option."

He wasn't about to contradict her. "Simon seems like the kind of person who would do the right thing. If you wanted to take responsibility for the child, I don't see that he would stand in your way. Is that what you want?"

"Yes." She answered automatically but then paused to let the idea sink in. It seemed impossible, but … "Yes, absolutely. God, I don't know the first thing about raising a child, but there's no way I could let anyone else have her. Or him. To have a small part of Ellie to love …"

Alex tightened his hold on her, nuzzling his nose into her hair and breathing in her sweet scent. "You'd be a wonderful mother."

She reached up and touched his cheek. The tenderness she saw in his expression slayed her. Stroking the rough stubble with her fingertips, she watched him close his eyes. The next moment his hand cupped her hand to his cheek, and he turned into it and kissed her palm.

"Lou," he whispered. He opened his eyes and saw she was still watching him but with such an open vulnerability that he wanted to wrap his arms around her and never let her go. Instead, he reached over and cupped her face, his gaze never leaving hers, and slowly leaned in. She had plenty of time to pull away, but didn't. He brushed his lips against hers, softly at first, then more insistently, and a tiny thrill went through him when she responded and kissed him back. They tasted each other, tentatively, sensuously testing the waters, until he finally pulled away. But he didn't go far. Resting his forehead on hers, he took a slow, deep breath, all the while stroking her cheek.

It scared him to be involved in this operation—even from a distance. Philippe Lemans did not seem like the kind of man who would easily accept defeat. In an odd twist of circumstances, he was suddenly very glad that Matisse was on his side.

By the time Etienne and Simon arrived back at Orly for an early flight to Avignon, a special-ops team from the French military was waiting for them at the hangar. By design, the leader of the group, Laurent Dubois, was well-known to Matisse from his own military service. In the way of a well-trained soldier, he didn't blink when Etienne told him he no longer using the name Moreau. The briefing took place en route.

To Etienne's surprise, Kaden had turned out to be quite a resource for sophisticated field com systems, micro cameras, surveillance software, and other interesting toys to supplement the standard equipment the special-ops team had brought with them. He was a financier, not an engineer, but his knowledge of technical functionality was impressive. Military units across the western hemisphere had significantly benefited from the results of his investments in the incubation of new ideas in the field. All of which, Etienne was sure, had helped to make Macallister a very rich man. But now, through his connections, the team had an impressive array of equipment waiting for them at the airport hangar in Paris.

Matisse, Simon, and the soldiers arrived in the Luberon well ahead of the others to reconnoiter and get themselves ready for the exploration and distraction that Lou and Alex would provide. Jérôme had a part that morning, too—his resemblance to Etienne was so close that he was the perfect decoy. He drove Matisse's SUV to the house, having ostensibly just been released from jail, went in, puttered around in the kitchen then left again, heading for the supermarket in Apt. If he was being watched, someone would likely follow.

Meanwhile, Dubois and his team completed their transformation into field hands, commandeering a flatbed truck carrying a tractor and another beat-up farm truck. They placed their weapons and other equipment in unremarkable canvas sacks alongside rakes and hoes in the back of the truck and covered their black mission clothing with loose canvas work pants and flannel shirts. With worn straw hats, from a distance they looked like any other field laborers in the Luberon.

It was just 9:00 a.m. on Wednesday morning, not ten minutes after Jérôme had driven off, when Dubois and his team arrived at the back of Matisse's fields, coincidentally fronting the same road that was the entrance to Les Prés. While four men made a grand show of maneuvering the tractor off the flatbed, two others managed to disappear into the fields across the wide drainage ditch, and within less than thirty minutes, succeeded in scrambling the surveillance cameras they found into loops showing nothing but random birds searching for whatever was still left from harvest.

Moving from the orchard to the back perimeter of the compound, for that was what it appeared to be, camouflaged as it was by tall hedges, with an iron gate at the front entrance. The men performed an electronic scan to ascertain the location of sensors, cameras, and any other monitoring devices, and as they'd been briefed to expect, there were many. Too many for the equipment they had. They needed a high-powered jammer. Tapping twice on his earpiece, Dubois waited for Matisse to acknowledge.

"*Oui.*"

"Grandma's house is heavily covered with eyes and ears. Is there any relief in sight?"

Etienne smiled. He'd just received word from Macallister that his contacts had come through with the delicate jamming device he had requested, along with another very delicate but extremely useful item. "On its way. ETA two hours, tops. Use the time to light up the neighbors." Meaning, scan for similar devices on his own property. He would not be surprised if they found one or two.

The van that had been waiting for them when they landed was a kitted-out communications center on wheels. By the time they pulled into an out-of-the-way dirt lot at the top of the village, after dropping the military team at their farm gear, Etienne had adjusted all the various settings to the secure frequencies used for INTERPOL operations. The lot was empty, and they parked underneath some untamed trees at the far end, where the van was all but invisible from the road.

And now they waited. Etienne used the time to sync the audio and video receivers of Dubois's team to the output monitors in the van. Almost immediately he had several video feeds of the Les Prés orchards and vineyards. Once synced, the real-time feed would come to the com van, while the loops would feed to the main monitors, presumably within the farmhouse itself. If the new jamming equipment was as good as advertised, it would do the same. It was still being tested, not yet on the market. At worst, it would interrupt the feed going to the main monitors, and that could alert Philippe's men. Matisse prayed the equipment was as solid as Macallister claimed.

He checked his watch: 10:00 a.m. The TGV from Paris should be arriving any minute. At that moment, Lou texted him that they were about to disembark. The plan was for them to come straight to the village, park in the student lot, and walk down together to the admin building to collect her mail. There was no security with the staff mailboxes. Rather, they were open for anyone to put things in or take them out, making the timing of their upcoming exchange critical. At this point, there was no evidence that Louise was suspected of anything other than having taken a ride from Matisse. And if they played their parts right, it would appear to anyone watching that she and Alex had become lovers.

Etienne pondered that, wondering if it would become true. Alex had staked a rather possessive claim last night, but Etienne found it interesting that the other man had not gone caveman when Lou had relied on both of them for comfort. It was as if he had understood their unique relationship and had respected it. Louise, on the other hand, had kept her feelings well masked. She'd treated them both with affection and had relied on them mutually. Etienne greatly admired her inner strength, and learning about her sister made him understand just how painfully she'd gained her grit. If he was truthful, he would admit that he was a little in love with her himself. And how ridiculous was that?

For the second time in a week, the image of another woman surfaced unbidden into Etienne's thoughts, one whose battle-tested strength and fierce independence he'd greatly admired. He'd never dared to even think it, but … if Lou could see beyond the surface, was it possible …?

"I still don't like using those kids in this," Etienne told Simon to distract himself from the direction his thoughts were going.

"Neither do I," Simon replied. "But stop thinking of them as kids. They aren't that much younger than you."

Etienne frowned but said nothing.

"They'll be safe enough," Simon continued. "It'll be broad daylight and our men are in position. And they are both highly motivated."

Etienne knew that, yet ... "That's part of the problem. It's too personal. Feels too much like we're using them as bait. I'm concerned about Lou's ability to be objective."

Simon smiled at his friend. "You're the one who told me how tough she is."

"That was before we knew about her sister."

"Which just proves your point, *n'est ce pas, mon vieux?*"

Eventually Simon wandered down into the village to have a coffee and keep an eye out, waiting for the right time to slip the small envelope containing two earpieces into Lou's mailbox. When Etienne alerted him by text that Alex and Lou had just pulled into the parking lot, he made his way to the admin building and stepped inside.

The office was busy with people coming and going. The attendant at the desk was none other than Pierre D'Arcy, whom Simon recognized from a photograph that Etienne had procured by hacking into the school's database. *This should be interesting,* he thought. Pierre was engaged in conversation with a group of people, facing away, at the moment, from the wall of mailboxes. Simon walked over to the boxes and, with his back to the front desk to obscure his action, quickly set the envelope inside the box for L. Marcel. Instead of leaving, he wandered over to the display of brochures in front of the window and made a show of reading one.

Alex parked his car and turned off the engine, then reached over and squeezed Lou's hand. She waited while he came around to open her door. Grabbing their overnight bags, they walked, hand in hand, toward the main office of the college.

Lou's heart was racing, and she tried to convince herself it was because they were about to step into a dangerous game. It had nothing to do with the man walking beside her. Nothing at all. *Right.* He held on to her hand like he meant it. Not casual. And *whew,* the way he spoke to her. *Whispered to her.* Held her and reassured her. But she was frightened. Not of him, but of herself. She had presumed that her heart had been ripped away permanently after she'd lost her sister, but here it was, beating hard and strong for him. *Crap,* she hadn't meant to admit that to herself. Now what was she supposed to do?

Alex pulled her to a stop, and out of her thoughts. It was a busy morning in the village with many people, mostly students, streaming by them, going up and down the steep cobblestone lane, but Alex maneuvered her over to the side behind a stone archway. "Are you okay?"

She looked up into his eyes and met that unbelievable tenderness again, edged with concern. How could she not be okay looking into those eyes? *Things happen for a reason,* her sister used to say. *Don't overthink it; just go with it,* another of her favorite Ellie-isms. "I'm fine. Just a little nervous."

He lifted his free hand and pressed two fingers lightly to her lips. His eyes held hers. "Me, too. But I trust Simon and, unbelievably, I trust Matisse, too."

She had to grin at that. "Told you," she teased.

He kissed her quickly. "Let's not keep Simon waiting."

Simon saw the couple as they stepped up to the door. He made brief eye contact with Louise but subtly shook his head as she entered. Her eyes darted away as she made a beeline for the mailboxes, her hand firmly curled around Alex's arm. Reaching them, she leaned in close and said something to make him laugh. They kissed briefly before she absently pulled the papers and envelopes from her box.

Observing her discretely from across the lobby, Simon thought she was either a damn fine actress or she really had a thing for Alex. He also observed Pierre, who didn't miss their entrance and certainly didn't miss the kiss, from the scowl on his face. Hopefully, he didn't notice the bulky little envelope she pulled from her box. They left hand in hand as soon as she had her mail, and it was with interest that Simon watched Pierre follow them with his eyes until they were out of site.

As he turned to replace the brochure he'd been scanning, he felt someone brush past him. Pierre, who pulled out his cell phone as he moved toward the door. Simon followed him out.

Inside her apartment, Lou shook the earpieces out onto her kitchen table. They tumbled out along with a folded piece of paper—instructions for how to insert and activate them. There was a handwritten note scrawled at the bottom. *Wear these at all times from this moment. Do not take them out for any reason, even at night. Tap twice to talk to me. Do this as soon as you get it inserted to test it.*

She handed one to Alex along with the note. He shrugged and fit the tiny device into his ear. "They're worried about you, *chérie*. If there was another way, Matisse would never let you go in unprotected."

"But you'll be with me."

He gave her a deprecating laugh at that. "I may be fit and strong, but as you pointed out the other night, I have no more training than you. And I have a bit of a disadvantage," he said wryly as he lifted his boot slightly. She rolled her eyes in response.

Earpieces in place, Lou tapped hers as instructed. Instantly it beeped and Etienne's voice echoed in her ear. *I'm here,* petite. *Everything is all right?*

When she hesitated, he instructed, *Just speak normally. I'll be able to hear you.*

"Ah, hi … we're fine. Sorry but this is just a little strange."

"I know, but you'll get used to it, and you will be safer this way. Two taps activates it. Make sure you don't let anyone see you fingering the earpiece. When we're done talking, I'll turn your receiver off from here."

"When should I turn it back on?"

"Not until you leave the village this afternoon, unless something comes up. You should also know that I can activate it from here, too. You'll hear a faint beep when I do. Now tell Alex to activate his so I can check it."

Their plan was to go to the property together later that afternoon, she under the cover of investigating what she'd found in the tax records, he as her photographer. It was perfectly rational, given their respective positions with the school. She just prayed she could pull off the diversion long enough for Matisse's team to get all their equipment tested.

Lou had an early-afternoon meeting with her team that she couldn't miss, a concession Simon had no choice but to grant her. They were nearing the end of the project, and she was anxious to see what the others had found in their separate assignments. She debated the wisdom of her bringing up the question of an old prison with the team—although it was unrelated to the Maison Basse it was relevant to castle history, if in fact it was true, and it was possible the aged villager on the team may have heard of it. But in the end, they decided it was too risky. The last thing they needed was for one of the town elders to go knocking on the door at Les Prés and give them a warning. *She* needed to be the one to knock on the door.

Alex wasn't happy about leaving her but took advantage of the free hours to work in the lab on the images he'd taken the week before at the Maison Basse. He was pleased with them. The lighting had been spectacular that afternoon as it had filtered inside the dim interior, and he decided to use them for his midterm project. He opened the image of Louise that he'd captured as she walked under the ancient archway—he'd been right about it being abstract. He began a delicate brush-up operation with the photo-editing program to push the contrast between her shadowed figure and the sunbeams streaming over her shoulders through the arch when he felt the back of his neck start to tingle. He glanced up and found Pierre standing almost directly behind him.

"*Très belle image,*" Pierre said. "It's Louise Marcel, I presume. When did you take it?"

Alex looked at him thoughtfully, wondering again why he was so nosy about Lou. "I took it last week," he said, declining to confirm the identity of the figure in the image. He turned back to the computer, hoping Pierre would take the hint and leave him alone. No such luck.

"She's a pretty girl. You certainly didn't waste any time, did you? I thought you had only just met her after your … accident."

Alex turned back around and faced the RA, his face expressionless. "That's really none of your business, Pierre. Was there something you needed? I'm busy here."

Pierre narrowed his eyes a bit before effecting a Gallic shrug. "Have a care with her, *mon ami*. I believe there is another in the village with his eye on her."

Knowing the prick was just prodding him to get a reaction didn't make it any easier *not* to react, but he managed to keep his voice just as nonchalant as Pierre's had been as he turned and reached for the mouse to go back to work. *"Merci pour les conseils."* *Now get the fuck out of here before I kick your skinny ass, friend.*

Pierre moved away but didn't leave the lab. He busied himself at another desk, and Alex did his best to ignore him. His concentration was shot, however. Before last night's interesting revelations, he'd thought the man was annoying but harmless. Now that he knew Matisse suspected him of being in league with the sinister Philippe, he guessed every piece of information the weasel gathered somehow ended up in his boss's ear. And Alex couldn't bear knowing that Louise might have come to that scumbag's attention. He'd already destroyed her sister. Though they had no proof—yet—no other explanation fit. They had to uncover that prison and expose the depraved enterprise that Philippe had perpetrated for too long.

His cell phone beeped with a text from Lou that she was ready to go. He downloaded his files onto a high-gig memory stick and also saved them to his private folder on the school's network before logging off the computer. Gathering his backpack and jacket, he glanced across the room. Pierre was watching him, looking like he wanted to ask another question. The look Alex gave him did not invite it.

As he stepped out into the sun, he was struck with a sudden intuition. Instead of heading down the cobblestones, he sidestepped, then backed up and leaned against the building just outside the open door. He was just in time to hear Pierre tell someone that he, Alex, had just left the lab. *Now isn't that interesting? The little prick is tracking my movements.*

It didn't make any sense but he wasn't going to be the judge of that. As he walked toward the parking lot he tapped twice on his earpiece and waited for the beep of connection.

"Que se passé-t-il?" Matisse sounded alert and ready for anything.

"It may be nothing, but I just left the photo lab. On my way now to rendezvous with Lou." He relayed his conversation with Pierre and then the one-sided phone call he'd overheard. "Why do you suppose he has any interest in following me?"

"I don't know. He's put you and Louise together, so perhaps by having you tracked, he thinks he'll be able to keep track of her as well. It is possible you will have some company at Les Prés," Matisse mused. "I've stationed one of Dubois's men in the parking lot to watch Lou's car. He's dressed as a laborer, reading a journal on the bench next to the phone booth. He'll see if anyone follows you. Proceed as planned." He paused for a moment and added, "And, Alex, don't let her out of your sight."

"*D'accord.*"

Twenty-One

Philippe waited for his flight back to Paris, in the first-class lounge at the Hong Kong airport, with the patience of a two-year-old. At least he'd been able to get out tonight, which meant he would arrive early enough in the morning to catch the first train down to Avignon. With luck, he could be in Lacoste before noon tomorrow—Thursday.

His absence could not have come at a worse time. He'd felt good about his meeting at the docks with Matisse, but it had all gone downhill from there. The girl had delivered that night and escaped shortly thereafter, only to be found dead in the churchyard the following morning. Matisse had been arrested and was awaiting arraignment. Checking his watch, he amended his thought. The arraignment had already happened, but he'd not been apprised of the outcome. Philippe thought it odd that Matisse had refused to see Bernard or accept any help from him, and had been astounded to learn that he'd found his own attorney. Did he not think Philippe would take care of him? He could hardly blame him, though, and wondered if Matisse thought he, Philippe, had set him up. He hadn't, of course, but he couldn't guarantee someone in his employ hadn't taken some misplaced initiative. Someone had sprung the girl out of the cellar but then abandoned her. Why? Was it the same person who'd pointed the finger at Matisse?

Philippe had his suspicions but couldn't trust anyone at this point, including Bernard, as much as that pained him. The man had been a loyal favorite of his father's. He'd always made sure the women had been treated carefully, understanding their value but also, perhaps, because he'd been raised to treat them well. It was all relative in their business, of course. But Bernard was getting old, and he needed to be retired from the game. Philippe had hoped that Matisse would take his place. He had hoped that he would be in a position to *force* Matisse to take his place. But in truth, he had no leverage, and Matisse did not seem to be swayed by money, a fact that made no sense to Philippe. He'd reviewed the criminal records that Matisse had racked up over the years after his rather disgraceful military service, and everything he'd seen pointed to someone who was looking for an easy *sou*. He wondered if he could somehow use that bitch Regina. Or perhaps that young damsel that Matisse had rescued from the ditch. Pierre seemed eager to attribute some relationship there. As Philippe pondered his problems and waited for his flight, he knew one thing for certain: they would not be expecting him in Lacoste so soon. Perhaps he could learn something with a surprise appearance.

Parking her car on the side of the road near the back entrance to Les Prés, Louise turned off the engine and looked at Alex. He nodded and she tapped her earpiece. "Showtime" was all she said after the *beep.* They both got out of the car, she grabbed her bag, and he looped his camera around his neck.

During her earlier meeting with the Maison Basse research team, she'd given her approach to this some thought. The academic setting had made her realize that the best way to go about it was as a professional historian—the way she would tackle any academic problem—and try her best not to think about the criminal activities that could be taking place underground here. She definitely had to block Ellie from her mind. *If only that were possible.*

She decided to walk the perimeter of the property first to get a feel for the setting before knocking on the door. It was not uncommon in France for people to walk through vineyards and orchards, and most of the time the owners didn't mind. She was curious to learn whether that was the case here. Distraction was distraction, after all, and they might have more time this way. She spoke her intentions to Etienne, who replied that he was opening her frequency to the entire team.

From the com van, Etienne did as promised. Logical, to be sure, but fuck if he'd let anything happen to her. Having six deadly soldiers within close proximity, knowing her every move, still didn't give him complete comfort.

Ignorant of the protective thought process of their team leader, Lou jumped the ditch, followed by Alex, and together they walked the hard-packed dirt between what she guessed were cherry trees. The farmhouse itself seemed to be obscured by a thick hedge so tall that they could barely see the top of the roof and a few chimneys.

"Huh," she mused. She'd seen trees planted for wind and sun protection, but that hedge looked awfully like they want privacy. "Let's walk along the edge of this field to see if we can find any evidence of an old foundation wall. I'm betting the house as it stands today was built in the last century, perhaps earlier, but definitely after the property ownership was transferred separately from the castle. I doubt there'd have been a need for much of a house with the prison. This one could be sitting on the original foundation, although that building technique isn't seen much past mid-nineteenth century, especially when the original foundation was all but ruins."

"Unless the original foundation included an underground prison."

"Point taken." Pulling out her notebook and a small GPS device, she slung her bag across her back and flipped the book open to look at her notes. By now they'd walked the length of the hedge and could see that it continued at a right angle to block the front of the house as well, but there was a break in the line of shrubbery where the wide driveway entered the surround. An imposing wrought-iron gate spanned the opening, with a smaller pedestrian gate set into the hedge.

She looked around to get her bearings. They were standing near a drainage ditch that marked the boundary between the orchard they'd walked through and a vineyard beyond. Both stretched out in front of them until the fields met the road on the far side of the property.

Looking to the north past the hedge-enclosed house, they could see another farmhouse that Lou knew to be Etienne's. It, too, was separated from the surrounding fields by a hedge, but that hedge was lower and looked more like the typical arrangement to keep animals out or to add to the aesthetics of the property, not to hide the house from view. Except for the south side, where the hedge gave way to a length of taller fence. She wondered if it blocked the view of Les Prés, then wondered if that had been intentional. In the field closest to Etienne's house, she could see men with a tractor and glanced around quickly to see if she could spot the rest of the security team.

She handed the GPS device to Alex. "See if you can get a fix on our position and I'll plot it on the sketch I made." While he fiddled with the unit, Lou walked over to the edge of the ditch. It was deeper and wider than she had expected, certainly more than something made with a backhoe. It was overgrown with weeds and grass, and there was water at the bottom where she could see through the vegetation.

Alex called out the coordinates, and she jotted them down then tried to make sense of where they were on her sketch, if they were even near it. *Bingo!* They were standing just inside the southwest boundary of what the old tax register identified as Les Presons. Excitement bubbled up inside her as it always did with new discoveries. Alex had walked up behind her while she'd been studying her notes, and she turned to him with a big smile.

"Good work, detective."

"Look at this," she kept her voice low as she gestured toward the unusually wide ditch. "Convenient to separate the fields, but I don't think this is an ordinary drainage ditch." She looked up toward the village that was visible through the trees. "It's possible that this is the original road leading into the property. Let's walk down farther and take another reading."

They continued in the direction they'd been heading, basically straight toward the road across the field, walking along the edge of the ditch that ran parallel to the long driveway. Lou was studying it carefully, thinking it looked remarkably uniform. She stopped abruptly when the vegetation thinned out enough for her to see the bottom of the ditch.

"Alex, wait! Get another reading on our position."

He did as she instructed while she sat at the very edge of the ditch, letting her feet dangle down. The ditch was about a meter deep and there was water in the bottom, but it was quite shallow and she could see flat stones just beneath the surface of the water—stones that fit together remarkably like paving stones. Unlike most ditches where the sides slope down when a berm is built up on each side, the sides of this ditch were quite straight.

Alex called out the coordinates. She wrote them down and then plotted them onto her sketch, pleased that they were exactly where she expected to be along the property line. She set the notebook aside and pulled out a pocket-knife. She used the blade as a shovel and started digging at the turf that grew on the lip of the ditch.

"What are you doing?" Alex came over and squatted next to her as she dug.

"Here, look at this." She'd managed to dig out a square of the turf about the size of her palm. She tossed it aside and brushed off the area she'd just uncovered, revealing a flat stone surface. She and Alex exchanged glances then she started digging some more. Alex reached into his pocket for his own knife, and together they uncovered a section at the edge of the ditch about half a meter long. After yanking out the weeds clinging to the inside edge of the ditch and brushing away the dirt on top, they stared at the stones beneath.

Lou reached for his hand to balance herself as she scooted into the ditch and stood in the shallow water at the bottom. With her booted foot, she rubbed the flat stones beneath to reveal the pattern of the paving. Alex wiped his hands on his jeans, pulled the lens cover from his camera and started taking pictures of what they'd revealed, including her in the ditch for perspective on its size.

"This is no ordinary ditch," she said unnecessarily as she ran her fingers along the neatly laid stones now revealed along the edge. "I'd say we might have found an old paved roadway. In my wildest imagination, this could be evidence of an old tunnel."

Movement caught her eye, and she looked back toward the house. A large man with a scabby, almost bald pate was striding toward them, having just appeared around the corner of the hedge. He was wearing a very unfriendly looking frown. "We've got company."

Alex helped her back up out of the ditch. Deciding that a good offense was the best defense in this situation, Lou smiled her most charming smile. "*Bonjour, monsieur!*"

The man was not charmed. In rapid French, he railed at them. "Who are you and what are you doing here? Don't you know you are on private property?"

In her best—slow—French, Louise stammered out her apology for intruding and then introduced herself and tried to explain who she was and what she was doing there. Alex noticed that if the man recognized the surname, he didn't react. Nor did he seem to recognize her. Lou had told them there was not a strong resemblance between her and her sister, other than blond hair and blue eyes. Alex stayed quiet for the moment, enjoying the lilt of her accent and hoping it had as soothing an effect on their new companion.

"You are American?" he asked in heavily accented and stilted English.

Lou smiled brightly. *"Oui, monsieur, je suis Américaine, mais, mon ami est Français."*

The man glared at Alex as if he didn't believe it. Alex held out his hand, which the man took, albeit reluctantly, then quickly introduced himself and explained in rapid French that they had intended to ring the bell to explain themselves and ask permission to investigate an extraordinary discovery the *mademoiselle* had made, but they wanted to confirm that they were in the right place first.

The man looked back and forth between the two with a bemused look on his face, so Alex plunged ahead, confirming everything that Louise had said and implying she was a rather important scholar of medieval architecture. Which was true, he supposed.

"Quelle découverte?" the man asked.

We're talking—that's good, Alex thought, but he felt he needed to hedge. Fortunately, Louise spoke up in English, and he served as translator between the two.

"I found a reference in the village tax records from more than three hundred years ago to what I believe is this property," Lou explained, throwing her arms wide in an attempt to be as dramatic as possible. While Alex translated, she frantically thought about what she could tell the man that might engage him without actually telling him anything.

He nodded for her to continue after Alex had translated. "You see, *monsieur,* I think that your property was originally owned by the inhabitants of the château." She gestured to the village in the distance for emphasis. "We—the faculty and staff at the college there—are working on an important documentation project that involves château properties." *True enough,* she thought as Alex translated.

"We hope to include this one in our documentation, if it turns out to be the real property." Before the man could answer, she continued. "You see this ditch?" Not waiting for an answer, she knelt down and indicated the patch of stone that they'd exposed. "From what I can tell, this ditch runs along the original property line and may have been the original road from the château to this property." She almost mentioned the tunnel theory, but something made her hold back.

Lou smiled gamely as Alex translated, watching the man's face for any sign … of interest or otherwise.

Suspicion was not what she had hoped to see, but it was unmistakable as the man's eyes narrowed at her. "And just what right does this … college have to investigate private property?"

Lou blinked up at him. "Our work is sanctioned by the Ministry of Culture." That meant nothing, of course, but she was hoping he didn't realize it.

"Ah, but the Ministry of Culture does not own this property, *mademoiselle,* and cannot give you permission to be here, and certainly not to dig around. You will leave at once. If you want access, have your *Minister* make a formal written request."

Lou flipped through her notebook as if looking for something. "According to the property tax records, a Monsieur Philippe Lemans is the owner. Are you he?"

Taken aback momentarily, the man blinked several times. "No," he finally answered. "Monsieur Lemans is not here. I am the caretaker and am responsible for the property in his absence."

"When do you expect him?"

"Soon."

Lou and Alex both appeared pleased with that admission, and the man looked as if perhaps he should have kept his mouth shut.

"Okay then," Lou said as she stood and brushed her hands on her jeans. "We'll just stop back real soon and ask him ourselves." She reached out her hand to him. "What did you say your name was?"

As Alex translated, he had to hold back his laugh when the man suddenly looked aghast. He stepped back without taking Lou's extended hand. "You should not come back here. Monsieur Lemans is a ... he is a very busy man and does not like to be disturbed."

Lou nodded, appearing unconcerned. "Then you'd best let him know we'll be calling on him so he's not surprised to see us. *Bonne journée, monsieur.*"

Twenty-Two

From his position behind the tractor, Laurent Dubois watched through field glasses and listened on his own com-link to the interaction between the care-taker and Matisse's friends. Although they had hoped the two would find an opportunity to get inside the compound, the fact that they had drawn some-one out and put them on notice that there was interest in the property was good enough for now.

The encounter alongside the ditch had given his team an opportunity to test their equipment, and it confirmed that the slick new items that had been delivered earlier in the afternoon were functioning as intended. This meant they had the capacity to override the compound's audio and video sensors into loops while they rerouted the actual images to their own monitors. The real bonus was that they had identified the well-concealed access door hidden in the hedge when the caretaker had exited to confront his trespassers. Once it became dark, they'd be able to move in closer and put the more delicate equipment to work.

It was late afternoon by the time Alex and Lou were escorted off the Les Prés property and the "work crew" next door wrapped up for the day. They left the tractor on the edge of the field beside the flatbed truck in case they needed it for cover the next day. Then the crew of four piled into the other truck and headed around the property toward the farmhouse. To any observ-ers, the crew would be checking in with the property owner at the end of the day—nothing unusual about that.

Matisse hadn't known to what extent—if at all—his house was watched, or if the work in his fields was attended to. To his relief, the only sensor their equipment had picked up on his own property was the one he himself had installed at his back gate. No hidden cameras in the vicinity, and nothing else to indicate his movements were monitored. Furthermore, their ploy of using Jérôme as a decoy had yielded no results. No one had followed him, and no one had appeared at the house upon his return. For someone as paranoid and in need of control as Philippe seemed to be, Etienne found that odd.

Thus Etienne and Simon had determined it was safe to use the house as their base for the brief amount of time needed to nail Philippe. They pulled the com van into the empty barn and, along with the two team members who had done the recon earlier, were busy setting up an array of monitors in one of the back bedrooms when Dubois and his team arrived.

"There's enough room for everyone to bunk down here for the night," Matisse told his men. "I assume you brought gear?" They all nodded. "Good. And thanks to Jérôme, we've got plenty of food."

"Never say you'll honor us with your culinary skills!" Simon teased.

The other man just shrugged. "It's less conspicuous than all of us going out somewhere. I doubt you'll be disappointed. Besides, we need to take turns at the monitors. I'll put on some coffee."

While Matisse started work in the kitchen, Simon went back to the monitors and Dubois got his men organized for sleeping arrangements. When he was done with that task, he came back into the kitchen, poured himself a cup of coffee, and leaned against the counter. "I think we need to keep watch outside as well as on the monitors."

"I agree. You, Simon, and I can cover the monitors if the rest of your team takes the exterior."

Dubois nodded. "What about Alex and Louise?"

Etienne stopped washing chickens to frown at him. "What about them?"

"Who's going to be watching them?"

"No one." He set the chickens into a large roasting pan then drizzled olive oil over the top of them, rubbing it in as he went. "But they've got their com-links, and I made it very clear that they should not take them out. Also, they'll be staying together at Lou's apartment tonight. Alex understands that he is not to let her out of his sight."

Dubois watched his old friend work for a few minutes in silence. Etienne quartered onions and lemons, smashed a handful of garlic cloves and rinsed some herbs he'd brought in earlier from the garden. He used it all to stuff the four chickens he'd prepared then seasoned them with salt and pepper.

"You care about her."

Etienne froze midway in his reach for the bowl of potatoes he'd already scrubbed. He glowered at the other man. "Not relevant to the mission, Laurent." He grabbed the potatoes and poked them a bit too aggressively with a fork before scattering them in the remaining space in the roasting pan. "And none of your business."

Dubois smirked as the big man slid the pan into the oven.

"She's very pretty. And she handled the caretaker quite well this afternoon."

Etienne poured himself a cup of coffee and leaned back against the counter, sipping it while regarding the other man. "Yes she is, and she did." They'd all been listening to the exchange in the field earlier, and he'd felt no small amount of satisfaction that she'd been able to confirm her discovery about the property before she'd been chased off. "I doubt there's much she can't handle. Anyone who knows her at all couldn't help but care about her."

"And how well do you know her?"

Etienne turned away and set his cup down. He opened the fridge and pulled out several heads of lettuce. "We're not having this conversation."

His friend just laughed. "Whatever you say, man. Need some help?"

It was Etienne's turn to smirk. "Can I trust you not to bleed in the salad if I give you the tomatoes to chop?"

Simon came back into the kitchen carrying his open laptop, set it down on the table, then pulled out a chair and dropped himself into it. "Lemans just boarded a flight in Hong Kong, nonstop to Paris. It's scheduled to arrive just after five o'clock tomorrow morning."

He and Etienne exchanged looks. "He'll be here before noon."

"Assuming he'll come straight here, yes." Simon nodded. "That means we've got to get inside there tonight. And we've got to get a look at that hidden doorway. If the girl was held there, it stands to reason that was the way she got out. If we're very lucky, we might find some blood evidence. Reynaud has a magistrate standing by for a warrant."

———————•◆•———————

After leaving Les Prés, Louise drove them to the supermarket in Apt, having the urge to cook for Alex. She didn't want to risk being caught at a restaurant if Etienne needed to contact them. It was a little strange having the com-link in her ear, knowing he could listen in on their conversation, but at least it gave a little beep in warning when it went active or inactive.

"You know, this is a little intimidating, with your father being a famous chef and all," she said as she pushed their cart down the aisle.

"Don't worry, he's not that famous," he answered deadpan.

"Great," she muttered, but then he caught her arm and stopped her forward progress. "I love the thought of you cooking for me," he said sincerely. "Anything you make, I'll like."

She eyed him skeptically, and he added, "Besides, it's been awhile since anyone has cooked for me—only Kaden and Annie for family meals in more years than I can count."

"Kaden cooks?"

Alex laughed. "*Mais oui, mademoiselle.* He learned from my father—and my great uncle Henri. When he and Annie first met, she couldn't boil water."

"No kidding! Wow." She put the cart in motion, racking her brain for what she could make him that would be different than what he was used to. Then it came to her. "What do you say to a little down home southern cooking?"

That accent just did things to him, especially when she looked at him with those smoky blue eyes. It was all he could do to keep from groaning out loud. He winked at her, and in a ridiculous attempt at a southern accent himself, replied, "Bring it on, darlin'."

She laughed all the way down the next aisle.

Back at her apartment, Louise changed into comfy sweatpants, an oversized sweater, and her favorite thick fuzzy socks. Alex had gone up to his dorm room to grab an overnight bag, promising to return quickly. She was a little nervous about having him spend the night, not entirely sure of his expectations. She liked him, *more* than liked him, enjoyed his kisses and his tender displays of affection, but she wasn't ready for it to go further—yet. But Etienne had been adamant about them staying together. When she'd started to protest, he'd pulled her aside. "You don't have to let him in your bedroom, *petite*," he'd said, "but I'd worry less if he was in your apartment." She'd relented, and now she was going to cook him dinner. The son of a not-so-famous French chef.

The loud knock on her door startled her. *That was fast.* She flung the door open, ready to speak her thoughts to him but was brought up short. Pierre D'Arcy stood in her doorway with a perky bouquet of flowers in his hand and a smarmy smile on his face.

"*Bonsoir, mademoiselle.* You were expecting someone else?" He pushed past her into the room before she could collect herself from her surprise to stop him. Before she turned around to face him, she lifted her hand to her ear, tapping the com-link twice quickly and making a show of smoothing back her hair. *Beep, beep.*

"Excuse me, Pierre, but I didn't actually invite you in. And yes, I am expecting someone." She glanced out the door into the narrow street. "He'll be here any minute. You need to leave. Now."

She heard a curse through her com-link, then: *Alex, get your bloody ass down there NOW.*

"Afraid to be seen with me? Then close the door, Louise."

She scoffed. "I don't think so," and as if to prove her point, she moved over and stood in front of the open door, arms crossed over her chest in an aggressive stance. "What are you doing here?" She spoke loudly, hoping someone was near enough to hear.

"I brought you flowers." He held them out to her as if to entice her away from the door, but she didn't move.

"Thanks all the same, but I'll decline. I barely know you. Why are you here?" She did her best to keep the fear from her voice, but his menacing look was making her pulse jump.

Keep him talking. Alex is almost there, Etienne said through the com-link.

"I thought it was time we got to know each other a little better. I've been watching you, you know." He smiled like a hunter at trapped game. "I think you've been watching me, too."

She laughed without humor. "You're delusional." At his confused look, she sneered. "Having trouble with English? *Tu es délirant.*"

Not bad, petite—from the voice in her ear. She could have sworn he was chuckling. *Damn it, where are you, Alex?*

Unfortunately, Pierre was not nearly as impressed with Lou's French as Etienne was, and her verbal jab might as well have waved a red flag in front of a bull. He stalked toward her, tossing the flowers on a chair, intent on grabbing her.

"Back off!" She thrust both hands out, the heels of her palms connecting with his chest just as he reached for her shoulders. He hadn't expected it, and he bounced back, catching himself on the couch.

"*Putain!*" he cursed, raising his hand as he came back toward her.

But he never got the chance to touch her, because at that moment Alex launched himself through the open door, growling as his fist connected with Pierre's face so hard, Lou heard the crunch. She gasped, then flinched, pressing back against the door.

About fucking time.

Pierre went flying backward over the couch, but Alex didn't stop. He stepped around it, grabbed Pierre by the front of his shirt, and hauled him up. As Pierre opened his mouth to protest and weakly brought his hands to his face, Alex punched him again, and again.

"Alex! Stop!"

No, petite, *let him beat the crap out of that bastard.*

"But ..."

"No buts," Alex snarled, breathing hard as he dropped Pierre's limp, unconscious body onto the floor. "God damn it, I wasn't gone ten minutes. This bastard was watching your apartment."

I'll send a cleanup crew, Matisse intoned into both of their com-links. *Find something to tie him up with. We'll turn his little game around on him. Expect two of my men shortly.*

Alex acknowledged the instructions as he walked over to Louise and pulled her into his arms, then reached behind her and pushed the door closed. They both heard the *beep-beep* indicating Etienne had deactivated the link. "Are you okay? Did he touch you?"

"No, I'm fine." She returned the embrace and laid her cheek on his chest. "Thank God for the com-links. I don't know what he was planning, but he was giving me the creepiest looks." She shivered just thinking about it. "Thank you for rushing back."

He tipped her chin up so she was looking at him. "I was just stepping out of my door when Matisse yelled at me. Quick thinking on your part to activate the link."

"What do you think he was doing here? He said—"

"I heard," Alex practically growled. "Come on, let's get him tied up before he comes to."

The only rope Lou could think of was the tie to her bathrobe, so Alex used it to secure Pierre's hands behind his back then pulled off his own belt to strap it around his ankles.

"Should we gag him?"

"If he starts to make noise, I'll shove a sock in his mouth." He laughed at her expression. "That reminds me, I dropped my bag at the bottom of your stairs." He turned to the door just as they heard a knock on it. Walking over, he spoke loudly enough for his voice to carry through the unopened door. "*Qui est là?*"

"*Matisse nous a envoyé.*"

Alex quickly opened the door. "*Entrez.*"

Two men dressed in black stepped over the threshold. One held out the duffel Alex had dropped. "*À vous?*" Alex took it and grunted his thanks then shut the door behind them. They introduced themselves as André and Claude, part of the team led by Laurent Dubois that was now ensconced at Matisse's farmhouse.

The one called André looked at the prone figure on the floor. "What can you tell us about your uninvited guest?"

"Matisse knows who he is," Alex said. "Name's Pierre D'Arcy. He does various jobs for the college here, so he manages to stick his nose in everyone's business. I originally thought he was just an annoying little prick, but lately he's been very keen on knowing Lou's whereabouts. It seems he's been watching her, or having her watched. He showed up tonight with flowers, claiming he wanted to 'get to know her better' but wasn't too friendly when she told him to leave."

"Matisse said he's connected to our target." André knelt down and studied the unconscious man, touching two fingers to his neck to feel for a pulse. Pierre's face was a mess, with a broken and bloody nose and one eye that had swelled up nicely. André looked up at Alex and grinned, nodding at his canvas boot. "Not bad for a gimp."

"It slowed me down some, but I was pretty motivated." He gave Louise a heated look.

André nodded in understanding. "We'll take it from here." He reached down and undid the belt from Pierre's ankles and handed it to Alex, then untied his wrists. "We'll just escort our drunken friend down to our car and let him sleep it off somewhere safe."

Louise spoke up for the first time. "What are you going to do with him?"

With a predator's smile, Claude answered. "We'll take him back to the house and get him cleaned up. If he's lucky he won't wake up until we reset his nose. When he does, we'll ask him some questions. Don't worry, *mademoiselle*, we won't hurt him any more than necessary. We'll just give him strong encouragement to answer truthfully."

She pegged him with a dark look. "Don't be gentle on my account." The men all smiled wide at that. With an arm slung over each of the other men's shoulders, Pierre was dragged down the short alley to their waiting car below.

Back inside with the door closed and locked, Alex and Lou stared at each other for a moment. Alex allowed a small smile to show. "I think I could use a glass of wine."

"Amen to that." Lou headed for her tiny kitchen. "Come on, I'm still planning on impressing you with some good ole southern cooking."

Twenty-Three

Pierre came back to consciousness with a jerk. He opened his eyes but saw nothing. He turned his head to the side and received a burst of pain in his skull for his effort, causing him to let out a muffled whimper. There was something scratchy and smelly over his head, and his whole face throbbed in pain, especially his nose. It felt swollen and stuffed up, making it difficult to breathe. He tried to reach up but found his wrists bound in place. He wiggled, tried to lean forward, then tried to put his foot out, but nothing gave. He was seated in a chair with his torso and all limbs bound tightly to it. Outrage momentarily won out over fear as he struggled against the bindings. *I'm tied to a fucking chair?*

"Relax, my friend." A man's voice came from somewhere over to his left. Pierre jerked his head in that direction and whimpered again, at the pain but also at the dangerous promise in the voice. Soft but lethal, the smooth tone sent an icy shiver up his spine.

"Who are you?" Pierre was unable to keep the fear out of his voice.

"I have a more pertinent question: why are you interested in Mademoiselle Marcel?"

Pierre squirmed in his chair, sweat breaking out on his forehead under the coarse hood. He struggled to pull his muddled thoughts together. *Louise?* As the pain centered at his nose throbbed insistently, he suddenly remembered what he'd been doing when that asshole jumped him. "She … she's a pretty woman. I like her."

"You like her, do you? Enough to smack her around? Didn't anyone ever teach you that no means no?" The voice took on a harder edge that made Pierre sweat even more.

"I-I-I, ah, I don't know what you mean." It came out as a high-pitched whine, earning him a disgusted snort.

"I don't doubt it, you slimy little shit." The sound of a chair scraping against concrete was followed by the whisper of footsteps coming toward him. Pierre trembled as he felt the heat of the man's body leaning over him, and felt, more than heard, the exhale of breath near his face. He cried out when a large hand roughly fisted his hair through the sack that covered his head. That voice was right next to his ear now. "When a woman tells you she doesn't want your company, it means you back off. You're lucky you got off with just a broken nose. If she was my woman, you'd be dead."

Dubois jerked the sack up, pulling a few tufts of hair with it. Pierre squeezed his eyes closed and yelped in pain, tensing his shoulders and ducking his head.

"What a pussy. Not so fun when the tables are turned now, is it?"

Pierre opened his eyes with dread. He winced and closed them quickly, trying to block out the image. *I'm in deep shit.* Crouched in front of his chair was a man that looked every bit as lethal as his voice had sounded, the dark, hard-edged face with pale-blue eyes as cold as glacial ice, menacing in its lack of expression. Pierre took a deep breath and opened his eyes again, trying not to panic. Even crouched, Dubois's size was overwhelming. His close-cropped hair gave him a military look, and the wide shoulders with sharply defined muscles bulging under the skin-tight black tee shirt enhanced the image.

"Learned your behavior from Philippe Lemans, did you?"

Captured in the icy stare, Pierre was unable to hide his look of horror. Too late, he realized his mistake. He sputtered, jerked to back away from the man, but all he could gain was about an inch before he smacked his head against the wooden post that his chair was tied to. "I-I, ah, I don't know what you're talking about. Who?"

Laurent grimaced. "You really are a worthless twit." Standing, he shoved the sack back over Pierre's head, knocking against the bandages across his nose and sending a stab of pain into his skull. Pierre barely heard the soft footsteps retreating across the room followed by a door opening then slamming shut. How could such a big man make so little noise? He heard the snick of a lock then footsteps crunching on gravel as the man walked away.

Fuck. *Fuck, fuck, fuck.* That was him—fucked. Fear iced up his spine as he thought of what might come next. He'd been so terrorized by the man that he hadn't even looked around. He closed his eyes and tried to visualize the background. Some sort of barn, but nothing he recognized. Who was this guy? Was he working alone? Did he work for Philippe? Had Philippe figured out what he'd done? But no, no one who worked for Philippe would care about how he treated a woman, so it had to be someone else. *Les gendarmes?* He definitely looked military, but this was France, for God's sake. Nothing happened without a committee, and Philippe would have been warned if something was going on locally.

Laurent Dubois was still shaking his head when he stepped through the back door into Matisse's kitchen. He met the gazes of his team, all of whom looked as disgusted as he felt, having watched it all on the surveillance monitors from the house. He threw an exasperated look at Simon as he headed across the kitchen to the coffee pot. "I can't believe Philippe has eluded you so long with idiots like that in his employ."

Matisse watched his friend carefully. As much as he'd wanted to beat the crap out of the little prick Pierre, he'd kept his cool, and his cover, and sent in Laurent for the initial interrogation. He was glad for the confirmation of his suspicion, but he didn't appreciate the criticism from the leader of his military team. "Pierre may be a coward, but he's a devious one. Keep him off balance and scared shitless—otherwise we'll get nothing out of him. His interest in Louise doesn't make sense, and I don't like it. We need to find out what he was up to, if it was personal or somehow connected to Philippe."

"Stands to reason he was acting alone, since he *was* alone." Simon leaned back in his chair and studied his friend. "Are you thinking he—or they—may have connected her to Elena?"

"It's possible. They were only three years apart. Two blond, blue-eyed Americans with a mouthful of perfect white teeth."

Simon couldn't help but laugh. "You just described half the American coeds traveling in Europe."

Etienne cursed. "Lou said there wasn't that close of a resemblance, but ..."

"The girl in those crime-scene photos looked like she'd been suffering for a while," Simon pointed out soberly, "not just from a traumatic end. I'm guessing she was kept drugged most of the time. Plus, we don't know how long she was under Philippe's control, and what happened to her prior to his ... possession of her. It's likely that four years of hard living wiped the shine off her fresh looks. Unless someone had studied both her and Louise carefully, I doubt anyone would make the connection."

Etienne nodded and turned to Dubois. "What is your plan? We don't have much time."

"We go at him hard. I'll take Claude and André with me." He offered a thin smile to his comrades. "They may have trouble keeping their hands to themselves. We'll assume he's been inside the house, and in the cells, if they exist."

"They exist—they have to exist, nothing else makes sense." Etienne's voice was hard.

"The ultimate goal is access. If he's as devious as you say, he'll know something."

Etienne was about to reply when the cell phone sitting in the middle of the table chimed. Grabbing it up, he smiled at the text message.

* * *

Bernard was in a quandary. First the college brats sniffing around, and now this, and he didn't have the first clue what to do, if anything. He'd never trusted that whelp Pierre, and now Philippe was suspicious of him, too, apparently for good reason. Bernard had put a man to watching him, as instructed, but hadn't been told what to do in the event something actually happened. And besides, the text he'd received from the man tasked to the job made no sense. For all his arrogance and insubordination, Bernard didn't ever know Pierre to be seen drunk. Why then, would he be in that state with two men who'd never been seen before in the village?

He'd texted Pierre to find out what was going on, and the reply he'd just received back made even less sense. What could the young fool possibly have to show him that he couldn't just call and tell him about? Bernard's shady but predictable existence was getting more and more confusing, and he could only hope Philippe would return soon and relieve him of the need to think too hard.

———— ✦ ————

The door opened with a bang, and Pierre heard those soft footsteps coming toward him. "You're in luck, punk. The boss thinks you have information we need."

Dieu merci, Pierre mouthed to a deity he'd never bothered with, but before he could relax, the hood was yanked from his head again. "Fuck!" he yelled as the material dragged against his bandaged nose. "*Fais attention!*"

Dubois glared at him. "You have one minute to tell me everything you know about accessing the underground facility at Les Prés."

"*Je ne sais rien.*"

"Uh-huh." Dubois stepped forward until he was right in front of Pierre and slowly extended his hand toward the bandaged and swollen nose of his captive. Pierre's eyes widened in fear, and he turned his head to the side, trying in vain to prevent the contact. He actually whimpered, and Dubois sneered. "Do you want to try again?"

"You're not supposed to hurt me!"

"I said you were lucky to have information that I want. I have no specific instructions about how to get it from you." His smile was menacing as he tapped his index finger twice on Pierre's bandaged nose, causing the bound man to cry out.

More footsteps crunched on the gravel outside the barn an instant before two more large men came in through the open door. Pierre looked relieved for a moment until he saw they were dressed the same as his tormenter, except for the black masks pulled down over their faces. *Putain de merde. I'm so fucked.*

One of the masked men, André, spoke as he indicated Pierre. "We don't need him anymore. We found the concealed entrance and can blow it open. Silence him and come with us now."

"No!" Pierre squealed. "I can help you! I'll tell you anything, just don't kill me." The tears came then, and he choked back a sob. "Please don't kill me!"

Dubois turned his back on Pierre when he couldn't contain his smile. He made eye contact with the man who'd spoken and rolled his eyes.

André growled at the prisoner. "Shut up, you sniveling little prick. It's too late for you." To Dubois, he made a slicing motion across his neck. *"Allez,* get it done and let's go."

"There's a keypad! I have the code."

Dubois turned around to face Pierre. André and his companion watched but said nothing.

"Well?" Dubois sounded bored.

"Will you let me go?"

Dubois unsheathed a large knife that was strapped to his thigh and stepped toward the bound captive. "No."

Pierre's eyes widened. "7-2-4-9-B. Press the pound key before and after the code. You'll hear a click and then you can pull the door open."

"And the code for the front gate?" Dubois held up the knife so his intention was not mistaken.

Pierre rattled off another code.

Dubois smiled. "That wasn't so hard, now, was it?" He stuffed a gag in the prisoner's mouth then turned and followed his men out, shutting the light off as he left, plunging the barn into darkness.

Twenty-Four

"It's simple, now that we have the gate code. Matisse will let himself in, go to the front door, and knock." Dubois looked at his friend. "They'll be expecting Pierre, so that will put them off balance. Tell them whatever you need to, but just make sure you get inside. We'll need you in place there, and it will buy us time to distract them while we breach the basement."

Simon studied his computer screen as he listened to the plan. It displayed a satellite photo of Les Prés with remarkable clarity. Using his mouse to manipulate the image, he was able to get a glimpse of what looked like a cellar door hidden behind the tall hedge at the back of the enclosure. He tapped the screen. "Look at this—right where Louise said it would be."

André was hunched over another terminal, his fingers clicking over the keyboard. He suddenly sat up and shouted in triumph. "Got you, you bastards!" The other men crowded around to see a digital outline of the farmhouse next door with a number of reddish-yellow splotches showing inside.

Matisse smiled thinly. "Well done, Macallister," he muttered to himself. Matisse had been skeptical about the success of the heat signature security software Kaden had provided, but it worked as promised. For the first time, Matisse felt like they could succeed in bringing down Philippe without getting the wrong people killed.

Simon pointed at the bottom of the screen. "Is that what I think it is?" The image of the structure was displayed at an angle, like a three-dimensional architectural drawing, and the edges of the building were wavy. In what appeared to be the basement of the house, there were five unmoving colored shapes spaced evenly apart.

"Fucking hell," someone muttered.

The level above had three more colored shapes, one moving in a pattern that could be someone working in a kitchen, but it was hard to tell. Nothing but the outline of the structure was distinguishable. Then there was a very small bright red spot on the upper level. Simon pointed to it. "Do you think that's the child?"

"Could be," Matisse agreed. "And out of the way if things go bad. Let's do this while we have the advantage. I don't know what the routine is there, but for now the odds look good."

———————

Louise was drying dishes when her com-link beeped twice. She glanced at Alex to confirm his activated, too.

"Lou, Alex, we're getting ready to move." Etienne's voice came through clearly, and he didn't mince words. "We think there is a child there, and we could use your help once we get it safely out."

Lou brought a hand to her mouth to stifle a cry. "Ellie's baby?"

Matisse heard the hope and anguish in her voice and felt his heart tighten. "It very well could be, *petite*. Can you come now?"

"We're on our way," Alex answered for her as he reached out and took her hand.

"Park next to the barn and come to the kitchen door. Simon will be here to let you in." He paused. "And Alex, bring your camera."

Simon watched the array of monitors as the team moved into position, making sure they were out of sight of the security cameras at the other property. He then disconnected the system from the loop they'd been feeding it so that Matisse's arrival would be picked up on their system. Once Matisse was inside, he'd reconnect the loop and give the signal to move in.

He tapped his com-link twice. "Everyone is in position," he reported. "Wait, hold up. I think the kids are arriving." He crossed to the windows and saw Lou's dented Fiat pull around back. "It's them. You're clear to move."

The affirmative responses came back over the link as Louise and Alex walked quickly to the back door. Simon opened it and waved them in with a smile. "You're just in time for the show," he whispered. They followed him back to the monitors. "This one is linked to their security cameras, and that one shows the body heat signatures inside the house. We can see the movement, but we can't identify them."

He motioned them to the chairs in front of the monitor with the heat signature software. "Keep an eye on this one," he said. "Matisse will come in somewhere around here." He pointed to the screen. "And Dubois and his four men will come in down here somewhere. If you see another body signature, alert them. I'll watch the outside monitors. We've got men stationed out there, too, but it's possible there's another entrance we don't know about."

Lou's eyes widened as she took it all in. "Holy crap," she whispered. "I can't believe this is really happening. What if they have guns?"

Alex squeezed her hand and glanced at Simon. "I'm guessing our team is packing more and they've got vests on, don't they?"

Simon nodded. "Yes, well, except for Etienne. It would be too obvious." He stole a look at Lou and saw her pale slightly. "He'll be fine. Don't worry."

I'll be fine, petite, *but thank you for your concern.*

Simon had forgotten the com-link was active. He didn't like it either but was glad he hadn't said anything more.

Outside, Matisse felt his heart tighten at the realization that Lou was concerned for his safety. He quickly shook off the distraction, signaled he was on the move, and then pushed through his back gate to walk across the field to the imposing gate of his maternal grandparents' home.

Trepidation tingled up his spine, not so much for the present danger but because it was all about to come to a head. Twenty years of waiting for justice. He'd never stepped foot in the house where his mother had lived for all those years, and the emotions that welled up inside were equal parts regret and rage.

Five minutes later, he approached the entrance to the house. The porch lights were on as if someone was expected—hopefully just Pierre. Tamping down the regret in favor of the more powerful feelings of rage and retribution, Matisse entered the code and felt a quick sense of relief when the gate clicked. He pushed it open and strode to the front door. He knocked loudly.

In the kitchen of the farmhouse next door, the trio watched as the red splotch indicating Matisse moved into the screen then paused. Almost instantly, the movement in what they presumed was the kitchen halted while the two formerly stationary spots of color moved quickly toward Matisse.

"There are two people coming toward the door, Etienne," Simon reported. "One moved to the side, so beware of someone behind you once you get in."

The door opened slowly to reveal an elderly man with a few thin wisps of white hair swirling around an otherwise bald crown that was blotchy red and scabbed in places. He had a comically large nose that protruded from a ruddy complexion, but his baggy, red-rimmed eyes were dark and cold as he regarded Matisse.

"How the hell did you get in?"

Matisse returned the man's glare with a sneer and stood a little taller. Although he hadn't seen Bernard in almost twenty years, he could never mistake that cruel stare, and hatred vibrated through his muscles. He allowed himself an instant of satisfaction at how much bigger than his childhood tormentor he was now. The bastard certainly hadn't aged well, with a disgraceful paunch falling over his belt, and stooped shoulders.

"How do you think? I'm here for Philippe."

"He's not here. Come back when he calls for you." The words came out on a sneer as Bernard moved back to close the door. Matisse stepped over the threshold to block it with his boot. His menacing presence filled the doorway, and he towered over Bernard.

"He did."

Bernard frowned, and Matisse could tell he was trying to sort out what would be the greater transgression—throwing him out or letting him in. "He's not here," he repeated.

"I know." Matisse pressed his advantage, seeing the uncertainty in the other man's expression. "I'm here in his place. He sent me to take a small burden from you."

Bernard gaped up at him. Matisse stepped farther into the room and shut the door behind him.

At the other house, Simon muttered, "Bloody well done, chap," and quickly tapped out a command on his keyboard, reactivating the security feed loop that would hide the team's movements. "All clear to move," he intoned to the men in the field.

Matisse kept his back to the door as he glanced around the room. Beyond the small foyer was a large room, presumably the main lounge. He could see the kitchen through an open door across the room, and a hallway leading off in another direction. He didn't immediately see the stairs to the upper floor. The door just to his left was slightly ajar, undoubtedly where the second person hid from his view. There was a slight illumination behind the door, and he saw a shadow move. *Idiot.*

But he'd just dropped a bomb, and he needed to keep them distracted with his unexpected appearance. He ignored Bernard's outraged look and strode toward the kitchen. "Where is it?"

Bernard snapped his jaw shut. Through gritted teeth, he struggled not to panic. "You're bluffing. I have received no instructions from Philippe."

"*Désolé,* old man. I guess he doesn't trust you."

Dubois and his team are in came a voice in Matisse's ear. At almost the same moment, he heard Louise chime in. *The person behind you is moving.*

Matisse turned and took a step toward Bernard, who had followed him across the room, placing the old man between himself and the door where the unidentified man was hiding. Bernard must have been confident the other man would have his back since he didn't take his eyes off Matisse.

"Don't be a fool. Philippe's unaccountable goodwill toward you will disappear, and I promise you, you don't want that. If you leave now, I'll tell him you followed orders."

Matisse scoffed. "I'm not the fool here, *vieil homme,* and I do not take orders from you. Now quit stalling. Where is the child?"

Three things happened at once. Lou's voice through the com-link warned him of someone coming up behind him, Bernard's defiant expression took on a look of triumph a fraction of a second before Matisse was jumped from behind, and the hidden man burst into the room brandishing a gun.

Matisse roared as small hands with sharp nails dug into the sides of his neck. His attacker was much shorter than he and flayed at his back while scrabbling to wrap legs around one of his. He grabbed the hands and wrenched them off his neck, then spun around and, while still gripping the hands, swung his attacker off and away like he would remove a coat and toss it aside. The woman, as it turned out, was flung straight into Bernard, knocking him over like a bowling pin. Without losing momentum, Matisse let his body swing full circle, ducking low as he reached for the knife sheathed at his hip. As he came back to his original position, he let it loose and watched it fly across the room where it lodged deep in the chest of the man with the gun. The man grunted as he clutched the knife and collapsed in slow motion, the gun discharging into the floor.

Matisse turned his attention back to the tangled pair on the floor, both of whom were trying frantically to sort themselves out, and calmly stepped toward them. The woman hissed at him then gasped as Matisse leveled his own handgun on her. She struggled to get up, but Matisse stopped her. "*Ne bougez pas,*" he barked, and she froze.

"But I am the midwife," she whined.

"I don't care if you are Mother Teresa. Stay where you are and keep your hands where I can see them."

A soft whistle behind him made him smile. "Just in time to take out the trash," he commented as four men in head-to-toe black filed in from the kitchen doorway. Their approach had been completely silent.

Dubois's team took control of the scene. Two of the men secured the midwife and Bernard, leaving them seated on the floor where they had landed, while the other two saw to the prone man with the fatal knife wound. They were less concerned about the state of his health—or lack thereof—than the growing blood stain on his torso threatening to spill onto the carpet in front of the door. It wouldn't do to alert their main quarry by being careless.

Matisse narrowed his eyes as he noticed Bernard surreptitiously inching to his left. Tracking his direction, Matisse caught sight of his target—a cell phone lay partially covered by the skirt of the couch. It must have flown from Bernard's pocket when he went down.

"I'll take that," he said as he stepped over and scooped it up, ignoring the curses from Bernard. "No need for you to notify the boss. He'll be here soon enough."

The front door opened, and Simon walked in trailed by Louise and Alex. "Hold up, Etienne," Simon commanded.

Matisse frowned but did as he was asked. Simon instructed Alex to photograph the dead man and ushered Lou away from the body. He pulled his phone from a pocket and fiddled with it, then held it toward the prisoners. With quick efficiency, Simon dispatched his police duty to advise both the midwife and Bernard of their rights, video-taping the short proceeding for the record.

Once so notified, both captives clammed up. With a shrug, Matisse looked at Lou. "Come with me, *petite*. Let's find the infant."

In an upstairs bedroom, they discovered that the tiny blotch of color they'd seen on the heat signature surveillance system was, indeed, a baby, wearing nothing but a diaper with pink hearts on it. The child slept peacefully, despite the commotion downstairs. Louise stared for a moment, then reached into the cradle and gently ran her fingertip along the soft skin of the baby's chubby cheek, touching the tiny birthmark at its temple. She looked up at Matisse and blinked, releasing the tears that had pooled in her eyes.

Matisse moved to her side and wrapped an arm around her, pulling her close to his chest. She leaned into him and hugged him tightly before he kissed the top of her head and gently rubbed her back while Lou sobbed into his coat.

"Shh, *petite,* don't cry. She's safe."

Lou nodded against him. After a moment she lifted her head and looked up at him, wiped her nose on the back of her sleeve, and peered back at the child. "You think it's a girl?"

He smiled. "There's only one way to find out." Then he frowned. "Do you have any idea how to care for a baby?"

Lou shook her head and let out a shaky laugh. She reached over to a nearby table and grabbed a tissue, blew her nose, then took a deep breath. "I have no idea, but I'm a quick study."

Downstairs, after transferring Mathilde and Bernard to the van that Simon had procured for just this purpose, the team retraced their entry route back down to the cells in the basement. Louise had been correct about the place—it had been built as a prison, complete with imposing wrought-iron bars caging in dark cells. But someone had expended both effort and expense to make the confines habitable, modernizing what amounted to a dungeon with electricity and plumbing.

There were six cells altogether, three on each side of a wide corridor. Five were currently occupied by women—girls, really—all white, in various stages of pregnancy, all of whom were asleep or, more likely, drugged. The cells were large but sparse, built of hand-hewn stone without windows, each furnished with nothing more than a metal-framed bed bolted to the floor, a table with a single chair, also bolted down, a sink attached to the back wall and a toilet. There was no privacy for the occupants. The medieval locking mechanisms looked intact but had been rendered moot by modern keypads welded and wired into the gates that posed an immediate challenge to the rescue squad.

"Alex," Simon said quietly. "I need to you document this entire set up, wide angle and close up. I want shots of each of the women in their cells with the keypads in the photo, all the equipment and supplies, and the back entrance as well as the upper entrance from the kitchen, closed and open."

Alex nodded as he looked around, mentally calculating the best angles and assessing the light. Before he could snap his first shot, Claude pulled a handful of plastic gloves from a pocket in his fatigues and handed a pair to Alex. When Alex looked at him in surprise, Claude pressed them at him.

"Don't touch anything without these. No walls, bars, cabinet handles, or drawer knobs. Don't even brush up against anything."

Alex tugged them on as Claude sauntered down toward the end of the passage, where Dubois and André were peering through a barred window cut into an ancient door.

"Check this out, boss."

Simon walked over and looked in, then smiled. "Well, hello," he said with satisfaction. Inside the room—what had likely been a guard's room at one time—was a wall of ledgers, a large desk with several computer screens, and a large safe, possibly a gun vault, taking up a corner. The old door fit the period of the prison, with heavy wood planks held together by riveted iron bars, but it, too, had been modified with a modern keypad lock.

Directly across from the ledger room was a low stone archway that led to a compact kitchen. With a gloved hand, Simon opened the refrigerator door to reveal a large quantity of vials organized in neat rows. Checking cupboards and drawers, he found first-aid supplies as well as all the paraphernalia necessary for injections and a multitude of medical tests. "Make sure you document the contents of the fridge and cabinets in here," he called to Alex, who was clicking away in the main corridor.

An alcove off the kitchen revealed an open shower stall. Simon grimaced when he saw the heavy chain and metal cuff hanging down from a bolt in the stone ceiling. *God forbid someone tries to escape naked from the shower.*

He glanced at his watch. It was now just past midnight, and they had a lot of work to do before dawn. "Okay, let's get to work. André, you help Claude with the cameras. Laurent, let's test the lock at the cellar door to see if someone sitting in that room can hear it open, or if there's some other kind of signal. We may need to get here in a hurry if Philippe suspects something."

Dubois had been studying one of the cell keypads. He'd tried the code Pierre had given them for the cellar door, but it didn't work. He turned from his task to frown at Simon. "What about the girls?"

Simon came over to where he stood and studied the keypad for a moment, then shifted his glance to the woman inside the cell. "We need to get them out of here, but it needs to look like an inside job, not a rescue."

Dubois grimaced. "Without the codes, the only way in is with a welding torch. And even then, it will likely take all night." He gripped the iron bars and tugged. "These were built to last."

Simon was still staring at the prone woman. "How the bloody hell did Elena get free? These girls aren't just asleep, they're in some kind of drug-induced stupor."

"An inside job," Dubois said, repeating Simon's words. "Do you suppose Pierre had something to do with it? Perhaps he has these codes, too. I didn't think to ask."

Simon looked at his watch. "We don't have a lot of time, and even if we find the codes, we'll need a female officer trained in this sort of thing, with an experienced recovery team. I won't be able to get anyone like that here before the morning, and that's pushing it. No matter what, we don't want to tip off Philippe. We need for him to incriminate himself."

Dubois didn't look happy about it, but he couldn't deny the truth of the situation.

"We need to leave them as they are, just for one more night. It will serve us better in the end, at any rate. If we take them now, Philippe may find a way to plausibly deny any knowledge. With our cameras in place, we stand a good chance of catching him with his hand in the cookie jar. Assuming he comes directly here, and assuming Matisse can get him to talk freely, we'll be able to nail him once and for all."

Simon understood the frustration in his team leader's eyes. "I don't like it either, but they'll be no worse off if we wait for a few more hours, Laurent. We won't let anything happen to them. But that reminds me, get the infrared light and check for blood on the stones outside the back door. We can't take samples from inside here yet, not without a warrant," he paused and looked into the empty cell. It appeared spotlessly clean, but he knew there would be some evidence the detergents missed. "But anything outside is fair game."

It was Laurent who found it.

"Purcell," he called. "You need to see this." Laurent was crouched down with an infrared light aimed at the junction of a rock wall and the floor in the narrow passage between the back exit and the records room.

Simon and André walked over to peer over Laurent's shoulder.

"What do you have?" Simon asked, seeing nothing but a stone wall.

"Look." Laurent pointed the light at the floor, illuminating an old trail of blood, one that abruptly ended at the wall, one large splat seemingly cut off by the wall.

"Fuck," André breathed. Pulling gloves from his back pocket, he tugged them on and began examining the wall above the blood trail. Laurent switched his lamp from infrared to bright white, and the outline of a well-concealed door was revealed.

"Mother of God," Laurent whispered. "How does it open?"

They all stood, studying the wall in both awe and outrage, when Alex came up behind them.

"What did you find?" Alex asked, then cursed as he saw the outline of the embedded door. "*Putain de merde,* do you think this is the entrance to the tunnel that Lou mentioned?"

For a moment longer, Simon studied the well-concealed crack denoting the outline of what had to be a door, then looked at Alex in speculation. "Perhaps." To the group he said, "Who knows anything about hidden doors?"

André ran his fingers along the barely visible crack, starting from the bottom left corner. When he reached the top right-hand corner, his finger hit a snag. Sliding his fingers back, he felt an indent, and instinctively pressed into it. A quiet *snick* sounded, and a portion of the stone wall pressed inward.

"Holy shit," was all Simon could say. With an almost silent hiss, like it was guided by hydraulics, the stone-covered door slid back and to the right, opening into an abyss as black as midnight. But within seconds, lights embedded in the floor beyond began to illuminate, revealing a hand-hewn stone passage that sloped gently downward.

The men stood transfixed, the implications of what they'd just discovered more terrible than any of them were prepared to speak aloud.

Simon broke the spell. "We cannot explore this now. There's no time, and we'll need a warrant for any hope of using this … Christ, if this is a tunnel to the village, Lou may have solved dozens of missing persons cases in one fell swoop."

Turning to Laurent, he said, "Figure out how to reseal the door. We'll investigate it fully tomorrow."

The military leader was unhappy with the directive but followed it nonetheless.

An hour later, tiny wireless cameras were hidden in crevices in the stone walls, and Alex had photographed everything he could think of. Two of the girls had come awake during the process, but both were nonresponsive and dull eyed. One sucked her thumb; the other sat on her bed cross-legged, rocking back and forth with her arms wrapped around her bulging waist, humming. It was then that Alex noticed the cuff around one of her ankles, attached by a chain to the bed. He cursed.

Alex used the video function on his camera to record the girls' odd behavior. The one sucking her thumb watched him with large, unblinking eyes with an intensity that made him uneasy. *This could have been Lou's sister a week ago,* he thought. *Thank God she's not here to see this.*

Louise had taken the baby girl, along with a bag of supplies from the bedroom and cans of formula from the kitchen, and returned with Matisse to his house. Alex knew that Lou wanted to keep the child, and Simon had promised to do everything possible to make her wish a reality, including facilitating the necessary DNA tests to prove the familial tie. He envisioned a vivacious little girl running through a vineyard with her blue eyes sparkling and blond hair flying in the wind, and was surprised to find he liked the image. Especially when he caught a vision of a laughing Louise chasing behind her.

Twenty-Five

The third and fourth members of Dubois's team, François and Sebastien, had taken the van with the two prisoners and the corpse to a nearby safe house organized by Reynaud. Help from the local *gendarmes* was not an option, it being unclear as yet if they were part of the problem or the solution, but Simon needed more men as well as a recovery team to deal with the girls. He spent the wee hours of the morning on the phone in the makeshift war room at Matisse's farmhouse, convincing his French colleagues of the urgency. Specifically, the head of the organization.

"Counterfeit wine labels are the least of our problems here, sir. We've uncovered a bloody baby factory and a human trafficking operation that dates back at least thirty years, judging by the number of ledgers, probably more." He didn't mention the tunnel, as he had no real intelligence about it. "We have an opportunity to solve decades' worth of MP cases and shut down a serious pipeline in the process."

"You found records?" The secretary general was used to receiving phone calls in the middle of the night, and Simon had to respect how quickly his mind worked at 2:00 a.m.

"A records room. We haven't yet breached it, so as not to tip off the primary target." Simon held his breath. "But from what I could see through the door, sir, there's a very high probability that we've got written documentation going back quite a ways. I've uploaded photographic images of the place, along with my formal request for manpower. The target is en route to Paris from Hong Kong as we speak, and we have reason to believe he'll come straight here as soon as he lands. I didn't want to compromise the acquisition of any of the data—every scrap must be admissible—but, I also want to make sure it's not destroyed when we take him down."

There was a moment's pause, and Simon held his breath while the SG reviewed the images. He thought he heard a soft curse, then "Good work, Commander. You'll have our full support. I'm authorizing your request now with an urgent tag, and I'll alert our China branch regarding your suspicions."

Simon expelled the air from his lungs in relief. "Thank you, sir. Sorry to have wakened you."

The SG mumbled something about going with the territory before ending the call.

Rubbing the fatigue from his eyes, Simon dialed another number. Within twenty minutes, thanks to the SG's authorization, he'd activated another half dozen men and a hostage recovery team that would arrive within the next six hours. That would give them just enough time to be briefed and take positions. By first morning light, the trap would be set. Now they just needed the rat.

At three o'clock, Simon emerged from the war room, intent on finding some coffee. *No use in trying to sleep at this point,* he thought. He was too keyed up anyway.

The sight that greeted him made him stop in his tracks. Alex was seated—slumped—at the kitchen table, his head resting on crossed arms, asleep. Etienne stood at the stove, the infant cradled in one arm like a football, fidgeting and making small mewling sounds, while a bottle of formula was heating up in a pan of water. Simon looked into the parlor and saw Louise stretched out on the couch, also asleep.

When Etienne looked over at him and smiled, Simon nearly fell over. He had not seen that smile on Etienne's ravaged features in years. It was contentment, pure and simple. And as he rocked the tiny babe and cooed softly to it, the look in his eyes said everything. For the first time since Simon had known him, his younger friend looked genuinely happy.

Simon cleared his throat and moved toward the coffee pot. "You'd better be careful, my friend. You look like you actually know what you're doing."

Matisse laughed softly, careful to hold his bundle steady. "I've never been more frightened in my life." The baby girl squirmed and fussed, so he raised her to his shoulder, holding her steady against his body with one huge hand while the other gently stroked her tiny back. "She's a helpless, mushy little thing, but one look from those glossy blue eyes and I was lost. Louise named her Ellie."

"Makes sense." Simon's gaze moved from the babe curled against Etienne's shoulder to the young man sleeping at the table.

Etienne followed his gaze, the smile lingering. "He's as lost as I am. Just doesn't have as much stamina." He turned his concentration back to the bottle at the stove and stuck his finger in the water to test the temperature. "We'll figure it out, Simon. Even with this fussy young lady taking over the house. For the first time in my life, I have a good feeling about the future."

The sharp *ding-ding* of Simon's cell phone jerked him from the sleep he'd been sure he wouldn't get. He grabbed for it and read the message.

Lemans cleared immigration; heading for TGV.

He checked his watch—5:45 a.m.

Simon scrubbed his hands over his face, stretched back his shoulders and looked around. He'd settled himself in the overstuffed armchair near the fireplace a few hours ago, thinking he'd get a little rest, but had apparently fallen dead asleep. His half-full cup of coffee sat on the table nearby, stone cold. Louise was still asleep on the couch, the light of dawn not yet penetrating the darkness outside.

He stood and stretched again. The kitchen was empty, and all was quiet. Slipping into the bathroom, he took a quick shower, and by the time he emerged, the house had come to life. Laurent and his men were up and checking weapons, a pot of coffee was ready, and Louise was stirring on the couch. Simon nodded to the men as he approached the coffee machine, refilling the cup.

"Where's Alex?"

Matisse walked into the kitchen at that moment, looking fresh from his own shower. "I dragged him into one of the bedrooms after you passed out." He smiled. "I was tempted to let him sleep on the table, but …" He shrugged. "I'm not that cruel."

Laurent let out a barking laugh. Then Ellie let out a piercing wail, and he cringed as Louise groaned. She sat up and stretched, then reached down into the makeshift bassinet Matisse had rigged and stroked the baby's soft head. "Shh, baby girl. You're okay, probably just hungry. Or wet." The baby let out another lusty cry, and Lou looked over to the men and grinned. "Sorry, guys, these things don't come with instructions."

The infant continued to fuss, so Louise bent over and picked her up, cradling her against her chest as she stood. "No rest for the weary," she sighed.

"Here, *petite,* let me take her." Matisse stepped over to her and reached out, gently plucking the child from Lou's arms. Then he surprised her by leaning over and giving her a quick peck on the cheek. "Did you sleep okay?"

Lou stared at him with a dazed look, bringing her fingers up to touch the cheek he'd kissed. "I, ah, yeah, I did. Thanks." Then she smiled as she watched him cuddle Ellie against his massive chest and kiss the top of her downy head. The baby quieted immediately, fisting her tiny fingers into the fabric of his tee shirt like he was her lifeline. Lou eyed him suspiciously. "You certainly seem to have a knack for that."

He shrugged, but his eyes sparkled as he met her gaze. "We've come to an accord, *la minuscule et moi.*"

"*Minuscule?*"

"Hard to argue with, don't you think? Besides, *petite* was already taken." He playfully tapped the tip of Lou's nose then turned back to the kitchen. "Take a shower, you'll feel better. I'll take care of Ellie."

She opened her mouth to protest but thought better of it. Simon was watching her thoughtfully while the other men ribbed Matisse about his magic touch with the baby, which he laughed at with good humor. She shrugged. No reason not to take advantage of all the help she could while it lasted.

The house was large—much larger than she'd realized that first time she'd been there, and as she made her way down the hall to the bathroom, she passed several bedrooms, the beds now neatly made up. *Military discipline,* she thought. The door directly across from the bathroom was slightly ajar, and she caught sight of Alex sprawled out on top of the duvet in the dark room, fast asleep. Glancing back down the hall, she quietly pushed the door open farther and stepped inside.

Her heart rate kicked up as she took in the masculine beauty laid out before her. He was fully dressed, but his shirt had come untucked, one arm flung above his head, and she could see a line of soft dark hair trailing down his lower abdomen to disappear beneath the fly of his jeans. She curled her fingers into fists to resist the urge to reach out and touch him. His long lashes formed dark semicircles on his high cheekbones, and his hair was tousled. Why was it that bed head always looked so sexy on guys?

She'd been fighting her attraction to him, trying desperately not to fall under the spell of those hypnotic hazel-green eyes and sensual kisses. Her initial impression of him had been of a cocky rich kid, taking nothing seriously, used to charming his way into women's beds with flattery and empty promises. Even so, she hadn't been able to help but like him a little. In the last few days, though, she'd seen another side of him. They'd been pulled into a dangerous drama that felt surreal, and he'd jumped in without hesitation. Despite their close proximity, he hadn't pushed her; he hadn't even tried anything but a few sweet kisses. He'd been a perfect gentleman. And he'd stuck by her side. He hadn't tried to distance himself when her own family drama was exposed, not even when it looked like she might end up with a newborn baby.

Of course, he hadn't made any promises, either. Heck, they hadn't even talked about anything beyond the immediate. He'd been strong and supportive for her, willingly taking on the role Matisse gave him to help her. And, well, maybe the fact that he *hadn't* pushed her for sex meant he *wasn't* all that interested. *Who knows what to think?* The last thing she needed was a fling with a sexy Frenchman, much less a broken heart.

Louise shook her head at her jumbled thoughts and quietly backed out of the room. She needed a shower, preferably one that would wash the cobwebs out of her head.

Pierre woke with a cry when Dubois kicked his feet to rouse him. He glanced around, seeing the light of day coming through the door that had been left open. He ached all over, and now that he was awake, he felt the urgent need to relieve himself.

"I thought you might be needing to take a piss," Dubois said with a smirk.

"Desperately," Pierre said with a grimace.

Dubois moved around behind him and started loosening the bindings. "Don't do anything stupid or you'll be pissing down your leg."

Pierre nodded. When the last of the bindings were off, he tried to stand up but couldn't. With an impatient sigh, Dubois grabbed his arm and tugged him up, then walked him to a grubby toilet in the corner behind a bamboo screen. He stood with his arms crossed over his chest as Pierre quickly did his business, zipped up, then started shaking out his arms and legs.

"Can you walk?"

"*Oui.*"

"Good. Go back to your chair and sit down."

"Could I ... could I have some water?"

Dubois stared silently until Pierre did as he was told, the fear clear on his face. He pulled out his cell phone and called Matisse. "Our guest would like some water," he said, without taking his eyes off Pierre.

"Do you think he's ready to talk?" Matisse wanted to be as prepared as possible, and they didn't have much time.

"Mm hmm," Dubois said carefully, but Etienne got his meaning.

"Excellent. We'll send over some bacon and eggs, they're just about ready. Kill him with kindness or smack him around if you want, just get me something useful, Laurent."

The call ended, and Dubois pocketed the phone. He walked over to an old workbench and snagged the stool beneath it, then carried it over and sat down on it, right in front of Pierre. The stool was bar height so it put him above his cowering captive.

Pierre didn't understand why he hadn't been tied up again, but he wasn't going to question it. It changed nothing, as he had zero chance of escaping from the large man towering over him. His whole head throbbed in pain, his nose felt like it was going to explode, and his stomach twisted in fear. The man had not been threatening this morning, but that could change at any moment.

"What, ah … what are you going to do with me?"

As Dubois studied the prisoner, trying to decide how to play this interrogation, he found he had no desire to hurt the young man any further. He was in enough pain as it was—Alex had done quite a number on him—and he was still scared shitless. *Kill him with kindness,* Matisse has said. He'd give it a try.

"I'll make a deal with you," Dubois finally said. "I'll be perfectly honest with you, and you tell me the truth as well."

Pierre started to speak but Dubois held up his hand and stopped him. "My name is Laurent Dubois, and I'm a colonel in the Armée de Terre, assigned to INTERPOL for a special operation." He pulled his wallet out of a pocket in his fatigues and flipped it open to his military ID. Pierre's eyes widened, but he said nothing.

"You are currently under arrest for the attempted assault of Louise Marcel. You may also be charged for your involvement in the illegal activities of Philippe Lemans, including but not limited to counterfeit, kidnapping, and human trafficking." Pierre's eyes got even wider.

"You have the right to remain silent, and you have the right to have an attorney present while being questioned. If you decide to talk now without one, make no mistake that anything you say can and will be used against you. If you choose not to speak with me, I will have no choice but to retie you to that chair until our operation is over. If you talk honestly, when we're finished here, you will still be restrained, but it will be in a more comfortable place."

Dubois kept his tone even and professional, like he gave people these choices every day. Pierre saw the truth of what Dubois said in his eyes and was trying to decide what to do when another tall man with a muscular build and a military haircut walked in carrying a tray.

"Put it over there," Dubois pointed to the workbench. The man did so, nodded to Dubois, gave Pierre a hard look, then left.

Pierre's mouth watered at the smell of bacon, and he prayed it was for him and not just a torture technique. Dubois watched him for a moment, then stood and pulled the stool back to the bench. He motioned to it.

"Go ahead," he said. "There's some aspirin there, too. I imagine you could use it."

By the time Simon's reinforcements arrived, Dubois thought he had most of Pierre's story. It was bizarre but strangely believable. Not that it would make any difference to his fate; Pierre's misguided actions had been the impetus for Elena's death, and he would be charged with manslaughter. It saddened Dubois to think about that young woman's end, but he hardened his resolve to finish this and take Philippe down. That monster had ruined enough lives.

With his hands cuffed behind him, Pierre preceded Dubois out of the barn and was led to a white van. He looked around, realized where he was, and stopped in his tracks. "But Matisse—"

"—is one of us. He's been working undercover for months. Get in." Dubois opened the back, helped a dumbstruck Pierre up, and indicated that he take a seat on the bench, then attached the handcuffs to a bar that ran alongside the bench.

"You'll be taken to a safe house until Philippe is in custody. One of my men will see that you get settled. I suggest you cooperate. Do not think about trying to escape—you won't be successful and will only get yourself hurt."

Pierre nodded his understanding before Dubois closed and latched the door, leaving him alone with his thoughts. *Matisse is an undercover agent! Incroyable!*

Dubois stepped through the kitchen door of the farmhouse and surveyed what was becoming a familiar scene: Simon tapping away on his laptop and speaking into a headset, Alex fiddling with his camera, and Matisse warming up a bottle of formula at the stove. In the other room, Louise sat on the couch with the baby bouncing on her knees, trying unsuccessfully to cajole her out of her fussy mood. *"Merde,"* he intoned under his breath as he beelined for the coffee pot.

"Did you listen to any of it?" Dubois asked Matisse.

"Enough to confirm my opinion of him." Matisse sounded disgusted. "What a stupid bloody coward. I'm not sure if I'm relieved or disappointed that we can't put the murder at Philippe's feet."

"You still can—indirectly. Reckless endangerment or some such. Does Louise know?"

Matisse shook his head as he looked at her through the archway that separated the kitchen from the lounge. "She needs to be told, but it's going to break her heart all over again."

Dubois thought Matisse had it just about right and didn't envy his friend the task. "I'll send Sebastien to deliver him to Reynaud. What is the ETA on the extra men?"

Simon looked up from his laptop. "They should be here momentarily."

With a resigned sigh, Matisse removed the pan from the stove and wiped off the bottle. When he tapped Alex on the shoulder and inclined his head toward Louise, Alex rose and followed him into the lounge. Matisse sat next to Lou on the couch and watched for a moment, the baby gurgling and squirming as she was bounced up and down, somewhere between laughing and breaking out in a great loud wail. Alex settled on the arm of the overstuffed chair on her other side.

"Pierre had an interesting story to tell," Matisse began as he handed the bottle to Lou. "One that I think you need to hear."

Louise studied his face, seeing the concern there, then looked to Alex, but Alex was watching Matisse, too. "Okay," she said warily but distracted herself by settling the baby in with the bottle.

"He apparently knew Elena. He, ah, claims he had strong feelings for her."

"So he was definitely involved with the business next door?" Lou shivered. "God. What do you think he had in mind for me?"

Matisse nodded in answer to the first question but let the second one alone. "If what he told Laurent is true, he believed that Philippe was actually helping those girls." He watched her carefully. "He said Philippe took in pregnant women who were destitute and living on the street, cleaned them up, and cared for them until they delivered their babies. He then arranged for the babies to be adopted and took the women somewhere to recover."

"He found them on the street?" Alex asked. "Doesn't that sound a little far-fetched?"

"Pierre also said that it was he who found your sister. He said she was digging through a trash bin in Aix. He was apparently quite taken with her, even in whatever grubby state she was in. He fed her, took her to the college gym to clean up, and discovered that she was pregnant."

Louise closed her eyes as she cradled the baby who was oblivious to the emotions swirling around her as she contently slurped at her bottle. "God damn it. She was alive and pregnant and eating out of a garbage can and she couldn't bring herself to call me?"

Neither man knew how to respond—it sounded unbelievable to them, too—so Matisse continued with the story.

"Pierre thought Philippe would help her, and in a way, I suppose he did. But he kept her drugged, like the others. Pierre said it was a mild sedative to keep them from hurting themselves and to help them detox from whatever drugs they'd been on. Many of the women they brought in were addicts, and Philippe was presumably concerned about the health of the babies."

"So he could sell them," Louise groaned. "An addicted baby would be undesirable in his world, I imagine."

Alex reached out and caressed her knee, then covered it with his hand. "So he became obsessed with Lou because she reminded him of the woman he'd found in Aix?"

"Something like that—but only after, well, only after Elena was found dead." Matisse could see the tears building in Lou's eyes but had to finish it.

"Pierre admitted to being the one who took her out of the cellar. He swore he thought he was helping her. He'd heard her screams and the midwife arguing with Bernard. By the time it was over, there was a lot of blood. They sedated her, and the infant was taken to the upstairs nursery, and Pierre was sent to clean up the cell, including all the bloody towels and sheets from the birth. He panicked, wrapped her in a bathrobe, and carried her out through the outside cellar door. He knew how to avoid the security cameras, apparently, and managed to get her through the hedge, but she was too heavy for him to carry any farther."

Louise felt the tears wet her cheeks as she listened to Matisse.

"He, ah, said he half carried, half dragged her through the orchard to the far road, then laid her down in the ditch, intending to go back through the cellar, leave as usual, and then drive around and pick her up."

"Oh, God, he left her in a ditch? That bastard!"

"I'm so sorry, *petite,* I know it sounds horrible and there's no excuse for what he did. He panicked. He thought he was helping her, but instead …"

Alex had moved from the arm of the chair to the cushion beside Lou and now had his arm cradled around her shoulders. He asked Matisse, "But how did she get to the village?"

Matisse shook his head. "Pierre didn't know. He claims he went back into the cellar, finished the cleanup then left as usual. It probably took at least a half an hour. By the time he drove around and reached the spot where he thought he'd left her, she was gone."

Louise sniffled and blew her nose. "She must have regained consciousness—she was probably freezing. God, she must have been so weak after all that blood loss. She had to have been delirious." The baby was asleep now, so Matisse leaned over and gently took her from Lou to set her down in the bassinet.

"It's possible she saw the lights of the village and managed to stumble her way there. It's unbelievable that no one saw her. *Merde,* I drove that very road when I went to meet you. I probably drove right by her," his voice held an unbearable sadness. "Pierre saw me drive by when he was out looking for her, which inspired him to pin her death on me when she turned up in the churchyard."

Tears flowing, Louise turned her head into the comfort of Alex's chest. "I can't believe I was so close to her all this time. *But why?* Why didn't she reach out to me for help?"

Alex smoothed his hand over her hair, as much at a loss for an answer as she was.

A commotion in the kitchen signaled the arrival of the secondary team. Matisse took her hand and gently caressed it, reluctant to let go but knowing he had to. She surprised him by leaning forward and hugging him. "Thank you for telling me," she whispered through her tears. He nodded to Alex then stood to join the group. As he turned away, the look of sympathy in his eyes was replaced by a hard glint of determination.

Twenty-Six

Philippe Lemans was sweating by the time he reached his car, but it had nothing to do with the temperature of the morning air or the exertion of wheeling his bag through the train station. He would never admit it to another living soul, but he was nervous. For the first time since he could remember, there was uncertainty on the horizon, and the foreign state did not sit well with him.

The back of his neck tingled, and he glanced behind him. He'd felt it on the train and now he felt it again—like he was being watched. But the only people around were tired businessmen like himself, finding their way to their cars. He stowed his bag in the trunk and got in, starting up the engine. He had to wait to back up for a man who managed to drop his overstuffed briefcase on the pavement directly behind him. He watched impatiently in his side mirror as the man retrieved the scattered papers, some of which had landed directly under his bumper.

The man stood and waived apologetically to Philippe before moving out of the way. Philippe wasted no time. Once he was through the exit gate, his thoughts centered again on Les Prés, anxious to capture whatever tableau of activity was happening there, and to assure himself that the infant, at least, was secure and healthy. It was too bad about the mother—he'd had a buyer for the pair, at an excellent price, since she'd been so young and relatively undamaged—but the priority was the baby. He was confident that his father would cover for him. Jean Luc had as much to lose as he did.

As he drove through the morning traffic of Avignon, he mulled over, again, the possibilities of what could have happened. It all came down to Pierre; he was almost certain of it. *That little shit could never hide his fascination for the girl*. On impulse, Philippe scrolled through the contacts on his phone and dialed Pierre's number. He would order him to the house and deal with him there. The number connected and rang, but the call went to voicemail. *That's strange.* Pierre normally answered on the first ring, even if he was working. He shrugged and tossed the phone on the passenger seat, not bothering to leave a message. Let him sweat a little when he saw the missed call.

Simon monitored the GPS signal coming from the tag on Philippe's bumper that their man had managed to affix at the same time he saw an incoming call from the man on Pierre's confiscated phone. *Interesting.* He signaled to his team leaders. "He's about thirty minutes out, assuming no traffic snarls. Let's get everyone in position."

He frowned slightly when it was apparent that no message was left on Pierre's phone. He watched for Bernard's phone to light up, but it didn't. *Even more interesting—Philippe contacting Pierre but not Bernard.* Did they have the order of things wrong? Not knowing the answer, and not having time to contemplate it, he passed the information on to Matisse and left it at that.

Right on time, Philippe pulled through the gate of his property, drove around to the back, and parked beside the truck that Bernard used. It was a cold morning, and the thin layer of frost that lay on the ground and covered the truck was still visible. Philippe noticed that it was undisturbed, indicating that no one had ventured out of the house yet. Satisfied that his people were where they should be, he went to retrieve his bag from the trunk, looking expectantly at the kitchen door. No one emerged to greet him. Then he noticed that there was no smoke coming from the chimney, and he frowned. Bernard always had a fire going on cold mornings like this, and he would most certainly have come to fetch his bag for him. He looked at the ground around the parking area more carefully, but his were the only tracks that marked the frost.

He shrugged, lifted his bag, and walked to the kitchen door. It was locked. The prickling sensation hit him again, and he looked around but saw nothing unusual. He used his key, calling out as he entered the house, but no one answered. He set the bag down and walked through the house. Nothing looked out of place—until he went upstairs to the nursery and found the child missing. *Fuck.* He checked the bedrooms where Bernard and Mathilde stayed, dreading what he might find, but the beds were made as if everything were normal. *As if they hadn't been slept in,* he amended.

Philippe hurried back downstairs, a sick feeling beginning to form in his gut. The kitchen was neat and tidy, no coffee cups or other dishes in the sink, nothing to indicate morning activity. No lingering smells of breakfast, or even coffee. The panel that hid the cellar door was in place as it should be and the lock and alarm were engaged. He let himself through and hastily took the stairs, not bothering to re-engage the panel. The girls were all in their cells. All but one was awake, looking surprisingly alert.

"*Bonjour, mademoiselles,*" he said carefully but received no replies. He glanced at the untouched tray of food on the floor just inside the cell of the girl who was still asleep, and he felt a jolt of alarm. It was not the usual breakfast fare, nor was it protocol to leave the trays on the floor. The women were supposed to be fed after they'd been given their medication. *What has happened here?*

After checking the rest of the cellar but finding nothing out of order, Philippe retraced his steps back up into the kitchen and stopped short at the site of Matisse looming large in the open doorway to the outside.

"What are you doing here?" Philippe demanded, stepping toward him threateningly. "You know it's forbidden!"

Matisse smiled without humor. "The rules changed after you had me arrested."

"I had nothing to do with that! I tried to bail you out as soon as I heard! I have no idea why you were pegged for murdering that girl."

Matisse smirked and took a step forward, feeling satisfaction when Philippe retreated a half step. "And what exactly do you know about the girl?"

The voice was full of menace, and Philippe felt ice creep up his spine. How did Matisse get through the gate, and where the hell were his men? He had no desire to have this conversation with Matisse without being protected by his thugs with their heavy metal. His stepbrother was too big, too strong, and at this moment, too intimidating. He tried another approach.

"The girl's death was an unfortunate accident, *mon frère.* She should never have been allowed to leave in that condition."

"Allowed? That's not the word I would have chosen, given the condition she was found in."

Philippe waved a hand in the air. "Postpartum women can go a little crazy." He tried to cover for the panic he heard in his own voice. "They can be hard to reason with, wanting to run here and there to accomplish some unfathomable purpose when all they should be doing is nursing their child."

"And exactly where is the child?"

"Out," Philippe replied quickly, glancing around the room and praying it was true. "She's out with her, ah, her nanny."

Matisse looked over Philippe's shoulder and indicated the open panel with his chin, the stairs visible. "What's down there?"

"Nothing, just the basement."

Philippe felt tiny beads of perspiration forming at his hairline as Matisse crossed his arms across his massive chest and glared down at him. He struggled with the urge to mop at it with his handkerchief.

"Now that I'm here," Matisse said, "tell me what you wanted to say to me."

"Are you willing to work for me under any circumstances?"

"Only a fool would agree to that, *mon frère.*" The slight emphasis on that last word made Philippe wince.

"Of course, but Etienne, this involves a business opportunity more lucrative than anything you could imagine."

Matisse looked skeptical. "Really."

"Relax, have a seat here," Philippe waived to the kitchen table. "Let me make us some coffee. I just got back, but—"

"I know; I've been watching for you ever since I was freed."

Philippe spun on his heels to face the larger man. "And why did you not accept my help?"

"Your help?" Matisse spat with contempt. "As far as I know, it was you who orchestrated my arrest!"

"Why would I do that?"

Ugly laughter broke through hard lips. "You tell me, *brother.* Perhaps to make me more pliable to your scheming? Make me grateful to you for getting me out?"

Well, yes, that was exactly what Philippe had hoped, but ... "I don't know what's gotten into you, Etienne. You came to me, remember? I thought we were working well together. I thought you wanted more."

"I told you I don't need more—the *more* was your idea. I'm perfectly happy where I am. And I don't like your attempt to humiliate me into submission." Matisse gave Philippe a withering look. "I was done with that a long time ago."

Philippe sighed as he turned back to the counter and prepared the coffee machine. He had too much to do now and didn't have the energy or inclination to spar with Matisse. Whatever was going on didn't involve him, and he needed to get him gone so he could figure out what that was.

"So tell me what this other business is."

The resigned acceptance in Etienne's voice gave Philippe a spark of hope. "Not unless you agree to be a part of it."

"That's a stupid condition—you can't make me do something I don't want to do."

Philippe turned back to him, his confidence restored. "No, but I could kill you."

Matisse raised his eyebrows. "You could try."

Seeing the confidence fade abruptly on Philippe's face, Matisse pressed, taking a step toward him. "You seem to be quite alone here, Philippe. Where are your devoted employees?"

"You've been watching the house—you tell me." This new, unyielding Matisse was beginning to make Philippe nervous. *What the hell is going on here?*

"You mean you don't know? I'm surprised they didn't have the coffee made and your house slippers waiting for you."

"They didn't know I was coming."

Matisse knew that, of course, but acted surprised. "Keep them guessing, eh? Well they obviously weren't expecting you, since they aren't even here." Then his eyes narrowed. "You wanted to catch them unawares. Why?"

Philippe had turned his back on Matisse and was fumbling with the coffee pot.

"What's really going on here? Why are you so nervous? What exactly are you hiding?"

"I'm not—" He caught movement out of the corner of his eye. "No! Don't go down there." But it was too late. Matisse had crossed the kitchen and slipped through the open panel leading to the cellar.

"Etienne! Stop!"

Philippe cursed and chased Matisse down the cellar steps, only to barely stop himself from slamming into his back at the bottom. Matisse had not seen the cellar the night before, although he'd heard all about it, but he didn't have to fake the shock on his face when he turned to look at Philippe. "Good God, what are you doing here?"

"Etienne, calm down. I can explain."

"The woman that died was your *prisoner?*" The rage that mottled Etienne's features was truly frightening.

"Er, not exactly, no," Philippe said coolly.

"Who are these women?" Matisse walked toward the cells. The captives sat on their beds and stared at him blankly. "*Mon Dieu*—they're pregnant." Even though he knew what happened here, even though he'd been briefed the night before, the horror of seeing it up close and personal turned him irrational, and his control faltered. He let all the humiliation of his youth and the suppressed hatred for the man before him come roaring to the surface.

"This is a God damned baby factory! *You bastard!* This is why you kept my mother a prisoner all those years—you used her to take care of pregnant women. She couldn't take care of me because she was taking care of them!"

Calm down, Etienne, came the voice in his ear. *Stick to the plan.* Simon. The link had been silent, and he'd forgotten his friend was listening.

Philippe had shifted slightly to the right while Matisse was raging and slipped his hand inside his jacket. When Matisse turned back to him with a look of pure hatred, Philippe calmly held up a large handgun and pointed it at his chest.

"Back off now, Etienne. You don't have all the facts." With a gun in his hand Philippe's confidence ricocheted back.

Matisse snarled but backed up a few steps. This wasn't going how he'd planned it—he had planned to be surprised, of course, but he needed to let Philippe explain it. He didn't need to get a hole in his chest before the recording device picked up all the sordid details.

"Then tell me," Matisse countered, his voice sounding much more calm.

"You are right, this has been going on for a long time. My father began it more than fifty years ago. There is profit in it—huge profits sometimes—but it's a humanitarian effort as well."

"Oh yes," Matisse nearly choked as he indicated the locked cells. "I can see that."

"I rescue them, care for them, see them through a painful experience, then give them a chance for a better life."

He's bloody delusional, Simon whispered through the com-link.

"What do you think becomes of women like these?" Philippe waived his hand at the cells. "And their bastards?" His eyes gleamed with an unholy light. "I'll tell you. The women are prostitutes and drug addicts, the babies— born addicts—get left at the doorstep of some underfunded charity, if they're lucky, or abandoned on a trash heap if they're not. There are plenty of places in the world where Caucasian babies are valued."

"You sell them to the highest bidder?" Matisse did not disguise the disgust in his voice. "And then what happens to them? Don't tell me they become the cherished children of wealthy families. More like pets or slaves would be my guess—or worse, sex toys to depraved men."

Philippe shrugged and lowered the gun. He still kept it in his hand with his finger on the trigger. "What difference does it make? They're no worse off than they would be otherwise."

Matisse bit back the insult that jumped into his mind. "What about the women? What's humanitarian about stealing their babies?"

"They hardly know after it's over." Philippe gestured to the women in the cells. "We keep them on a mild sedative that does no harm to the baby and maintains a dream-like atmosphere for the mother. Once she's safely delivered and recovered, we take her to a women's shelter. The good Christians do wonders for downtrodden women."

"How convenient for you." Matisse sneered. "But what about the women who weren't drug addicts? The ones who were not pregnant when they were snatched from the village?"

Philippe flinched. "We only process destitute women, Etienne. It's not cruel. The mother has a chance to get on with her life, unburdened by an unwanted child, and the child ends up in safe hands somewhere far away."

He actually believes his actions are justified. Incredible, Simon commented.

"Only destitute women? Are you sure?"

Philippe raised his chin in defiance. "*Oui,* only those who cannot care for themselves."

Don't dwell on it, Etienne. Get him to say the rest, Simon whispered.

"And no one ever looks for the children?" Matisse asked. "What about the adoption papers, or do you forego that step? And who exactly takes these babies? Jesus, Philippe." Matisse ran a hand roughly over his face and turned away, his gaze going to the unconscious girl in one of the cells.

"The children grow up to be well cared for. Perhaps it's a different life for them than they would have had here, but for the amount of money it takes to purchase one, I can guarantee they are not harmed."

"Nor are they allowed to make their own choices."

"Choices are dangerous for a child too young to understand the consequences. Getting stuck in the quagmire of indifferent social services is even worse." Philippe made an impatient gesture. "Let it go, Etienne. It is an ugly fact of life, perhaps, but trust me, these women are better off with our … help."

The contacts, Etienne, whispered the voice in his ear.

"Whatever became of Jean Luc? You say he started this … business, but he disappeared and left my mother with you. Why?"

Philippe smiled. "Jean Luc emigrated to Hong Kong soon after his marriage. From there, he orchestrates the placement of the children. He married her for me, you see; she refused me, but we needed her—and more importantly, we needed this property. I loved Juliette in my own way. You must understand this, Etienne. She was a good woman, and she cared for the girls."

"Don't patronize me. You didn't give a fuck about my mother or you wouldn't have kept us apart." Matisse was barely holding on to his sanity.

You have enough, Etienne. Get out of there before you lose control.

Matisse heard the words, but it was too late. His control had slipped beyond his ability to rein it back in. "You're a sick bastard, Philippe. I hope you've enjoyed your run. It's over."

"The problem with Juliette," Philippe said softly, ignoring the danger in Etienne's tone, "was that she never stopped loving your father. I tried everything to get her to come willingly to my bed, but …" He shook his head in regret. "You were the key. Fortunately by the time you ran off she was losing her appeal." He shrugged dismissively. "It was easier to scratch the itch another way than to go after you."

The casual way Philippe talked about using, then discarding Matisse's mother pulled the final pin that held together his sanity. Matisse roared his hatred, and in a fluid motion, he pulled a knife from a sheath under his coat and flung it at Philippe. Just before it buried itself in his target's gut, the gun in Philippe's hand discharged. Matisse cursed as the force of the bullet hitting his chest knocked him backward against the bars of a cell.

"I'm hit," he hissed, then closed his eyes as he lost command of his body and slid down to the floor. He weakly pressed his hand against the hole below his left collarbone and felt the thick, sticky fluid pulsing out of him.

Etienne! It was Lou's voice, sounding sweet but distant. *Etienne, hang on! God damn you, you big jerk. I'm not done with you!* He smiled despite the agony in his chest and thought he heard the pounding of footsteps on the stairs above him as his consciousness faded.

Twenty-Seven

"I can't believe you were there when it all went down," Spencer told Alex over the phone the next day after the entire INTERPOL team had been debriefed. "I'd give anything to be in the field like that."

"I didn't do much—just took some photographs. Mostly I listened to the action from the house next door."

Spencer let out a sigh. "At least you were *there,* not stuck in some office to hear about it afterwards. And I saw the photos that Simon uploaded for the SG—they were very good. Especially your shots of that old tunnel."

"*Merci,* I'm glad I could help. I imagine it will take a team of forensic investigators some time to unlock all the secrets of that place. Do you really think they used the tunnel to snatch women from the village?"

"We may never know. Depends on what they find in there."

"So what will happen with Philippe and the others?" Alex wasn't interested in reliving the final scenes—it was all a little too personal with Lou's family connection.

"Philippe will be very uncomfortable for a long time. Matisse managed to stick his liver with that knife, and that's a messy organ to damage. He's in the ICU under lockdown being monitored for infection. The bloody bastard deserves all the pain he can get as far as I'm concerned. And when he's done with the physical pain, we'll do our best to exert another kind of pain."

"What about that records room? Did they find anything?"

"Oh, yeah." The excitement in Spencer's voice was evident. "A chartered accountant couldn't have kept better records, and Simon's handed the analysis over to me. The whole collection should be arriving here tomorrow, and from what I've heard, they go back a long way."

"And Jean Luc? Will they be able to get to him, too?"

"That may be a little tricky, but with luck, he'll be implicated in the records. I've done some checking on him. He's had an interesting career. It turns out that he founded a legitimate export business to Hong Kong back in the sixties that specialized in luxury food products like caviar and foie gras, and of course fine French wines. There was a huge demand for the stuff among the British colonials. I won't know until I see the records, but the women and babies probably started shortly thereafter, along with the counterfeit wines, and that line has grown significantly in the last ten years. He left France for good, to live in Hong Kong, just after he married Juliette Matisse, but he didn't take her with him."

"He left her with Philippe." Alex had heard the story through the com-link.

"Right. I'm guessing that he connected with people there who wanted to open a pipeline for trade in women and children. There are some serious perverts with lots of money in China. I'm sure that's why he relocated himself. He needed someone on the ground he could trust, and he evidently couldn't trust anyone more than himself."

"So will you be able to shut him down?" It made Alex ill to think the sick bastard would get away with it.

"It's no longer a British colony, so it'll be tricky, but we are the international police, and our directives aim squarely at counterfeiting and human trafficking, so if anyone can do it, we can."

"Well, good luck with that. Louise and I will be rooting for you."

"Ah yes, the lovely Louise." Spencer's smile could be heard through the telephone connection.

Alex stiffened. "What about her?"

Spencer just laughed. "I've seen her photograph—she's a looker. Have you, you know …"

"Louise is a friend." Alex said irritably. "Don't read any more into it than that. And keep your mouth shut about her. She has nothing to do with any of this."

"Nothing, except it was her sister who ended up dead in the churchyard, and her niece who was recovered from that prison. Not to mention, if I read the reports correctly, it was *she* who connected the dots to identify the hidden cells."

"Spencer—"

"All right, all right, chill out, mate. I'm just giving you a hard time." He paused, then more seriously added, "I think you care about her."

Alex didn't hesitate. "I do." Spencer was one of his closest friends, and they'd seen each other through lots of women. "But I don't know how she feels. At first I didn't think she liked me much. Ever since we met, we've been somehow tied up with Matisse and, well, you know. I thought he was a crook, but she kept defending him, and … we had a bit of a rough beginning. When I finally think she's changing her opinion of me, we're suddenly in the middle of a murder investigation where the victim turns out to be her sister, Matisse turning out to be one of the good guys, and then there's the showdown at the farmhouse where he ends up getting shot."

Alex ran a hand through his hair in exasperation. "And now she has a newborn baby to take care of. I have no idea where we stand. Where I stand."

Spencer couldn't help it—he laughed. "I don't envy you, mate. But I hope you work it out. Just take it easy with her. It sounds like she's got more shit piled up at the moment than you do."

———◆———

Louise stepped into the dimly lit hospital room, getting a strong sense of déjà vu, and she thought of the hospital visit less than a month ago that started this whole roller-coaster ride. Etienne was asleep, dwarfing the narrow bed with his huge body. His upper left side was covered with thick bandages, but otherwise his chest and arms were bare, and she couldn't help but be impressed with the action-figure bulk of his muscles. His hair was combed back from his face, which looked pale in the artificial light, even with the few days' worth of unshaved whiskers. There was a sensor on his right hand attached to a heart monitor, and an IV drip was connected to his arm.

It was touch-and-go for several hours after they'd rushed him to the hospital; thanks to Simon's thoroughness, an ambulance had been on standby next door. The bullet had glanced off his ribs and ricocheted out through his shoulder, rather than through a vital organ, but he'd lost a lot of blood. His size and strength had saved him, the doctor said.

She leaned over him and softly kissed his brow, then took the seat beside his bed and reached for his hand. She marveled at how dear to her he had become in such a short period of time, and how strange their relationship was. She was barely aware of the tears of relief that wet her cheeks as she gently caressed his fingers.

"*Petite,* why are you crying?"

She looked up at his face and smiled. "I didn't know you were awake."

"I'm fine, *chérie.*" He tilted his head toward the bandages wrapped around his shoulder. "This will heal."

"I know, but I could have lost you." She swiped the back of a hand across her face, but her eyes were still watery. "I couldn't bear it if I'd lost you, too."

He watched her but said nothing, not sure at all what to say, returning her caress by running his thumb over the knuckles of the hand that held his. That she truly cared about him no longer bewildered him. He'd been getting used to the idea since Paris, and now it seemed natural that she felt as protective of him as he did of her. She was a beautiful woman, fresh and vibrant, fragile yet strong, as if her spirit had been honed by the tragedy of her sister. He felt deep affection and admiration for her; there was no doubt in his mind that he loved her, but …

Years ago, Etienne had known a woman … had fallen in love with a woman that he knew he could never have. At the time, it was ridiculous to even think it—he was a big ugly brute with a secret, sordid past, out for retribution … for justice. He'd admired and loved this woman, worked alongside her, in fact, and the only thing that saved his dignity was that he was sure she'd never been aware of his regard. She'd been kind to him, but, in his own defense … in his desperate attempt at self-preservation … he'd made it a point to be contrary in her presence, if only to confirm to himself and to her the impossibility of the situation.

But Lou … the lovely Louise … she'd reminded him of this woman from the very beginning. Her looks, her kindness, her very spirit. But unlike the woman in his past, Louise had not taken the hint. She had not backed down, she had not relented, and she had not believed he was the bully he had so carefully cultivated himself to be. Had it not been for his past, his feelings ... the love he had felt ... Lou could have easily been the sort that stirred his loins and made his heart beat faster.

His odd relationship with Lou, however, had had an unexpected effect. It had made him realize that perhaps, just maybe, he was worthy of the honest regard of a beautiful woman. There was no question that he loved Louise, but it would never be a romantic love because his heart had been captured so many years before by another woman ... and still was, he admitted to himself. With Louise, it was a comforting sort of love, accepting, unconditional, and protective—like a brother for his beloved little sister.

"I'm not going anywhere. But what of you? What of *la minuscule?*"

A beautiful smile lit up her face. "She's such a little sweetheart. We had the pediatrician here check her out. She's slightly malnourished, but otherwise, she's perfect." She frowned and shook her head as she wiped her eyes. "Thank God we got her out."

He waited.

"I want to keep her. I never thought I wanted kids, but ... Simon said he'd help me with the paperwork. I've been granted temporary custody, but nothing can be finalized before DNA tests prove that Ellie is my sister and little Ellie is my niece. I'm the closest thing she has to family here, so Simon doesn't think it will be a problem."

"So you'll take her back to America." The tightening of his heart hurt more than the bullet hole in his chest.

She looked down at their entwined hands, biting her lip as she hesitated. "Actually, I'm thinking of staying here."

It was Etienne's turn to frown. "I thought your job was temporary."

"It is, but Ellie is a French citizen, and if I'm her legal guardian, I'll be allowed to stay as a resident."

"What will you do?"

She laughed, sounding slightly hysterical. "You mean besides care for an infant? I thought I'd talk to the college president to see if there's a part-time position I could fill. We're almost finished with the documentation project at the Maison Basse, but the next phase is just as important and they'll need someone familiar with the history as the project moves forward. I'll need to find another place to live, of course—my apartment is too small for me and Ellie, and anyway it's owned by the college. I doubt they'd let me stay there."

Etienne watched her, overjoyed with the possibility of Louise remaining part of his life but afraid it was too good to be true. He cleared his throat. "I, ah, I wouldn't mind having a couple of roommates. My house is big enough."

She looked startled. "Oh." She searched his face for the truth, chewing on her lip in uncertainty. "I'm not sure that's—"

"It's not a marriage proposal, *petite,* just a practical offer from a friend who cares about you."

Louise felt a flash of hope along with her relief. She had—inexplicably—come to care deeply for Etienne, although not in a romantic way. She'd felt something special between them since the night of the storm, and she thought he'd felt it, too. She wanted him in her life, and in Ellie's.

"And it's a self-serving offer as well," he continued when she didn't respond. "I enjoy your company, but I could also use your help."

"My help?"

He nodded. "I'm retiring from INTERPOL."

She raised her eyebrows, letting a small smile curve her lips, but said nothing.

"It's served my purpose. Philippe has been exposed. Whatever becomes of him, it's no longer my concern. All I ever really wanted was justice, and to stop the humiliation." He hesitated, wondering if she would understand. "I find I have no appetite for vengeance, and I'm tired of living my life in anticipation of it. My mother is long gone, and … I've come to understand that she made her own choices, choices that affected us both."

"What of Les Prés?"

He shrugged. "She signed it over to him. As her stepson, he was arguably a legal heir. I could fight for it, I suppose, but in truth, I don't want it. I have my own property, one that has been in the Matisse family for almost 250 years. It's time I stopped playing detective and embrace my birthright." He smiled at her. "I wish to become a farmer. The land is rich and there is a lot of it. I have some ideas that can improve the vineyards, replant the other fields with crops that are in demand, and who knows? Perhaps I'll make a little wine."

"And you want a roommate because …?"

He laughed. "Beside the fact that it's a big empty house in need of some life?" His eyes twinkled. "Well, let's see. I'm good with computers, but I hate accounting, and I'll need organized finances to implement my plans. I'm a decent cook, but the idea of coming home from a long day in the fields to a lonely table of one is not enticing. But the idea of sharing those duties, and those meals …"

At her look of shock, he winked. "I don't expect you to clean up after me, and my housekeeper can extend her duties to child care as needed, but I wouldn't mind trying your southern cooking, *petite*." His eyes softened. "And I would very much like to help you with *la minuscule*."

She laughed. "I was right about you all along," she said as she leaned over to give him a hug.

Alex chose that moment to knock on the open door and step inside the room. Etienne and Lou both looked up at him with smiles. Alex saw how cozy they looked, holding hands and sharing secrets. He felt a stab of jealousy so intense it angered him, and he turned around abruptly. "*Pardon*," he said as he retreated.

"Alex, wait!" Lou glanced at Etienne, who nodded. She jumped up from her chair and dashed after him. She caught up to him at the stairs. "Alex, stop!"

He stopped but didn't turn around, doing his best to tamp down the despair that washed over him. She tugged on his arm, trying to turn him around to face her. He resisted momentarily but finally acquiesced. He felt like an idiot—a lovesick idiot. And as it had been with her from the beginning, he was unsure if she returned even a fraction of his feelings.

"What's wrong with you?"

"I didn't mean to intrude. I, ah, I know you two are close and, well, it looked like you needed some privacy." He looked down at his feet as he spoke, not risking eye contact.

"What are you talking about?" She gripped his arm harder, but he backed up a step, pulling her hand off her arm. She closed the gap with a step. "What is it that you think you saw?"

He swallowed, not able to keep the bitterness from his voice. "What am I to think, *mademoiselle?* You allow my kisses, yet you cozy up with him like you want to crawl into his bed."

"Alex," her voice softened. "Etienne and I are friends, nothing more, and you know it. I care for him like a brother. I was hugging him because he just made me a very generous offer."

"I can only imagine what that might be," he muttered.

Louise squared her shoulders and planted her hands on her hips, equal parts joyous and impatient with his hurt-puppy behavior. "Listen to me, you big baby, and listen good. You're being an ass. You think I've been leading you on? That my affection has been an act?"

He cocked his head and watched her. *God, she's beautiful when she's feisty.*

"Well let me tell you something." She poked a finger at his chest. "Despite how stupid you were initially about Etienne, I like you. I like your family. I think you're a decent man, but I think you've got issues to resolve, same as me and anyone else. The thing is, you know what some of mine are now. But I've yet to learn yours."

Alex started to speak, but she held up her hand.

"Those kisses of yours? I like them." She smiled. "I like them a lot. They make me feel warm, make me want more."

He held her gaze, kept his expression as neutral as possible, forcing the burgeoning hope down as he waited for the *but.*

"And I like that you haven't pushed me. Where I come from, we appreciate gentlemanly behavior."

And here it came, he was sure.

"But it takes more than sweet kisses to know the heart of someone. It takes time, and it takes trust. It means you have to be open and honest It means you have to let me in. How can I trust you if you don't trust me? I know you a little bit, a little below the surface, but I don't know much more."

He stepped toward her, closing the gap, reaching for her hand. She let him twine his fingers with hers. "I'm afraid you might not like what you find there."

With her free hand she touched his jaw, traced the edge of it up and down, then ran her fingertips across his lips. "I might not. But I could say the same for you. How do you feel about dating a woman with a newborn baby?"

His eyes widened. "Part of me wants to hold her in my arms and cherish her, and part of me wants to run for the hills."

She smiled. "Well, that's honest."

"But you're right, I do have unresolved issues. Some I've come to terms with, others ..." He shrugged. "I'm working on them. Accepting what I can and can't change is part of that."

He traced her smile with his own fingertips. "You are so brave and beautiful. Matisse deserves you," he said ruefully.

She frowned. "He's no more in love with me than I am with him, but he's like the big brother I never had. I think he'll make a wonderful uncle to my little girl."

"I don't understand," he frowned.

"I'm staying in France, Alex. I have no idea what the future will hold, but I'm no longer interested in avoiding it."

"What about your parents? Surely they'll want—"

"They'll want to see little Ellie, of course. And I'm sure they'll be on the next flight out as soon as I call." She studied his face for a moment. "But I can't go back, at least not yet. For the first time in four years, I feel like I'm moving forward, and I like the feeling. I like the new friends I've made. A couple of them have become very dear to me."

Alex swallowed the lump in his throat at her sweet sentiment, since he agreed with it. "I feel the same way," he whispered as he leaned down to kiss her. He wrapped his hand around the back of her head and snuck the other around her waist and pulled her to him. Her arms wrapped around his neck as she smiled up into his face.

She kissed him, and it felt like spring bursting in his soul. "I trust you, *chérie,* and I have all the time in the world."

Happily ever after?

The dynasty that began with *Falling for France* and *French Twist* is about to be tested.

Gabrielle Walker is lamenting a life unraveling, the result of having loved and trusted a scoundrel, when a letter arrives from the other side of the world declaring that a distant cousin she had never met has bequeathed her an estate in the heart of the Dordogne River Valley in France.

Gabrielle arrives to claim her inheritance amidst a brewing land fight with a disgruntled local, distracting her from emerging headlines that a murder has taken place at the Ministry of Agriculture in Paris. She has no reason to think the events in Paris could interfere with her happily-ever-after. The charming Michel Bouvier, Alex's brother, knows otherwise. Why is he so secretive? Is it only his desire for Gabrielle that he conceals? Another scoundrel?

Gabrielle is determined not to be the moth to his flame. There is something other than wine fermenting here.

Can she find a way to trust again? Join her as she herself is *Finding France*, the next adventure in Nancy Milby's series *A Foreign Affair,* available now through Amazon.

A word about

A Word with You Press
Publishers and Purveyors of Fine Stories

In addition to being a full-service publishing house founded in 2009, *A Word with You Press* is a playful, passionate, and prolific consortium of writers connected by our collective love of the written word. We are, as well, devoted readers drawn to the notion that there is nothing more beautiful or powerful than a well-told story.

We realize that great writers and artists don't just happen. They are created by nurturing, mentoring, and by inspiration. We provide this literary triad through our interactive website, www.awordwithyoupress.com.

Visit us here to enter our writing contests and to become part of a broad but highly personal writing community. Improve your skills with what has become a significant, *de facto* writers' workshop, and approach us with your own publishing dreams and ambitions. We are always looking for new talent. Visit our store to buy from a distinguished list of our books, which include the work of a Pulitzer Prize winner, an award-winning poet, and first-rate literary fiction. Attend our seminars and retreats, and consider joining our growing list of published authors.

A writer is among the lucky few who discovers that art is not a diversion or distraction from everyday life; rather, art is an essential expression of the human spirit.

If you are such a writer, join us on our website, www.awordwithyoupress. com. If you have a project to discuss, we will assess the first thirty pages you send us *pro-bono*. Send your inquiries to the Editor-in-Chief, Thornton Sully, at thorn@awordwithyoupress.com. Be sure to indicate in the subject line *"pro-bono assessment"* and send your submission as a word doc attachment.

A Word with You Press
Publishers and Purveyors of Fine Stories
310 East A Street, Suite B, Moscow, Idaho 83843

Available or coming soon from

A Word with You Press

Almost Avalon
by Thornton Sully
A young couple struggles with love and life on the island
frontier just twenty-six miles west of Los Angeles.

The Mason Key
Volume One
A John Mason Adventure
by David Folz
A street urchin in England about the time the Colonies declare independence cheats the hangman to begin this historical adventure series. He discovers that his father's death may not have been an accident at all, but part
of a broader conspiracy.

The Mason Key II
Aloft and Alow
A John Mason Adventure
by David Folz
The historical saga continues as young Mason becomes
a mid-shipman on the very ship on which he was as
stow-away at the conclusion of *The Mason Key, Volume One.*

The Mason Key III
The Return
A John Mason Adventure
by David Folz
Mason and Marie fend off pirates en route to her father's plantation. John struggles with the Third Principle, Honor, and the Cruelty of Slavery while making his way back home.

Angus MacDream and the Roktopus Rogue
by Isabelle Rooney-Freedman
Young adults on a mythical Scottish island save the world. Delightfully illustrated by Teri Rider

The Wanderer
by Derek Thompson
A stranger wakes up on a deserted beach and embarks on a journey of discovery. The first in our *Magical Realism* series.

The Coffee Shop Chronicles, Vol. I,
Oh, the Places I Have Bean!
An anthology of award-winning stories inspired by events that occurred over a cup of coffee.

The Coffee Shop Chronicles, Vol. II,
A Jolt of Espresso
Stories condensed to exactly 100 words each, inspired by our favorite brew.
Visiting Angels and Home Devils
by Dr. Don Hanley, Ph.D.
A discussion guide for couples.

The Courtesans of God
by Thornton Sully
A novel based on the real life of a temple priestess in the palace of the King
of Malaysia.

Bounce
by Pulitzer Prize winner Jonathan Freedman
A nutty watermelon man, a spurned she-lawyer, a frustrated carioca journal-
ist and a misanthropic parrot set out to Brazil to change the world.

=Left Unlatched
in the hopes that you'll come in…

A Book of Poetry
by R.T. Sedgwick
Winner of the 2012 San Diego Book Awards – Poetry.

The Boy with a Torn Hat

by Thornton Sully
Debut novel was a finalist in the 2010 USA
Book Awards for Literary Fiction
"Henry Miller meets Bob Dylan in this coming of age romp played out in
the twisted alleyways and smoky beer halls of Heidelberg. Sully is a cun-
ning wordsmith and master of bringing music to art and art to language.
Excessive, expressive, lusty, and once in a blue metaphor—profound. Here
is what I mean: 'Some women are imprisoned like a tongue in a bell—they
swing violently but unnoticed until the moment of contact with the bronze
perimeter of their existence—and thenthe sound they make astonishes us its
power and pain and beauty, and its immediacy' —Wunderbar"
—Jonathan Freedman, Pulitzer Prize winner

Raw Man
by Pulitzer-Prize nominee Fred Rivera
This lightly-novelized Vietnam memoir, now required reading at major
universities, derives its title from the author's epiphany: "Twenty-seven years
after I got on the flight home, I saw that Nam war was just *raw man* spelled
backwards. I'm pretty raw today."

A Word with You, Vol. I
The best from A Word with You Press
An anthology of select winners from the literary contests of *A Word with You
Press* from 2009 to 2015

Falling for France
by Nancy Milby
The first in *A Foreign Affair* series finds Annie Shaw having to choose
between a successful career and real romance with a French aristocrat, and
wanting both.

French Twist
by Nancy Milby
The saga continues as American archeologist Louise Marcel becomes en-
tangled in nasty business on French soil, as she conceals her own hidden
agenda.

Finding France
by Nancy Milby
The third in *A Foreign Affair* series finds Gabrielle Walker lamenting a life unraveling when a letter informs her she is the inheritor of a large estate in France. Then it gets complicated!

Finding Home
by Nancy Milby
Etienne, the recurring enigma in the series *A Foreign Affair,* is brutal to his enemies but a gentle giant to those he loves. Can the secret woman in his past enter his life again? Perhaps, but not with complications—some predictable, but some…

Max and Cheez go to Spain
by Naureen Zaim and David Ulrich
A delightful illustrated children's book finds two cats on the first of many adventures, stowing away in a suitcase to Spain. What other countries will they investigate, now that they have the travel bug? A great way to introduce young children to the cultures of the world.

A Word with You Press
Publishers and Purveyors of Fine Stories
310 East A Street, Suite B, Moscow, Idaho 83843

www.awordwithyoupress.com

About the Author

Nancy Milby lives in Laguna Beach, California, with her husband, Steve, and their lovable cats Beckham and Boo. After finding her own way out of the corporate world, Nancy founded the local cooking school, Laguna Culinary Arts, which, for twelve years was synonymous with great fun, great food and wine, and great culinary adventures to destinations around the world. Currently, Nancy runs the breakaway division, LCA Wine, a boutique wine shop and wine education center, where she shares her passion by teaching wine classes and leading small groups of food and wine enthusiasts on overseas adventures.

To check out the fun, go to www.lcawine.com or www.nancymilby.com.

www.ingramcontent.com/pod-product-compliance
Lightning Source LLC
Chambersburg PA
CBHW031325170626
46807CB00002B/574